Undying EverGreene

Visit Jo Cook's website and subscribe to her newsletter to receive a FREE novella, A Rose for Carter, as well as news about upcoming releases.

AuthorJoCook.com

Also by Jo Cook

World of Eoroe: Bryten series:

A Rose for Carter (novella)
Prince John's Lost Love
The Guarded Heart
Undying EverGreene

Undying EverGreene

World of Eoroe: Bryten
Book Three

Jo Cook

Table of Contents

Dedicated to the Prologue Writing Group

Thanks for keeping me on track and motivated!

Once upon a time in the world of Eoroe,

On the continent of Bryten…

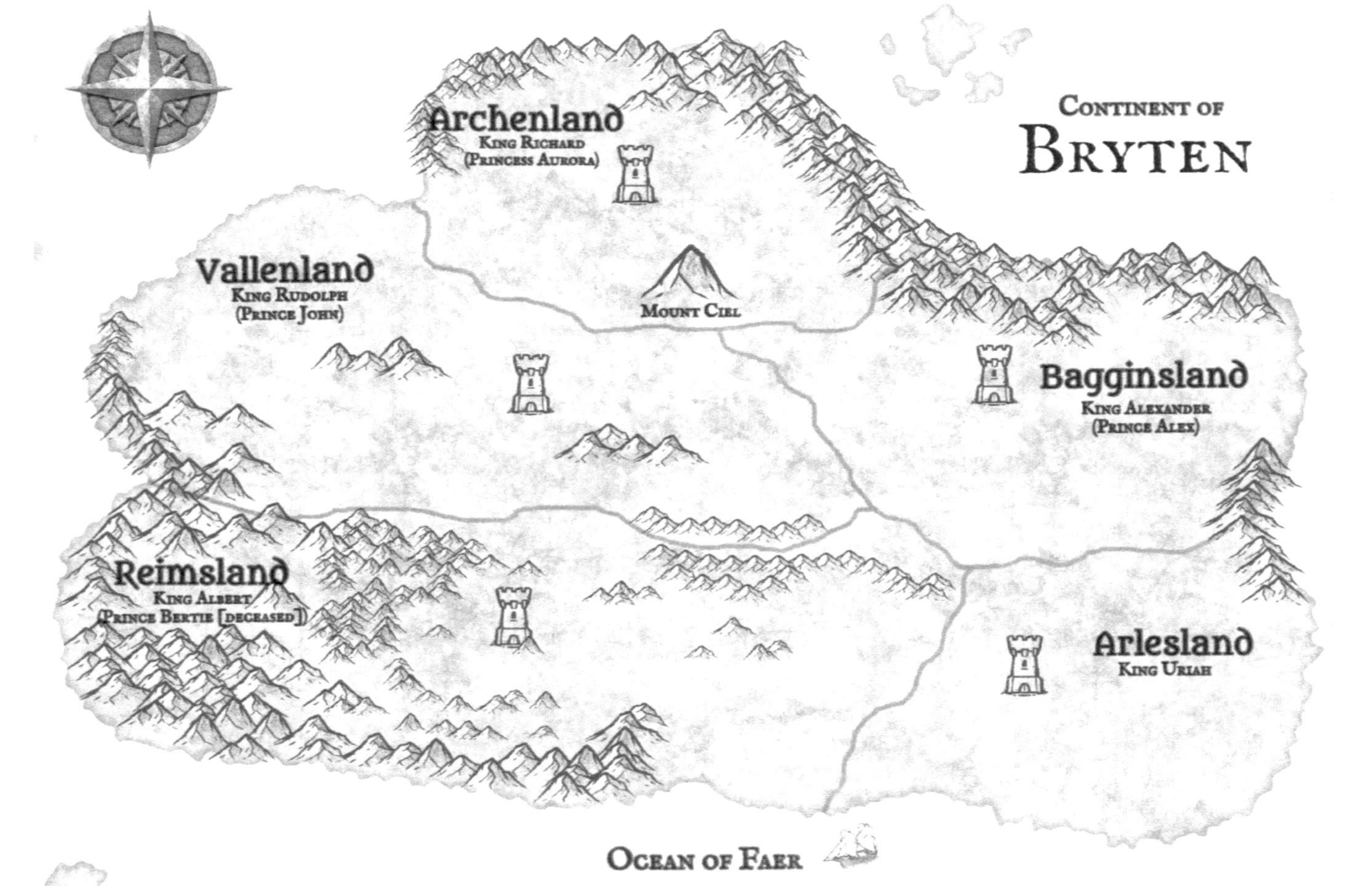

Continent of
Bryten
Archenland
King Richard
(Princess Aurora)
Mount Ciel
Vallenland
King Rudolph
(Prince John)
Bagginsland
King Alexander
(Prince Alex)
Reimsland
King Albert
(Prince Bertie [deceased])
Arlesland
King Uriah
Ocean of Faer

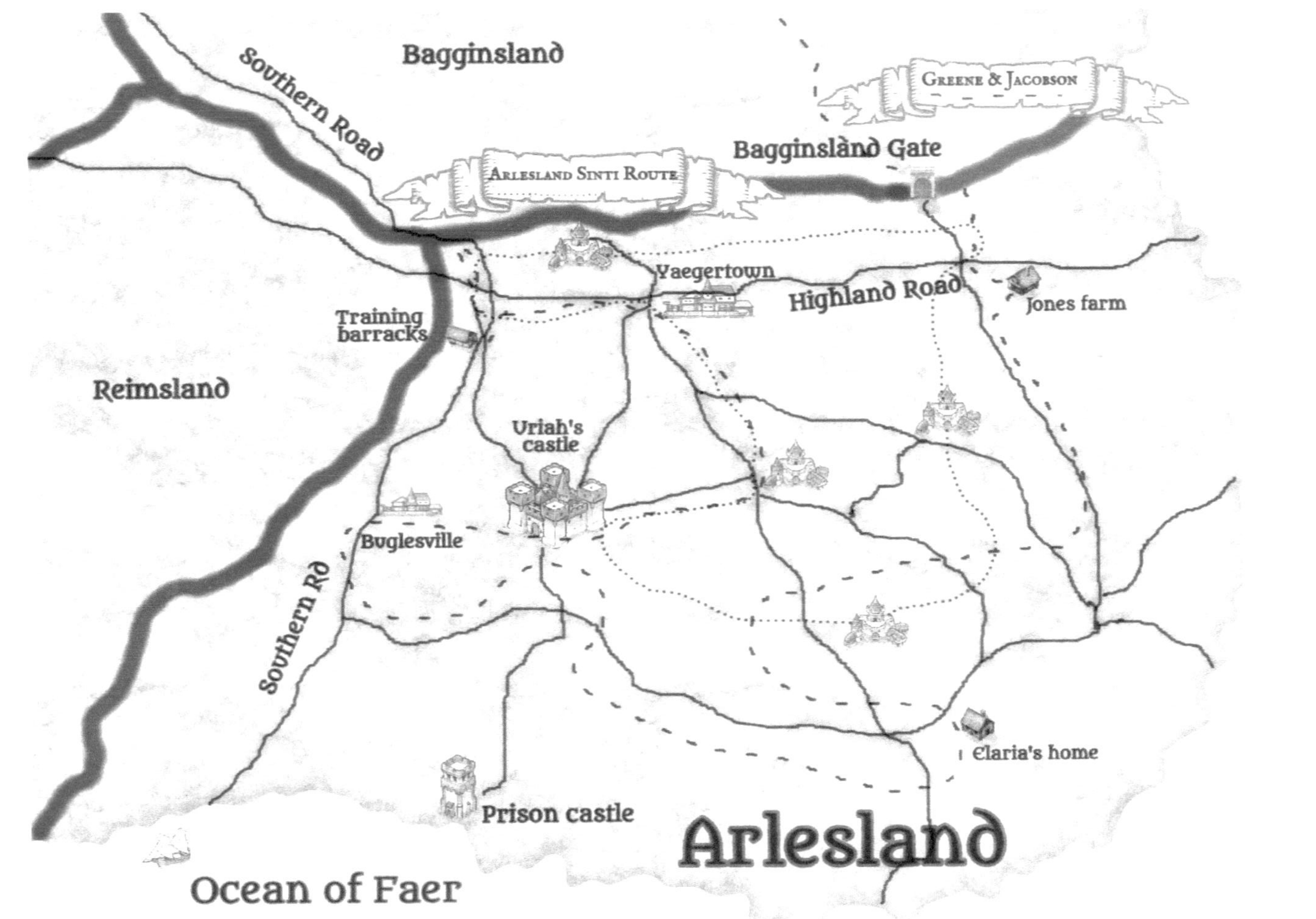

Bagginsland
Southern Road
Greene & Jacobson
Arlesland Sinti Route
Bagginsland Gate
Training barracks
Yaegertown
Highland Road
Jones farm
Reimsland
Uriah's castle
Buglesville
Southern Rd
Elaria's home
Prison castle
Arlesland
Ocean of Faer

Pronunciation Guide

Bryten: Bri´-ten
Eoroe: Eh´-row
Gaemedden: Gay´-med-un
Grauta Beadu: Grau´-tah Bay´-doo
Heol: Hee´-ol
Heolcnihts: Hell´-kuh-nites
Reimsland: Rimes´-land
Saiwola: Say-woh´-la
Skaeweer: Skay´-weer
Sutherne: Soo´-thern
Ungesewen Weraldi: UN-guh-su-wen Weh-RAHL-dee

Bitter Sand

Charla stood on tiptoe, raising the lantern to cast a circle of light in the dark barn. There! Hanging the lantern on a hook, she pulled a small block of wood over so she could climb onto it to reach the very back of the cabinet where her grandfather's old chest was stored. Some things belonging to her dead mother were stored in the chest, and Charla was hoping to find something she could use for her wedding in a few days.

Her fingers brushed the chest, but she couldn't quite pull it to her. She climbed precariously onto one of the lower shelves to extend her reach, and slowly eased the chest out from its dark corner. It was heavy, but Charla was determined and she managed to pull it off the shelf without dropping it.

Placing it on the ground, she swung her long black braids over one shoulder and unlatched it. The chest was full to the brim of old baby clothes that Charla and her brother David had worn, along with some of the colorful, flowing robes their grandfather Old Dan had worn in the village where he'd grown up, the same village where Charla and David's parents had died.

Old Dan had been a strong presence in Charla's life, even after a sickness several years ago left him with twisted, almost useless legs. He could walk after a fashion, but it was very painful, so he mostly relied on his grandchildren to be his legs. He also relied on them to help him communicate, since his lack of teeth made his words difficult for others to understand.

Charla had always wondered about the village where she was born, where her mother was raised and married, but Old Dan had never taken them back for a visit. He wouldn't even say where the village was located. He just shook his head and mumbled "It doesn't matter" whenever Charla and David pressed him for information.

Charla laid aside the colorful robes and kept sorting through the detritus of her grandfather's ninety or so years.

There! The beautiful beaded bag had belonged to Charla's mother. Charla had always loved the bag and wanted to carry it to dances and other special occasions, but Old Dan shook his head and looked like he was going to cry each time she asked. She'd reluctantly left it in darkness on those other occasions, but she was determined to carry it for her wedding.

As Charla pulled the bag out, she saw there was a thin cord tangled around the bag's drawstring. She picked at the knot but it was too tight, so she pulled on the other end of the cord, hoping to create some slack in the knot. The cord was firmly attached to something, though, and wouldn't budge.

Annoyed, wishing she had a knife so she could just cut the cord, Charla dug down through the jumble of things to find the other end, which was caught under a small bundle of cloth. Charla tugged on the cord, but it still didn't budge. Sighing in frustration, she picked up the bundle and was surprised to find it was much heavier than its size would indicate. And it wasn't just a bundle of cloth… it felt like several layers of cloth wrapped around a small, solid object.

Curious, Charla began to unwrap the bundle. As she did, the air got heavier and hard to breathe, and a mist came over her eyes. She looked toward the faintly lit door of the barn, wondering if someone had started a fire outside, but the light from the lantern seemed undisturbed by smoke.

She blinked and rubbed her eyes, but that didn't help, so she shook her head and went on unwrapping the bundle.

It was much smaller than she'd expected, a tiny metal chest about the size of the palm of her hand and only a couple of inches deep. Charla picked at the clasp but it didn't move, so she wedged her thumb under it and pushed hard.

"Ow!" she cried as the clasp bit into her flesh, puncturing the skin so that a drop of blood seeped along the edge of the box. Charla pulled her thumb away to see how deep the cut was, and barely noticed when the lock sprang open. She forgot her thumb quickly, though, when a pale-yellow dust began to drift from the box. Puzzled, Charla ran a finger through the powder-filled box and then lifted it to her nose, sniffing. She didn't recognize the scent, which was bitter, but the powder was gritty, like sand…

Into her mind burst the image of a small village baking under a fierce yellow sun. Behind the village rose a snow-capped mountain, all jagged edges and cruel drop-offs. In the village she saw dark-skinned people like herself going about the chores of gathering water from a well and cooking over open fires.

Suddenly, all the people looked toward something that Charla couldn't see. A young man ran into the midst of the villagers, panting, with sweat dripping from his black skin. He spoke to them quickly, and their voices rose in surprise, questioning him and calling out to an old man in a brightly striped robe who was making his way toward them from the largest hut. When the old man reached the group, he listened carefully to what the boy said, turned to confer with some of the men around them, and then quickly gave some orders. Charla couldn't hear what he said, but the sharp tone of his voice and the vigor in his arms as he directed the villagers was urgent.

As the villagers scattered to do his bidding, the old man turned and looked straight at Charla. This time Charla heard him clearly, the words echoing in her mind.

"*Skaeweer*, come!"

The village disappeared and Charla was back in the barn. She saw everything around her plainly for a moment, then her eyes rolled up and she collapsed on the hard ground.

The Note

I'm getting married in two days!

Laughter lit Timothy Greene's blue eyes as joy ran through him, just as it had done ever since he realized he loved Charla. This type of love, this happiness, was new to him, traumatized as he'd been growing up with a violent father who regularly beat him, his mother, and sisters. His father's anger problem had come violently into the open when he'd attacked the king's daughter a few weeks ago, which earned him a special place in the Kingham Castle dungeons.

Greene shook his head firmly, determined not to let those painful thoughts intrude on such a glorious day, especially so early in the morning.

But a small part of him, a part he resolutely ignored, wondered if the same seeds of violence would ever cause him to strike out at Charla.

Reaching the house where Charla lived with her grandfather and brother, he knocked lightly on the back door, then pushed it to enter, but the door was locked. Frowning, Greene knocked a little louder and waited a moment before putting his ear to the crack of the door. He could hear no sounds of Charla moving around in the kitchen like she normally did at this time of day. Puzzled, Greene reached into his pocket for the extra key Charla had given him, which he'd never had cause to use before.

As he unlocked the door and stepped into the kitchen, he was surprised by the quiet. No food on the table, none cooking on the stove, no sounds of the inhabitants moving around in the back of the house.

"Hello?" Greene called, taking two long strides to the back of the house, calling for Charla as he went, but there was no one back there. Heart pounding, Greene circled Charla's bed to open the wardrobe. Her two daily dresses were gone, along with a lightweight cloak and her traveling bag. Glancing at the floor, Greene could see a gap in the row of shoes and boots. Her daily pair was gone.

Clothes missing, shoes missing. Greene's breath hitched in fear.

He quickly stepped across the small hall into the other bedroom, opened the wardrobe, and saw some of Old Dan and David's clothes were missing as well. His breath was coming fast now.

Two leaping steps took him back into the kitchen, where he searched for a note of any kind. Nothing on the kitchen table… but there, on the counter by the sink, lay a piece of paper.

Greene snatched it up and read it rapidly. He read it again slowly, trying to understand the message, then read it a third time disbelievingly. He sat down hard in one of the chairs and put his head between his knees until the dizziness passed.

The note didn't say where Charla had gone, but it did give a reason.

There was one other person who might know where Charla was. Greene stood up, note clenched in one hand, stumbled to the door, and ran toward the castle. He didn't notice the surprised faces that turned to watch him speed past, didn't hear the murmurs of concern.

He ran through the castle gates, straight up the hill to the castle, bursting through the closest door and up the stairs to the third floor.

He was breathing hard when he finally came to a stop and pounded on an ornately carved door. After a moment, the door opened to show the surprised face of a tall man with a mop of dark curly hair and gray eyes. Prince Phillip Martin had married Princess Aurora just two days previously. The prince was the former Captain of the King's Guards, so, like Greene and the other guards, he was known simply by his last name.

"Is Princess Aurora here?" Greene gasped, looking over Martin's shoulder. He saw the red hair and startled green eyes of the princess peeking around the door of the dressing room.

Pulling him into the room, Aurora insisted that Greene take a seat before he told them what was wrong. Greene opened his mouth, but the concern on their faces undid him. He buried his face in his hands as sobs wracked him.

"Greene, what in the world happened?" Aurora murmured, her hand stroking his wavy brown hair. Her worried eyes met Martin's, which reflected her concern. She turned back to Greene and noticed the note he was still clutching in one hand.

"What's this?" she asked, tugging on the paper.

Greene's sobs lessened for a moment and his hand gripped the paper tighter, then he let go and began to rock back and forth, moaning in pain.

Terrified, Aurora opened the note and scanned it quickly. "What is this?" she asked. "Where did you get it?" She read it again, frowning, then handed it to Martin.

Greene just continued moaning.

Martin read the note, but like Aurora, he didn't know what to make of it. He surveyed Greene for a moment, then said sternly, "Greene! Stop that noise and tell us what happened." The voice he used wasn't Martin's kind voice, but the stern voice of the captain who'd once ruled over the King's Guards. Aurora started to protest such unfeeling treatment, but then realized it was having the desired effect.

Greene stopped rocking in his chair and slowly straightened, his blue eyes full of tears. Silently taking the handkerchief Martin offered him, he said, voice breaking, "Charla and her family have disappeared, and all I could find was that note." The pain in his voice made Aurora's stomach clench. "She's left me. She's called off the wedding and left me."

Shocked, Aurora said, "Greene! Surely not! She loves you so much!"

Martin was re-reading the note. "What makes you think it's a note for you? It's addressed 'Dear friend.' Surely that's not the way she addresses you."

Greene said dully, "It's how she used to start our letters when we were first courting, before we said we loved each other. It makes sense that she'd use that now, when she's breaking off our engagement."

Aurora reached for the note in Martin's hand and read it again, slowly.

Dear friend,

I am so sorry, but it's just not working. Everything we do seems to make it worse instead of better! I need to take a break, put it aside for a while, so I can clear my mind.

Just let me think it over for a while, see if I can come up with something that works.

C

Aurora shook her head. "There's absolutely no *way* Charla wrote this note to you, certainly not to break off your engagement! She would *never* do that in a note! It doesn't even sound like that's what she's talking about!"

But as she read the letter for the third time, she could almost see how Greene was interpreting it. Charla wouldn't have left without letting someone know, so this note must be a reference to her absence. What else could she be talking about, if not her engagement?

Aurora couldn't make sense of the note, no matter how she read it.

Greene looked at her with dead eyes. "I was never good enough for Charla. I was sure one day she'd realize that, and decide she wanted nothing to do with me."

Martin studied him a moment and said, "Forget the note for a moment. Tell us exactly what you saw at Charla's house."

Greene said dully, staring at the floor, "Their clothes were missing along with their traveling bags. I looked for a note and I found that by the sink." He pressed the heels of his hands to his eyes, stood up and turned to leave, shaking his head. "I'm sorry, but I just want to be alone right now. I need to think everything over."

Aurora reached out to stop him, opening her mouth to argue, but Martin pulled her back. Shaking his head, he gently reached out to close the door behind Greene.

He said, "Greene can't hear you right now. He needs time to calm down. I agree with you about the note, though. It makes no sense the way Greene is interpreting it." He pondered a moment. "I think we need to go to Charla's house and see if there's anything Greene missed. Surely she wouldn't have just left without a word to *you*, even if she was upset with *him*."

Aurora and Martin searched the house and found clothes missing, but there were no signs of *why* the family had left so abruptly.

"Where in the world could they have gone? Especially just before the wedding?" Aurora asked in exasperation.

Martin shook his head and shrugged, frowning.

Sighing, Aurora said, "Well, I can send word to all the villages and guard outposts to let us know if they see Charla."

"Good idea," Martin said, pulling her close and kissing her forehead.

It's better that she left you now, when you still have good memories.
Greene could still faintly remember a time when his parents had been happy. In his childhood, there had been times of laughter in his family instead of the miasma of fear that filled the house in the later years.

He had once been surprised to see a look of immense sadness on his mother's face as she watched her husband rage through the house, breaking furniture and throwing beloved books in the fire. It was the first time Greene had considered that his mother must have once loved his father very much.

As much as he loved Charla.

So maybe it was better that she'd gone now, before the love turned to hate.

Cathy Greene looked up with a smile when her son walked in the door of her small house. She was surprised when Greene fell to his knees with a groan, his head dropping into her lap. "Mum," he whispered. "Mum…"

"What in the world, Timothy?" She stroked his hair, smoothing the waves down absentmindedly.

Greene only shook his head, but his whole body was shivering as if he were ill.

After a few moments, Cathy instinctively began to hum a lullaby, one that had soothed the young Timothy many times. Gradually, the shivers ceased and Greene lay quietly in her lap as her hand continued the gentle movement across his hair and down his back, the wordless hum bringing him a measure of peace.

Cathy stopped humming but continued stroking his hair. After a few moments, Greene said dully, "Charla left me."

The movement of her hand paused, then resumed. "What happened?" Cathy asked gently.

"I went to her house this morning but they were all gone. Charla, Old Dan and David. Bags packed, food missing, and a note in the kitchen saying she needed to take a 'break.' A break from *us*."

The most frightening thing to Cathy was the complete lack of tone in Timothy's voice, as if all his emotions had shut down. Timothy had always been so full of life, his laughter ringing through the house and almost banishing the shadows of his violent father.

Cathy remembered the joy and relief she'd felt when Greene introduced them to Charla, and later on shyly told her that Charla had agreed to marry him. From the very beginning, Cathy had felt a deep affection for Timothy's beloved. The girl's long-lashed eyes, the braided black hair falling down her back, the curve of her sweet mouth and her lovely figure made Cathy worry that her son had merely fallen for the girl's beauty. The warmth in the honey-colored eyes and the peace and strength in Charla's low voice had drawn Cathy to her, though, and they had become fast friends in the following weeks.

She just couldn't imagine the girl leaving Timothy with only a note. It made no sense, but her son was absolutely convinced it had happened, so right now all she could do was try to comfort him.

Greene stayed with his mother and younger sister Deirdre for lunch, but as soon as he was finished, he kissed his mother and walked out the door without a backward glance. He felt a sudden urge to run away from all this pain, but there was nowhere in Kingham Village that wouldn't remind him of Charla.

Greene Volunteers

Later that day, Anderson, the new Captain of the King's Guards, saw Greene go by the window of his office and called out, "Greene! C'mere a minute."

Greene appeared in the doorway, his body oddly stiff.

"Greene, we're looking for some guards to go to Arlesland on a special mission. You did some covert work on Princess Aurora's village tour, so I thought you might have some insight into the guards who accompanied you. Which would you recommend to go disguised into another kingdom?"

Greene asked, his lips as stiff as the rest of his body, "When would they have to leave?"

Anderson replied, "As soon as possible."

Greene stared at him for a moment, then mumbled something.

Anderson asked, "What?"

Greene stared at the ground, then looked up and said, "I can go."

Anderson frowned. "But the men will be leaving in just a few days. Charla surely won't want you to leave so soon after the wedding…"

Greene cleared his throat, shook his head and sighed. "The wedding's off." He paused, then went on. "Charla called it off."

Anderson sat back in his chair, speechless.

Martin looked up from the papers he was perusing when Anderson knocked on the door of his study. He'd recently turned his duties as Captain of the Guards over to Anderson, but the new captain valued his input.

He sat back in his chair and grinned as Anderson gave a bow and entered the room.

"I'm not sure I'll ever get used to being treated like a prince," he admitted with a light chuckle.

"Well, I'm sure there's at least one person who doesn't treat you like royalty," Anderson teased.

Martin laughed at the reference to his new wife. "Very true. In fact, she's been at pains to remind me she'll always outrank me!" He shook his head in mock frustration, then said, "So… what can I do for you, Anderson?"

"I just had an interesting conversation with Greene," Anderson said, taking a seat by Martin's desk. "He told me about Charla calling the wedding off, and he volunteered to go on the Arlesland mission.

Martin raised his eyebrows and whistled. "Really?"

Anderson continued, "I'm not sure he's in the right mental state, but I'm having a hard time finding the right guards for this mission. I need two, so if Greene could go, I'd only have to find one more."

Martin pondered a moment, then leaned back in his chair and called down the short hallway at the back of the room. "Aurora?"

A faint reply was heard. Martin raised his voice. "Would you come in here a minute?"

The princess walked into the room and made her way to Martin's chair, settling on the arm and leaning against her husband.

Martin told Aurora that Greene had volunteered for the Arlesland mission and she immediately began shaking her head. "No. Absolutely not. I've sent out messages via carrier pigeon to all the villages as well as the guard outposts about Charla and her family, and until we hear back from them, Greene isn't going anywhere."

Martin watched as she spoke, the determination on her face making him smile internally. Once Aurora got that look, it was hard to change her mind.

Personally, Martin wasn't as sanguine as she was about Charla's disappearance. It seemed clear to him that the family had been under no duress from outside forces when they packed up. Martin had the highest regard for Charla's grandfather Old Dan. His intellect hadn't suffered one bit from his advancing age, and although his lack of teeth made his speech hard to understand, Martin had carried on many highly detailed and complicated conversations with the old man over the years. If Old Dan had gone with Charla and David, Martin had no doubt they had a good reason for leaving.

He asked Anderson, "When are you planning for the guards to head to Arlesland?"

"King Richard wants to send them with King Alexander's entourage when they head back to Bagginsland so they can be disguised as King Alexander's guards. There's no evidence that King Uriah is watching the comings and goings between the kingdoms, but it makes sense to take precautions."

Martin was nodding. "That's good thinking."

Anderson continued, "King Alexander is planning to leave in a couple of days, probably on Thursday."

Aurora said, "That's when Charla and Greene are getting married." Her tone brooked no argument. "That gives us two days to find Charla. I *know* she'll be back."

She was quiet a moment, then turned back to Martin and searched his face. Ever since she'd been a child, she'd trusted his judgment absolutely. Now she saw patience and love on his face… and regret that she was probably going to be proven wrong about

Charla's wedding. She took a shaky breath. "You don't think she's coming back."

Martin took her hand and rubbed it gently. "I think she and Old Dan and David left for a good reason. I think it's doubtful they'll be back in time for the wedding. I don't understand that note Greene found… but the king said time is of the essence in this mission to Arlesland."

Squeezing her hand, Martin turned to Anderson. "As far as another guard to send with Greene… What about Jacobson?"

Anderson's eyebrows shot up and Aurora said in disbelief, "*Jacobson?* But he's such a chucklehead! He'd never be able to do a mission like that!"

Martin said slowly, "I disagree. I know Jacobson comes across as a bit lacking in brains, but I think he plays up the chucklehead persona to keep people from looking too closely at him. He doesn't like being the center of attention." He looked up at Aurora. "And you have to admit that he and Greene have become very close."

Greene and Jacobson both had violent fathers, and had inherited that anger. They'd bonded when Jacobson taught Greene some techniques to control his anger.

"And," Anderson added thoughtfully, "Greene and Jacobson are some of our strongest guards, so they can take care of themselves pretty easily."

"And when he forgets himself," Martin reminded him, "Jacobson is one of our best fighters."

It was true. Jacobson lost a lot of fights, but it seemed to be because he didn't like hurting the other men, not because he was a bad fighter.

Martin looked at Aurora, who grudgingly admitted, "King Alexander would probably be willing to leave Friday instead of Thursday, so if Charla isn't back by then…" She shrugged.

Anderson smiled, relieved to finally have a good plan. "Alright, I'll let Jacobson know he's definitely going, and I'll make a decision Thursday about Greene."

Martin nodded in agreement, and Aurora nodded in reluctance.

Greene, waking in his mother's house Wednesday, surveyed the blue sky outside the window with dull eyes. Part of him wanted to hope, along with Aurora, that Charla would return today in plenty of time for their wedding tomorrow, but it was a part that was easily silenced. Greene had had years of believing himself to be irreversibly broken, and the two months of joy he'd had with Charla couldn't overcome the ingrained belief that he wasn't worthy of love.

Greene heard his mother and sister Deirdre moving around in the other bedroom, and knew that soon they would be getting up to draw water from the well and begin their day. The least he could do was get the water for them.

He forced himself to sit up, get dressed and go out into the bright sunlight, trying to ignore the dark clouds in his heart.

By late that afternoon, Aurora had gone to the tower where the messenger pigeons were kept no fewer than five times, hoping to hear word about Charla. As soon as the pigeon keeper saw her coming the last three times, he'd shaken his head before she got all the way up the stairs, and she'd turned, defeated, and made her way back down.

It was getting too late to send out pigeons now, and of course the pigeon keeper already knew to alert her immediately if any word came of Charla. Her trips to the pigeon coop had just been a way to work off some of her nervous energy.

With tears in her heart, Aurora acknowledged that Charla wasn't coming back in time for the wedding.

Aurora knocked softly on Cathy Greene's door and raised her eyebrows inquiringly when Deirdre answered. The girl shook her head sadly, and stood back to let the princess in.

Nodding to Cathy Greene, who was preparing supper, Aurora went to the backyard and made her way to the darkest corner, where Greene had hidden himself away. He sat on a bench tucked under a heavy flowering vine, head down and shoulders slumped. Aurora had never seen anything so pitiful in her life. A small thought flitted through her mind, wondering if that was what she'd looked like years ago when a misunderstanding with Martin had broken her heart. Remembering the desolation she'd felt, Aurora sat down beside Greene and pulled him into her arms, rocking him like a child. He laid his head against hers and leaned into her, seeming too exhausted to hold himself up.

Aurora had no idea how long they sat that way, but the evening was darkening when Greene's mother called him into supper. Cathy invited Aurora to stay for supper, but she shook her head and said, "I need to get back, but thank you." She motioned for the older woman to follow her to the door, where she said in a low voice, "Let me know at once if he needs anything during the night. That's an order," she said, looking firmly into Cathy's eyes. The woman nodded and closed the door behind her.

Aurora made her way to the castle, up the stairs to the third-floor suite she shared with Martin, and dissolved in tears in his arms.

Wedding Day

Thursday. The day Greene and Charla had planned to marry.

The sun was fully up when Aurora found Greene sitting in the pavilion by the stream where he and Charla had planned to say their vows. The birds were singing, and butterflies and dragonflies flitted through the tent.

It was the most beautiful autumn day.

As Aurora walked up the aisle, Greene turned in his chair to face her. To her surprise, the misery, the shock, the blankness of the previous two days was gone. His face was calm, his eyes clear. He was even able to give her a small smile, although it was more a matter of muscle memory than an actual smile.

"How are you?" Aurora asked softly, sitting down beside him and taking his hand.

"Alright," he responded and turned back to look at the front of the tent where the arch that Charla had planned to cover in white roses and pink sweet peas stood bare, a shaft of sunlight making the wood gleam like gold.

Aurora's eyes followed his and she murmured, "It would've

been so beautiful…" She glanced at Greene in time to see a tear slip down his cheek. Turning away to give him privacy, she said softly, "I'm glad to see you looking better."

Greene nodded. "I couldn't seem to help myself the past couple of days. It felt like I was drowning. But a few minutes ago, when the sun came over the top of the trees and shone into the pavilion, it was like I'd finally managed to reach the surface."

His eyes slid to the side of the pavilion, where an old apple tree with a deeply gnarled trunk leaned its branches over the creek, some of the leaves touching the water.

"That tree has seen so much," he mused. "It's survived all these years, through storms and lightning. It's twisted, and the trunk is covered in burls so you almost can't see the original shape. And yet, somehow, it's so beautiful… hard times have made it so."

He was silent a moment, then he turned to Aurora and said, "Charla's note said she needed to think things over. She didn't say she'd definitely made up her mind that we couldn't be together." He took a deep breath and said, "I love her too much to let her go without a fight. I have to become the man she wanted me to be, the man I wanted to be *for* her. I thought I had done everything I could, but I realize now that I didn't dig deep enough. I don't know how long it will take, but I can do it, and when I do, I'll find her and beg her to give me another chance. I won't give up. I'll become a better man."

Aurora felt tears start to her eyes. She remembered the night he'd tried to protect her and had almost killed a man. That had been the first time Greene had tried to change himself drastically.

"I know you can," she whispered, cupping his cheek in her hand. Her throat was too tight to do more than whisper, but she said, "You've come so far in just a few months, Greene. You're already more in control of your emotions. I know how much you love Charla, and I know that if you set your mind to it, you can become the man you want to be."

Greene smiled and turned his head to kiss her palm. Then he turned back toward the front of the pavilion. "I need to get right away in order to do this. I need something to take my mind off missing Charla, something to challenge me. I want to do the

Arlesland mission." He turned toward her again. "Will you support me?"

Aurora sighed and nodded. "Let's go talk to Anderson."

Meeting with Princess Morgana

A few hours later, Greene and his fellow guard Jacobson were walking toward the king's weapons room. This meeting with the king would give Greene and Jacobson the information about Arlesland that made the mission imperative.

When Greene walked into the room behind Jacobson, he was surprised to see a woman chatting quietly with the king and Captain Anderson. She turned toward them and Greene recognized her as a woman he'd seen at Aurora and Martin's wedding. She'd been with the royal family of Vallenland, the kingdom southwest of Archenland.

He'd only gotten a glimpse of her that night, but now he could see that her hair was dark brown and her eyes a warm golden. She seemed to be a few years older than him, in her late twenties or early thirties.

King Richard said, "Princess Morgana, allow me to introduce you to King's Guards Greene and Jacobson." To Greene and Jacobson he said, "Princess Morgana is the adopted daughter of King Rudolph and Queen Valeria of Vallenland."

Greene and Jacobson bowed to the princess and murmured greetings as the king motioned for them to take their seats.

The king continued, "Did either of you meet Morgana's adopted brother Prince John at Aurora's wedding?"

Greene nodded. "I met him just for a moment, when Princess Aurora introduced Charla and me to Prince John and his wife." Greene's voice hitched a moment when he said Charla's name, but he managed to keep talking.

Princess Morgana asked, "Did you hear how my brother John and his wife Ceci came to fall in love?"

Puzzled, Greene shook his head.

Morgana smiled. "It's rather a long story, so I'll just tell you that Ceci was kidnapped and grew up as a commoner in Arlesland. My brother John went to Arlesland to find her, and had to pay a visit to King Uriah while he was there. He said Uriah was incredibly rude, and almost seemed to be trying to force a fight with him."

King Richard interjected, "Which doesn't surprise me. Uriah is a slippery one. He promises things and then acts like he doesn't remember. Acts like you've insulted him grievously on every concession he has to make, that sort of thing." King Richard shook his head. "But please continue, Morgana."

She took a deep breath. "Another important thing for you to know about John's trip to Arlesland is that he deeply offended King Uriah, and Uriah later attempted to kill him."

Jacobson's mouth dropped open as Greene exclaimed, "The man must be mad!"

King Richard nodded. "Exactly. Something is terribly wrong with Uriah's judgment and he seems to be trying to force a war, so we want to be as prepared as possible. Your goal in Arlesland is to gather all the information you can about the state of the kingdom in general, but especially about Uriah's military strength. We certainly have no desire to start a war with him, but he's giving every indication that he has no such qualms.

"Uriah is notorious for how horribly he treats his subjects, but one of the most troubling rumors we've heard is that he tells his people that their hardships are the direct result of the northern kingdoms' refusal to trade with him. We believe he may be using these lies to foment hatred for the north that will lead his people to die for him in a war."

The king looked sternly at Greene and Jacobson and said, "Do not mention what I'm about to tell you to Aurora or Martin. I will tell them in a few days, but I want them to have another day or two as newlyweds before they're thrown back into the intrigues of royal life."

Surprised, Greene and Jacobson nodded, faces serious.

King Richard continued, "I won't go into all the details, but on the evening of Aurora and Martin's wedding, I received information that Uriah was involved in attacks on Aurora and Martin which were meant to put a puppet of Uriah's in succession for the thrones of both my kingdom and Bagginsland."

Greene and Jacobson were stunned into silence.

King Richard said, "That's why this mission to Arlesland is so important. We have to find out what else Uriah may be planning, and we *must* find out how powerful his position is for open war."

King Richard continued, "Morgana, tell us what John told you about the general conditions in Arlesland."

"It was like something you'd expect to see in Sutherne," Morgana said.

The kingdoms of Bryten didn't have much communication with the southern continent of Sutherne because the Ocean of Faer between the continents was prone to violent storms and dangerous currents, making travel treacherous. What *was* known was that for many centuries Sutherne had been far behind Bryten in terms of civilization. The kingdoms of Sutherne were engaged in constant internal strife, rarely coming together long enough to choose leaders who would work to make their lives better. There were constant wars, burning of villages, pillaging, rape and killing.

So comparing Uriah's kingdom to Sutherne was a serious insult.

Morgana continued, "John said the people of Arlesland were suspicious of strangers, dirty, terribly thin, and seemed unused to kindness. But it was the information we learned from John's wife Ceci that gave us real insight into Uriah and Arlesland.

"Ceci said Uriah is mercurial. He'll have a favorite noble one week, and the next week they're locked in his dungeon. That kind of giving and taking of approval makes his subjects constantly on edge, never knowing whether what they do will bring his approbation or punishment, or even when the punishment will come. Uriah is known to hold grudges for decades before he finally takes revenge."

Greene asked King Richard, "Has he always been that way?"

The king shook his head. "No. I remember my father telling me about a visit he'd made to Arlesland when Uriah was a teenager. He said young Uriah was thoughtful, not at all hotheaded like his father."

King Richard shrugged. "From what I've heard, that all changed when Uriah was about nineteen or twenty. By the time I met Uriah five years later, he was unrecognizable as the thoughtful young man my father had met. I don't think anyone knows for sure what happened, but it had something to do with a friend of Uriah's getting killed."

Morgana was nodding. "The story John uncovered while he was in Arlesland was that Uriah was at a local tavern one night when a man with an ax burst into the room and killed one of Uriah's good friends in front of him. The madman cut off his friend's head, which must have been horrific to witness. That's apparently what changed Uriah, making him distrustful and wary of everyone."

King Richard said, "Something certainly wrought a terrible change in him. So," he turned to Greene and Jacobson, "you must be on your guard at all times when you're in Arlesland. A paranoid king makes for paranoid subjects. Find out what you can, but don't put yourselves in deadly danger. We're depending on your report."

A Worthy King

As his valet dressed him, King Uriah unrolled the letter he'd received some weeks ago and re-read it.

If you want my help, you must prove you deserve it. No more of your prevarications and delays. You say you want to conquer the northern kingdoms, to rule all of Bryten as I rule Sutherne. But you've done nothing to achieve that goal.

You say you're capable of leading this war. Where is your army? What horses, armor and battle gear do you have?

I refuse to commit my men until you prove your worth.

-R-

Uriah scowled. How did she expect him to get those things when his kingdom was full of hungry mouths and farms that barely produced enough to pay his taxes?

He stalked to the window and looked out at the market in the square below. Scrawny cattle, puny vegetables, dirty people. *That's* what his kingdom consisted of.

He frowned down at the letter. Did he really want to abase himself in order to win her support? Did he really need her to conquer the north?

Yes. He did.

Furious, the king slapped away the hand of his valet, who was attempting to fasten a silk cloak around his neck. "Enough!" he barked, screwing up the note from the Sutherne queen and throwing it into the fire as he left the room.

As he strode down the hall, anger and humiliation in every step, he barely saw the castle servants bowing and curtsying to him, barely noticed the fearful love in their eyes before they dropped their gaze respectfully to the floor.

He stopped in front of double doors covered in carvings inlaid with gold and silver, and waited impatiently for the guard to unlock the doors. As they were thrown open, light spilled out.

Sunlight from windows too narrow to admit a thief fell on heaps of gold spilling from sacks on the floor, caskets full of jewels, golden suits of armor inlaid with jewels, ropes of pearls. Uriah's father's treasure room had been impressive, but Uriah's was three times its size. The guards in charge of it had initially attempted to keep the gold coins in their chests, the jewels in their caskets, but one day the chests would no longer close. In frustration, the guards simply dumped the bags of coins on the floor, and since then organization of the treasure had given way to simple expedience. It was all they could do to record the steady stream of contributions that came in from commoners and nobles alike.

Uriah stood in the doorway, looking around in satisfaction. He felt no love for his people, no love for the nobles who professed to be his friends, no love for his army, and certainly no love for a woman. But he was sure the warmth in his heart as he gazed at his treasure was true love.

With a snap of his fingers, he demanded the latest record of contributions. He frowned down at the list, noting that the amount given in the past month had fallen significantly from the previous month's.

His people had been squeezed until they were almost dry. That was the main reason he wanted to control the northern kingdoms. The thought of all the gold waiting for him in the treasure rooms of the north made his heart race and his mouth water. Those kings could never appreciate their bounty the way he could. It was only right that he take it.

He left the room, the doors slamming behind him, and set off for his audience chamber. He had to convince his people to somehow dredge up the capital he needed to outfit his army.

The audience chamber was full. There were no commoners, because of course Uriah wouldn't let any of his filthy, starving people near him. Being surrounded by noble sycophants was bad enough.

Uriah climbed the steps to his throne as a phalanx of guards, led by their captain, surrounded the platform.

A servant intoned, "Hear ye now. Our gracious and loving King Uriah has come to listen. Approach him in supplication."

And they came, nobles dressed in velvet and silk, all bowing and cringing, ready to bore him with their whining requests. Inwardly scowling, Uriah thought that if he had to listen to them, he'd be sick.

But as they raised their eyes, he showed them only the benevolent face of their beloved king. Leaning forward with a smile, he motioned for the court scribe to take down his words and said, "My dear children. I know you chafe under the burdens I have placed on you, but our goal is very near. This morning I received a note from the Queen of Sutherne, pledging her support for our war against the north. We must make one more push for the capital we need in order to raise our army. To this end, I am increasing your taxes, but by only a small amount. I assure you that the end is near, and that all your sacrifice will be rewarded. Bear with me a little longer, give everything you can, and I assure you we will be successful."

As he looked around the room, he saw confident nods from his most loyal nobles. They trusted him completely. There were one or two, however, with frowns on their faces. Uriah signaled to his captain, who nodded and quietly ordered his men to delay those nobles for questioning.

While the nobles were still focused on his words, Uriah left the room, ignoring the protests from those alert enough to realize he had no intention of hearing their supplications that day. Uriah motioned the court scribe to follow him to a balcony that overlooked the marketplace, below which commoners gathered each day, hoping the king would grace them with a wave. He had something more important than a wave in mind that day, though.

As he walked onto the balcony, a cheer went up, catching the attention of the commoners in the marketplace, who left the stalls to stand looking up at their king.

At a motion from Uriah, the court scribe held up the parchment on which the speech to the nobles had been recorded, and Uriah read it word-for-word to the commoners below. For them, though, he added a special message.

"My children, I have a request for you. As you know, everything I do in preparation for war with the north is for your benefit. It is cruel for the northern kingdoms to refuse to trade with us, cruel of them to keep the riches of the northern mines to themselves. You are my precious children, and you deserve better!"

A cheer went up from the malnourished people below him.

"To conquer the northern kingdoms, I must prove to the Queen of Sutherne that my people believe in the cause. I need an army of you, my beloved children, to do that. As you love me, I ask that you send your young men to join this effort to ensure a prosperous future for our land, a future for your children's children. I trust you will not fail me in this time of need. I bless each of you for your sacrifice!"

As Uriah gave a gracious wave to acknowledge the cheers following his lie, he noticed the adulation seemed a bit ragged. It was possible his children were starting to think their continued sacrifices came at too high a cost.

But he could milk them a little longer. They were not yet at the point of rebellion. One of Uriah's most important acts as a king was to give his people just enough affection to ensure that when he was displeased, they would desperately try to regain his love. They thought it was their fault he was angry, and that if they gave him more of what they could ill afford, eventually he'd realize how deserving of love they were.

He wouldn't, of course.

Timmy and Johnny

The morning after their meeting with Princess Morgana and King Richard, Greene and Jacobson set off with the Bagginsland entourage, and two nights later they were sliding down ropes from the Bagginsland cliffs into Arlesland, where smuggled horses and supplies awaited them.

They bedded down a couple of miles south of the border, lighting no fire to reveal their presence, simply tying the horses securely to trees, pulling out some dried meat and flat bread to make a simple meal, and falling into an exhausted sleep as soon as they were prone.

The next morning, Greene awoke to a laughing voice calling, "Timmy! Wake up! It's time for a delicious meal of dried meat!"

Greene groaned and sat up, shooting a look of mock disgust at Jacobson. They wanted to act like commoners, which meant they couldn't call each other by their last names, as guards were wont to do. Jacobson had reluctantly revealed that his first name was Johnny, and when Greene had smothered a chuckle at the boyish moniker,

Jacobson declared his determination to call Greene "Timmy," rather than Timothy.

Jacobson used every opportunity to use Greene's new nickname, with Greene returning the kindness, so after a few hours they were quite comfortable answering to the "new" names.

After breakfast, they rubbed some dirt into the shaggy coats of their horses to make them less respectable looking, and made their way to the main road south into Arlesland.

Jacobson turned to look at the empty, potholed road behind them, and then at the empty, potholed road before them. "Doesn't seem a very popular route," he said.

"No," Greene replied, but at that moment a pair of horses trotted around a curve ahead of them. As the horses approached, Greene could see that the men astride them were wearing jackets with a royal crest on the shoulder. The men's matching scowls completed the uniform of Arlesland guards.

"Halt in the name of King Uriah!" the younger of the two soldiers called.

"Get down!" the older soldier commanded, waving an arm at them.

Greene and Jacobson obeyed and stood holding the reins of their horses as the younger soldier dismounted and walked over to them. His eyes met Greene's and he snarled, "Eyes on the ground, fool," and buffeted Greene about the ears. It was all Greene could do to feign weakness as he hunched away from the blows.

"Where are you from?" the older soldier sneered from atop his horse, looking them over from head to toe as the younger man searched their packs.

Greene, eyes on the ground, replied sullenly, "Bagginsland. On the way to visit family in Reimsland."

"Bagginsland, eh? What were you doing up there?"

Greene shrugged. "Looking for work."

The man barked a laugh. "Well, if you didn't find any in Bagginsland, you certainly won't find any here in Arlesland!"

The younger soldier had finished his search. He closed up the last sack on Jacobson's horse and moved away, tossing a bag of silver in his hands. Jacobson made a sound of fury and started toward him.

"Ah! No, no, no!" The soldier shook his head and drew his dagger. Jacobson stopped and the soldier mounted his horse, tucking the silver into his saddlebag. "This is just a toll. A toll on strangers, you might say," he snickered and the older soldier laughed.

Greene's blood was boiling. He and Jacobson had some silver in their pockets, but that bag was most of what they'd been planning to live on during the mission. A glance at Jacobson showed him that his fellow guard's face was bright red, his jaw clenched. But neither of them said a word.

"Smart. Very smart." The younger soldier nodded. "Stay out of trouble now, *strangers*."

And they rode off, leaving Greene and Jacobson seething in the middle of the road.

"Well, I guess it could've been worse," Jacobson muttered as they remounted and followed slowly after the soldiers. "They could've taken the horses, too, or thrown us in jail."

Greene nodded, but his jaw was still clenched. He told himself to relax, that it didn't really matter, that dwelling on it wouldn't change anything. "I already hate this place," he said, and Jacobson nodded agreement. They rode on in silence.

They stopped at a tavern that night, using one of their precious silver coins to buy two tankards of beer and a meal so they could listen to the local gossip. They didn't hear much, though, except how badly the harvest was going on the local farms (too little rain this year… and the year before).

Listening with one ear, Jacobson was mostly thinking about the pitiful quality of the food when he noticed a pair of eyes floating in midair over by the fireplace. Blinking, Jacobson squinted and realized the eyes were attached to a small boy who crouched among the soot. The boy's bare feet were completely black, as were his hands, and his clothes and face were almost as dirty.

The boy was staring at him, eyes wide. Jacobson surveyed him a moment, then tried a smile. The boy stared at him, then hesitantly smiled back. Jacobson made a silly face and the boy grinned. After a few more silly faces and grins, Jacobson surreptitiously flipped one of his precious coins toward the fireplace. The boy darted out to grab it before disappearing back into the shadows.

Jacobson grinned and went back to his sad mashed potatoes.

From Greene's point of view, the evening was a bit of a waste. The food wasn't worth the precious coins they'd spent on it, nor had they picked up any important gossip. Greene was just getting ready to suggest they leave when Jacobson nudged him, nodding toward a group of men at a table in the far corner.

Greene looked over and saw a young barmaid struggling with a man who had pulled her down onto his lap. Greene's heart began to race at the look of fear on the girl's face as she tried to break free. Her captor, a burly middle-aged man, was holding her tightly clamped to him with one arm, his other hand cruelly gripping her jaw as he pulled her face around to his.

Greene had seen men in their cups make unwelcome advances to women, but usually the men could be easily hauled out of the tavern and sent home to sleep it off. This man seemed completely sober, not sloppy drunk.

The most terrifying thing about the whole scene was that it was done in complete silence except for the girl's whimpers of fear. It wasn't a stupid, drunken assault; it was a cold-blooded one.

Even worse, the man's friends were sitting back in their chairs, watching with grim smiles, as if waiting for a turn.

Greene glanced at the bar and saw that the tavern owner was studiously ignoring what was happening, for which he couldn't much blame him. All the men around the girl looked to be strong and tough, unlikely to back down from a fight.

Greene sighed inwardly. He and Jacobson were about to blow their low profile.

The girl managed to wrench her head away, which made the man snarl and grab the neck of her blouse. It ripped, making the girl cry out and redouble her efforts as Greene and Jacobson pushed their chairs back with a screech and stood up.

The men around the girl looked toward Greene and Jacobson. There was a pause, then they shoved their own chairs back, menace in their scowls and bunched fists.

Greene and Jacobson had talked about situations like this, intense moments when their blood boiled. The most important thing in the next few minutes was that they not lose their tempers and kill anyone, so they needed to lighten things up.

"Well now," drawled Jacobson, casually crossing his arms over his chest so his biceps bulged beneath the sleeves of his shirt. "Seems like the lady doesn't want to kiss you, for which I can't blame her, seeing as I can smell you from here." He curled his lip and sneered.

Greene laughed as his heart rate steadied. Jacobson could always make him laugh. He said, "And even if you didn't smell like a pigsty, I'm pretty sure the lady wouldn't want to put her mouth anywhere near those mossy teeth of yours." He grimaced.

The insults had the desired effect. Fury on his face, the man swung the girl off his lap and she stumbled against the wall as he surged toward Greene and Jacobson.

"You ain't from around here, are ya?" Mossy Teeth sneered.

"No, for which we're grateful," Greene said sincerely.

The men snarled and moved forward as one. Greene felt his blood pressure rising again, but fortunately the men in front of him were menacing, but not very bright. They set up the next punchline themselves.

"Well, if'n you *were*, you'd know not to mess with us," Mossy Teeth said viciously. "We do *what* we want, *when* we want, to *whoever* we want."

"Well, that makes life easier, which is probably good, judging by your low forehead," Jacobson said sympathetically.

That did it. There was no more gay repartee, just punching and kicking, and beer steins slung against heads.

When the melee was done, Greene and Jacobson grinned and shook hands over the unconscious bodies on the floor, and turned toward the door just as an unwelcome voice spoke.

"Now, I thought I told you boys to stay out of trouble."

Help from a Small Friend

The grins slid off their faces as Greene and Jacobson turned to face the young soldier who'd stolen their silver. The man was smiling as a couple of his fellow guards followed him into the tavern.

Greene and Jacobson glanced at each other, then simultaneously picked up chairs, threw them at the soldiers, and ran for the kitchen. A small figure darted ahead of them and held open the back door as they raced through, Jacobson throwing a grin at the boy as they passed.

Greene and Jacobson crouched motionless in the darkness of a stable they'd found down several twisting alleys.

Listening carefully, they heard no sounds of pursuit, only distant shouts. After a few minutes, even those died away, making them sure that the guards had returned to their liquid refreshment.

"I bet they'll put the word out to arrest us now, though," Greene whispered. Jacobson nodded and dropped onto a bench in the center of the stable. All around them, horses quietly enjoyed their evening repast, a few heads with liquid eyes peering over the stall doors to regard the interlopers calmly.

"Of all the things we didn't need," Jacobson griped softly. "No bag of silver and now no horses." Their horses, along with their saddlebags, were back at the tavern.

Jacobson looked at the horses around them and turned back to Greene with bright eyes. "Hey! We could…" Then his face fell as he got a better look at one of the horses, which had a brand on its shoulder. No way could they sneak branded horses out the village gate.

Greene sighed. They'd known the mission in Arlesland would be rough, but they'd hoped to keep their precious supplies.

"But what else could we do?" Jacobson asked. "We couldn't leave that barmaid to those men."

Greene nodded. "Just our bad luck that soldier showed up."

Jacobson grunted.

Captain Anderson had mentioned how glad he was that Greene was going on the mission. He'd said, "We need someone who can think quickly on their feet and not get distracted by whatever happens. You have to do whatever it takes to go unnoticed and make sure the mission succeeds."

Well, they hadn't done a very good job so far. Two run-ins with Uriah's soldiers on their first day.

Sighing, Greene followed Jacobson up the ladder to the loft and bedded down in the pile of hay there.

The sounds of the stable lads woke them early the next morning. Sunlight was streaming through the cracks in the walls as Greene and Jacobson sat up, brushing hay from their hair and clothes. Looking out a window in the back of the loft, they saw that the stable backed up to the woods that surrounded the village. One large tree had branches that almost brushed the stable wall.

The sounds of the stable lads faded below. Jacobson carefully looked down and confirmed that the stable was empty. In a town this size, the lads would look after more than one stable, so Greene and Jacobson surmised they wouldn't be back, but the lads would still be nearby, so they couldn't risk leaving the barn by the front door.

After an argument about who should have the honor of raiding the chicken coop they could see from the window, Jacobson lost and resignedly squeezed through the loft window and made an awkward leap into the nearest tree, clutching branches and shimmying his way down to land with a soft thump on the ground. Glancing side to side, he ran hunched over to the chicken coop and quickly extracted several eggs from the softly clucking hens. As he ran back to the stables, he suddenly stopped and crouched down behind a broken-down wagon.

Placing the eggs carefully on the ground, Jacobson slowly stood up, his attention fixed on something Greene couldn't see, then darted out of view, coming back a few minutes later grinning ear to ear.

Puzzled, Greene leaned out the loft window and caught the eggs Jacobson threw up to him one at a time. As Jacobson threw the last egg, a bird startled out of the tree next to Greene, making him miss the egg, which plummeted straight back down onto Jacobson's upturned face. Greene managed to smother his laugh, but it was a close thing.

Grinning, he watched as Jacobson wiped the egg off and turned to glare up at him before leaping to catch the lowest hanging branch of the tree. By the time Jacobson reached the top, he'd regained his normally sunny disposition and was grinning as he wormed his way back into the window.

Dropping softly to the floor of the loft, Jacobson grinned bigger, then unbuttoned his shirt proudly. A bounty of small potatoes, carrots and onions poured forth, and Jacobson reached around inside the back of his shirt to produce a couple of ears of corn.

Greene's mouth was wide open. "It's a feast!" he said, lifting shining eyes to Jacobson.

"Yeah, well, you'd better not eat it all, *Timmy*, because who knows when we'll be this lucky again," Jacobson growled. "There was a lot more, but I was afraid to take much. I left one of my coins to pay for it."

Greene had started to tuck into the meal when Jacobson froze beside him, staring over his shoulder at the hay bales.

"What?" Greene whispered, not daring to turn around.

Suddenly, Jacobson's face cleared and he said softly, "It's alright. You can come out."

Turning, Greene saw a small, dirty face peeking out of the hay bale. As the child slowly crawled out, Greene realized it was a soot boy, in charge of taking care of the fires at public establishments.

"He was at the tavern where we ate last night," Jacobson murmured.

"Oh, right! He opened the back door for us!"

Jacobson nodded as he held out a potato to the boy, who devoured it in a few bites and looked hopefully at Jacobson for more. Chuckling, Jacobson handed him vegetables and eggs and watched them disappear into the small mouth.

Greene watched Jacobson give away a large portion of his share of the food, shooting a rueful glance at Greene as he did so. Greene grinned and continued eating his own share.

When the child's chewing slowed and he stopped halfway through his third carrot, Jacobson asked, "Where are your parents?"

The child shrugged as he stared down at the carrot. "Dunno. Never had a Pa, and me mam disappeared." His face screwed up as he said the last part, but he ducked his head and didn't cry.

Greene glanced at Jacobson, who said, "Where do you live now?"

The child shrugged again.

Jacobson persisted. "Do you live at the tavern?"

The child hesitated, then said, "Not supposed to, but sometimes I hides until the old man goes to bed, then I sneaks out to sleep by the fire."

Frowning, Jacobson asked, "Does he feed you?"

The child nodded. "I eats whatever's left on the plates. Maybe there's food, maybe there's not." He suddenly glanced up ferociously at the men. "But I can take care of meself!" he scowled.

Greene nodded earnestly, but his heart broke for the boy. He exchanged a glance with Jacobson and knew what the other man was thinking, but they couldn't take a little boy with them. The child's life wasn't perfect here, but it was his home and he had someplace where at least he was warm and fed at semi-regular intervals. He didn't look any thinner than the majority of the Arleslanders they'd already seen, and if he went with Greene and Jacobson, he might end up in terrible danger.

So Greene shook his head at Jacobson, whose face fell before he reluctantly nodded in agreement.

"What's your name?" Jacobson asked the boy gently.

"Tommy," he said.

Jacobson laughed. "Well, you fit right in with us. I'm Johnny and this is Timmy. Johnny, Timmy and Tommy!"

The boy gave a delighted laugh, his smile wide and white in his dirty face.

"But you have to promise not to tell anyone where we are, alright?" Greene said seriously, holding the little boy's gaze intently.

The dirty head nodded, eyes wide. "Wouldn't have no one to tell, even if'n I wanted to," he admitted. "Don't nobody care what I say. 'Just do your work, Tommy, and no mumbling!'" he quoted, scowling.

Jacobson tousled his hair. "Well, *we* care. You're a good kid, and we appreciate the help you gave us last night."

Tommy's small shoulders shrugged as he regarded the half of a carrot he still held. "Don't worry 'bout me. Won't tell nobody nothing. I'm true to you," he added gruffly.

Jacobson cast another pleading glance at Greene, who shook his head firmly.

As Tommy listened with wide eyes, Greene and Jacobson talked over their options for leaving without attracting the attention of the guards at the village gates.

"We'll have to split up to have any chance of making it through the gates," Greene said. "We're taller than most of the men in this town, but if we slouch and walk out with several people who are leaving, we might manage to go unnoticed."

Greene didn't like the idea of splitting up, and he really didn't think they'd manage to go unnoticed either way, since they were obviously more well fed than the vast majority of the Arleslanders. They'd rubbed dirt into their hair and clothes, but they couldn't do anything to disguise their muscular build.

Scooting forward, little Tommy said hesitantly, "You need a way out of the village?"

Greene and Jacobson nodded.

"I might know a way," the child said. "Wait here." With that, he climbed through the hay loft window, launched himself into the same tree Jacobson had used, and shinnied down the trunk like a monkey, running into the woods as they watched.

An hour later, Greene and Jacobson were about to give up on Tommy and try to make their own way to the village gate when they heard sounds coming from the ladder up to the hayloft. Quickly, they ducked behind some hay, only raising their heads when they heard a soft call. "It's me! Come out!"

Tommy's head was sticking up over the loft floor. He waved them to the ladder. "It's safe. I found a way out of the village." He motioned them urgently when they hesitated.

Greene and Jacobson exchanged a glance, then followed the child down the ladder.

The boy led them through narrow, deserted alleyways until they reached the other side of town, then held his finger over his lips for silence and crept slowly toward the marketplace ahead of them. As they approached the end of the alley, Tommy stopped and indicated they should stay where they were while he went ahead. A few moments later, he was running softly back to them, motioning them to follow.

Tommy reached the end of the alley again, glancing casually side to side, then motioned them forward, emphatically pointing to the other side of the alley opening. Crouching, Greene carefully looked around the corner of the alley and saw a wagon only a few steps away. The high sides hid the marketplace from view.

His sense of danger still on high alert, Greene glanced to the other side of the alley, where another large wagon stood. Tommy urgently pointed them toward the first wagon, then darted around to the front of it.

Greene and Jacobson crept from the alley just as a man stepped to the back of the wagon, making Greene's heart pound in fear. As he was readying himself to fight, the man unhooked the flap of a deep shelf in the side of the wagon where supplies were often stored. The exposed space was long enough for Greene and Jacobson to climb into, which they promptly did when the man gestured impatiently.

The flap was raised and latched, and Greene and Jacobson found themselves in a space a couple of feet high which stretched the entire width of the wagon, leaving a couple of feet on either side of them. There were gaps in the planks both above and below them, so they could easily hear the conversation of the people coming to buy vegetables, and could even feel a bit of the breeze which swirled through the marketplace.

Tommy's face briefly appeared at one of the cracks in the planks on the back side of the wagon. He grinned as Jacobson slipped him a small coin, and waved before disappearing.

Jacobson turned his head to see Greene looking at him with a knowing smile. He shrugged. "I know, I know. But he needs it more than we do. More than *you* do, anyway. Scoot over so your big belly isn't crowding me so much."

Chuckling, Greene moved his flat belly and the rest of him a scant inch to the right.

Being the first time in a couple of days that they'd felt safe, it wasn't much of a surprise that after an hour both Greene and Jacobson drifted into sleep. They were awakened once by the man opening the flap to the shelf and quickly pressing some apples into Jacobson's hand before he shut the door again. Jacobson passed half the apples to Greene and they munched the meal quietly before again falling asleep.

When Greene next awakened, he noticed there was significantly more light in their hiding space. Pondering, he realized that the crates of vegetables above them that had filled the wagon earlier were mostly gone.

Turning his head, he saw that Jacobson was awake as well. Jacobson said softly, "It looks like they've sold most of their wares for the day. We'll probably be moving on soon."

Just as Greene nodded, the shelf door opened and the wagon owner peered inside. He hissed, "Shift this way as far as you can."

Jacobson shifted toward the closing flap and Greene followed. In a moment, the flap next to Greene opened. Some bound cornstalks were shoved into the space he'd recently occupied. Narrow crates were then stacked on the other side of the cornstalks, and the flap was shut. A moment passed, and then the flap on Jacobson's side was opened again and an impatient hand waved them to shift to the other side, whereupon the same process with the cornstalks followed.

Greene and Jacobson were now squashed against each other by the cornstalks on either side, but not enough to be uncomfortable, and they were happy to be squashed if it meant they would go undiscovered at the village gate.

Additional cornstalks were loaded into the empty wagon bed above them so that the light in the space where Greene and Jacobson lay was completely blocked out. A few minutes more, and the wagon started moving.

Noises around them indicated that the other sellers in the market were also packing up and heading for the village gates. The buzz of conversation grew louder and Greene and Jacobson knew they must have reached the mass of people who were slowly passing through the gate under the eyes of watchful guards.

There was a heart-stopping moment when the guards halted their wagon, casually questioned the driver as to the contents, and opened the flaps of the shelf in which Greene and Jacobson were hiding. Greene held his breath and squeezed his eyes shut, the childish urge to hide overcoming logic for a moment.

The guards must have given only cursory glances at the cornstalks and other items, because the flaps were almost immediately shut, a shuffling above their heads indicating a similarly cursory exploration of the supplies above them.

One of the guards was talking to the wagon's owner. "Remember the king is increasing quotas next month, so be sure you bring extra vegetables."

A grunt of assent came and the wagon rolled through the gates.

As his heartbeat returned to normal and the sweat dried on his forehead, Greene sent up a heartfelt prayer for the good fortune they'd had that day in the form of a little boy named Tommy.

The wagon eventually turned off the main road and entered a very lumpy track. At each bounce and tilt that rolled him and Jacobson back and forth against the cornstalks, Greene thought longingly of the potholed road down which they'd ridden the day before. At least the potholes on the main road had been mostly filled in, so that even if a wagon swayed and pitched as it passed over them, it was unlikely that a wheel would be irreversibly damaged. But this road… Greene imagined holes as large as the span of the wheels and boulders as tall as the footboard. After they'd jounced along for a while, the wagon stopped, the driver got down, and the flap next to Jacobson opened.

"You can get out now," the driver said as he began to unload the crates of supplies and cornstalks.

"We can't thank you enough for your help," Greene said as he and Jacobson slid to the ground.

The man grunted. "Well, you may not be able to thank me enough, but you can pay me." He set the last crate down and turned a scowl on them, holding out his hand impatiently.

Greene and Jacobson froze, Greene cursing himself internally for not having foreseen this. In Archenland, folks helped each other as a matter of course, but he never should've expected that in Arlesland.

Keeping the smile on his face, although it was a bit grim now, Greene dug into his pockets and pulled out most of his remaining coins.

The man weighed the coins in his hand, scowled again and held out his other hand. After staring at him for a moment, Greene pulled out the rest of the coins, not bothering to smile this time.

The man jerked his head to the right. "There be the south. You can figure the rest out yourselves."

Silently, Greene and Jacobson helped him load the crates back into his cart, whereupon he turned away without a word, returned to the wagon seat, and clicked his horses to move on.

As he rode out of sight, Jacobson said, "Well, that was fun."

Greene said grimly, "At least we aren't in jail," and turned to lead the way back to the road.

Alice

Princess Aurora had taken to wandering down to Charla's house in the village every few days, hoping to find signs that her friend had come home, or discover some clue as to her whereabouts. So far those visits had been unfruitful.

One morning she made her way to the back door of Charla's house and was about to enter the kitchen when she heard someone calling her name.

"Princess! Princess Aurora!"

She turned to see a smiling face peering through the shrubby trees between Charla's house and the one next door. The face was surrounded by a crown of brown braids and enlivened by large dark eyes and a sweet smile.

Aurora's face lit up. "Alice! How are you? How is your aunt?" Charla's neighbor had been away for a few weeks nursing a sick relative.

"She's doing much better, thank you! All she needed was some time off her feet without having to worry about her family. Her oldest children were helpful, but her husband… well, he needed a bit more attention." Alice screwed her face up and laughed with Aurora.

Alice asked the princess, "How was your wedding? I'm so sorry I missed it! I'm looking forward to hearing about Charla's, too!"

Aurora hesitated. "Well, I'm afraid I have some bad news. My wedding was perfect, and I'll tell you all about it later. But Charla's... she and Greene didn't get married."

Alice's face fell, the smile sliding off it. "But... what in the world happened?"

Aurora shook her head in frustration. "We don't know. Greene came down here about a week ago, just a few days before their wedding, and he found Charla, Old Dan and David gone, and just a note from Charla to say that she needed some time to think things over, but that she was afraid it wasn't going to work out between them.

"I can't believe it!" Alice said, horrified. "She loved him so much!"

Aurora shook her head. "Me either. The note that Charla left was so odd, too. It didn't sound anything like her. It was so casual and offhand, dismissive of any love or affection between them."

Alice thought a moment. "I'm sure you checked their belongings to see what was missing..."

Aurora nodded. "Yes, I've looked through everything several times. Come take a look yourself, though. Maybe you'll see something we missed."

She and Alice looked through the house, and Alice agreed that the packing the family had done seemed to be methodical rather than under duress.

Alice asked, "And Charla left a note?"

Aurora nodded and pulled the note from her pocket. She'd taken to carrying it around and reading it at odd moments, trying to make sense of it. She handed it to Alice, who frowned as she read it.

Dear friend,

I am so sorry, but it's just not working. Everything we do seems to make it worse instead of better! I need to take a break, put it aside for a while, so I can clear my mind.

Just let me think it over for a while, see if I can come up with something that works.

C

"That doesn't make sense," she said, looking up at Aurora.

"I know! That's what I kept telling Greene! Charla *never* would've broken their engagement in a note, and she *certainly* wouldn't have done it with a note like *that!*" Aurora kept talking, but Alice was re-reading the note.

Dear friend… Everything we do seems to make it worse instead of better!

"… Greene said he found it on the counter by the sink, and there was nothing else in the house to indicate why they'd left…" Aurora was saying.

Alice glanced over at the sink, her mind still trying to make sense of the note. Her gaze sharpened, and she quickly looked back down at the note. "Greene found the note by the sink?" she asked, looking up Aurora with a frown. "Here?" she asked, walking over to the counter.

Aurora nodded. "Yes, that's where he said it was."

"*Here?* By the jars of jam?" Alice's voice was insistent.

Aurora nodded slowly. "Yes… why?"

Alice looked back down at the note, read it a third time and shook her head in dismay. "I think Charla wrote this note to *me*, not Greene! She was probably planning to leave it on my door for me to find when I came home."

Aurora snatched the note from her and read it frantically. "Why do you think it's for you?"

"The jam!" Alice said, pointing at it in frustration. "Charla was helping me with my grandmother's recipe. Our first batch didn't taste right, so Charla said she'd keep working on it while I was gone. But she must not have been able to figure it out!"

"Oh no…" Aurora said, reaching behind her to find a chair to collapse into. "Oh no…" she repeated, reading the note.

The note that had puzzled all of them made perfect sense now.

Aurora dropped her head into her hands. "And Greene… Greene thinks she broke off the engagement!"

"We have to let him know! Is he up at the barracks?" Alice asked.

Aurora stared at her, stricken. "He left a few days after Charla disappeared! He's gone on a mission for my father, and there's no way to get word to him!"

Alice dropped onto a chair. "Oh no," she echoed, eyes wide.

Aurora's horror for Greene dissipated as an even worse thought filled her mind.

"But… if Charla didn't leave because of Greene… *where is she?*"

Charla Awakens

Cozy beneath the colorful blankets of the wall bed, Charla didn't want to open her eyes. Last night had been her first full sleep since they'd crossed into Vallenland, and she wasn't ready for the day to start.

As the sleep left her, though, she suddenly remembered the horror of the past two days and sat up with a gasp. The curved wooden roof and painted walls surrounding her surprised her for a moment, before she remembered how Mother Tarni's Sinti had rescued herself, Old Dan, and David the day before.

She felt a hand touch her shoulder and turned quickly, the trauma from her time with the Dark Ones making her heart pound.

But it was the Sinti girl from the night before, the one who'd assisted Mother Tarni with the ceremony to remove the bitter sand from Charla's clothes. The girl's eyes were kind, unoffended by Charla's recoil. "I didn't mean to frighten you. Mother Tarni has requested that you attend her. Your grandfather and brother are already with her."

Reluctantly, Charla swung her legs from under the covers and stood up.

The Sinti girl said, "I welcome you to our Sinti camp," and dropped into a graceful curtsy, which Charla, slightly flustered, returned. "No, no," the girl laughed, reaching out to pull Charla up. "You are guest; you do not curtsy to me."

Charla nodded and looked down at her clothes, which were covered in sweat and blood, and most likely tears as well.

The Sinti girl patted Charla's hand and said, "I will help you change into clean clothes later, but for now you may wear this scarf." She draped one of the Sinti scarves around Charla's shoulders, putting beautiful colors over the stains.

As the blood and dirt disappeared from view, a wave of relief swept through Charla, and she felt ashamed of how reluctant she'd been to trust the Sinti thus far. Her treatment at the hands of the Dark Ones had scarred her more than she'd realized.

She took a deep breath and turned to the Sinti woman. "Thank you for your help. I'm ready to see Mother Tarni now."

Charla stood before Mother Tarni, clinging to her brother David and willing her legs not to give way. The Sinti were building up a fire to cook breakfast, and Mother Tarni was seated beside the campfire in a carved wooden chair as large as a throne.

When Charla had stepped from the wagon, she'd seen Old Dan, her disabled grandfather, being carried toward Mother Tarni on the arms of two Sinti men. As she'd watched, her grandfather attempted a bow from atop the arms of the Sinti men, which was received by Mother Tarni graciously. One gesture from her and another chair, less regal but full of cushions, was placed close to hers. Old Dan thankfully settled in it and looked around him. His eye caught Charla's and he smiled and murmured to Mother Tarni, who looked up and saw Charla.

Charla paused awkwardly, but her grandfather motioned her forward.

Mother Tarni sat very still, waiting, her eyes steady on Charla. The woman, neither young nor old, was imposing with her piercing eyes. Charla tried not to show how nervous she was as she walked toward her, but she was having a hard time keeping her chin from wobbling and legs from shaking. Her defenses were very low and this new situation was overwhelming. She wanted to go back to bed, rather than spending the day talking to strangers, but she kept moving forward. Thankfully, her brother David came to steady her.

Mother Tarni surveyed her carefully, head to toe, then murmured a word.

Charla asked sharply, "What did you say?"

The Sinti woman didn't answer the question. Instead she said, "Welcome, Charla, David, and Dan." She looked carefully at each of them as she said their names.

Charla corrected automatically, "Old Dan" but the Sinti woman smiled as she looked at Charla's grandfather.

"I do not see the age of which you speak. I see the soul inside, and it is strong." She said seriously to Old Dan, "You must stay with us rather than continuing your journey alone."

Charla shook her head in confusion. "Why would we stay with you?"

The woman didn't seem disconcerted by her blunt question. "You would stay with me for protection from the Dark Ones. I was called by Oynos to assist you."

Charla was silenced. This woman thought *God* was talking to her?

The Sinti queen studied her for a moment. "Your grandfather has told me of your collapse in the barn. Tell me what has happened since then."

Charla glanced at Old Dan, who nodded. She glanced back at Mother Tarni, whose face was calm, neither curious nor bored.

Charla gathered her thoughts, thinking back to that night when she'd seen the vision of the village, and heard the old man call "*Skaeweer*, come!" She took a deep breath and began. "After I fell unconscious, all I remember is waking up in the wagon…"

Charla slowly drifted back to consciousness, shifting on the hard surface beneath her. There was an exclamation somewhere nearby, and she opened her eyes to see her grandfather's black face peering down at her, his curly gray hair a nimbus in the daylight. "You're awake!"

Charla sat up and saw she was in the bed of a wagon, which her grandfather was driving. Her brother David sat beside him.

Puzzled, she asked, "Where are we?"

Old Dan replied, "In the forest south of Windham Village."

"South of *Windham?* Why?" Charla frowned. Windham Village was where she'd grown up, where she'd met and fallen in love with Greene.

Old Dan hedged. "What's the last thing you remember?"

Charla wrinkled her nose, a bitter smell rising up in her memory. "I was looking through your trunk and I found a little box wrapped up in the bottom of it. I opened it and…" She frowned and shook her head, her eyes looking off into the distance as she tried to remember.

"There was… an odor." She paused. "There was some kind of sand in the bottom of the box, and it had a sharp, bitter scent. And then…" Her voice drifted off. "Then… I saw something. I must have been dreaming, I suppose…"

"What did you see?" There was a slight tremble in Old Dan's voice, but Charla didn't notice.

"A village. It was in a desert, but there was a big mountain behind it, and trees at the foot of the mountain. The village was on the edge of the trees."

"What else did you see?" Old Dan's tone had become urgent, but again Charla didn't notice.

"A boy came running up to the villagers. He was sweating as if he'd run far. The villagers started talking and arguing, and then an old man turned toward me and said some word I've never heard before."

"What was it?" Old Dan's tone was hushed.

"Skay… skay weird? It didn't make any sense."

"Was it *skaeweer?*"

"Yes! That was it! He said, '*Skaeweer*, come!'"

Old Dan nodded as if she'd confirmed something.

"What did it mean, Grandpop? And where are we?" She knew the woods around Windham pretty well, but nothing looked familiar.

Old Dan was silent a moment, then shook himself. "We've just crossed over the Vallenland Border."

"*What?* Why in the world are we in *Vallenland?*"

Old Dan smiled at her sadly. "I'm sorry, child. This isn't what I wanted, but it's imperative that we do this."

"Do *what*? Where are we going?"

He said again, "I'm sorry child. I can't explain right now. I must ask you to trust me. It is very important that we make this journey, but I can't explain why."

Charla looked at David, who shook his head and said, "It's no use. I've been trying to get him to tell me what's going on ever since we left two days ago."

"*Two days ago?*"

Charla was overwhelmed. For a moment, her brain didn't fully register what David had said. But then... horror flooded her body.

"Are you telling me that today is *Thursday?*" Her eyes were huge as she stared at David. He reluctantly nodded, dropping his eyes as hers blazed. "Oh my *God. I'm supposed to be getting married today!*"

Old Dan looked over his shoulder, about to berate her for taking Oynos' name in vain, but the words died on his lips at the look on her face.

Charla finally managed to pluck another coherent thought out of the swirling chaos in her mind. "*Where is Greene?*"

Old Dan's look of rebuke changed to shame. "I'm sorry, child, but I didn't even think of telling Greene we were leaving."

"*What?*" Charla's voice was shrill, just like the panic bells in her mind.

Old Dan made shushing motions. "Keep your voice down!"

Charla looked around them, at the empty woods in front of and behind the wagon, at the looming rock walls to either side. "Why? There's no one around! Absolutely no one to hear! *And I feel like yelling!*" Charla felt the panic rising and fought to beat it down.

"Charla, you must keep your voice down!" Old Dan insisted.

She barely heard him. Breathing in sharp bursts, she went back to her main grievance, directing her comments equally at

David, who looked increasingly put upon, and Old Dan, who hunched his shoulders in defense.

"So… you just packed up in the middle of the night and left without saying a *word* to *my betrothed?*" Her voice was rising in pitch and tempo and her grandfather opened his mouth remonstrate again. "Alright, alright!" she hissed, dropping her voice to a furious whisper. "So as far as Greene knows, I've just *run out on him?*"

Charla was appalled. Greene already had enough problems believing that she loved him. He always talked about how grateful he was that she wanted to be with him. In that moment, Charla didn't care one bit about whatever reason her grandfather had for this journey. All she could think about was what Greene must have felt when he found her gone.

She suddenly began to push her way to the front of the wagon. "Stop!" She tried to pull the reins out of Old Dan's hands. "We have to go back! *Stop!*" But her grandfather was pulling her back, trying to make her listen.

"We can't go back. We *can't.* Not only will you put yourself in danger, but you'll bring danger to Greene and Princess Aurora and *everyone* in Archenland. The only thing we can do, the *only* way to keep the people you love safe, is to continue on this path."

Charla was sobbing now, struggling against Old Dan and her brother. "What is *wrong* with you? This doesn't make sense! Please, Grandpop, please! I *have* to go back!"

Old Dan halted the wagon and grabbed Charla's hands, which were still trying to pull the reins from him. "You can't, child. You *can't!* I wish I could explain, but you must trust me!"

"Can't I at least send Greene a message? Surely I can do that!" Tears were pouring down Charla's cheeks.

"No, my darling girl. I know it breaks your heart, but this is the way it must be."

The sincerity, the controlled fear, that Charla saw in her grandfather's eyes finally broke through her anguish. She focused on the only thing that made sense: he truly believed she would put Greene and her friends in danger. Old Dan had never led her wrong before. If he said there was danger, she had to believe it.

It didn't make it any easier to think about what Greene must be going through, though, and she spent the rest of the day weeping quietly in David's arms while Old Dan drove them silently through the woods.

It was only that night, while Old Dan slept on his pallet on the other side of the campfire, that the siblings were able to talk.

David whispered, "I found you passed out in the barn, and when I brought you inside, Grandpop examined you and then made me show him where I'd found you. He found that box you were talking about, the one with the sand in it, and told me to pack our bags. We left that night after the village was quiet. He wouldn't tell me where we were going. We drove south from Kingham Village and just before we got to the border, we turned onto an overgrown track. We went a few miles along it, but then found it blocked by a landslide. Grandpop insisted that I try to move some of the rocks out of the way so we could get the wagon through, but the rocks were too big for me to move alone."

Charla frowned. It was unlike her grandfather to insist on an obviously futile exercise, so his desire to travel that path must have been great.

David continued, "Finally he agreed to give it up. I thought we'd turn around and go back to the main road, but he said we needed to stay away from other travelers as much as possible, so he insisted we go west, toward Windham Village, where we found an even more overgrown path through the woods along the Vallenland border. Sometimes I had no idea where the path was, and I'm not sure Grandpop knew either. But he kept saying that going back to the main road would be dangerous. He said people would be looking for us. *Bad* people."

"What? Has he gone completely insane? What 'bad people' could possibly be looking for us?" Charla asked.

David shrugged, shaking his head.

She said bitterly, "None of this makes sense! He's in a terrible rush to go wherever we're going! Such a rush that he didn't even tell Greene we were leaving, but then he decides to wander around on some overgrown path? And now we're in Vallenland, and we're *still* wandering through the woods?"

That wasn't really accurate. They'd come to a road that afternoon, and traveled down it for a few hours before stopping, but before making camp, Old Dan had insisted that they make their way through the woods until they could no longer be seen from the road. They found a large fallen tree, and Old Dan agreed it was safe to build a small campfire on the other side of it, but he'd kept looking around at the forest as they ate, and insisted afterward that they bank the fire so only the embers glowed.

"It doesn't make sense to me either," David said, shrugging. "But he said the area where the borders of the three northern kingdoms meet was the most dangerous place for us to be, so we had to avoid that area."

Charla shook her head. "Are you *sure* Grandpop is in his right mind?" It was a question that had occurred to her many times that day.

"I..." David struggled to explain himself. "I don't understand his plan, but as far as I can tell, he's as lucid as ever. And..." He hesitated. "When I found you lying on the ground in the barn, it really scared me."

Charla nodded. "Yeah. That whole thing was weird." She pondered a moment, staring down at her hands. "It's the only thing that makes me believe maybe Grandpop isn't crazy. What I saw didn't make sense, so maybe that's why what he's doing doesn't make sense, either!"

David asked, "So... tell me again what happened?"

Hesitantly, Charla explained how she'd suddenly been... *somewhere* else and had seen a village she didn't recognize, full of people who didn't seem to see her, except for an old man. How the people had suddenly seemed afraid and started running, and how the old man had shouted one word at her.

"*Skaeweer*?" David repeated. "Grandpop recognized the word. What does it mean?"

"I have no idea!" Charla said, throwing her hands up. "I've never heard the word before in my life! But I must have collapsed right after that, because that's all I remember until I woke up in the wagon this morning."

At that moment, Old Dan woke up and saw them talking. Scolding them as if they were still small children, he insisted that they go to their pallets on either side of him, which put an end to their conversation.

Thinking things over before she fell asleep, Charla realized her anger at Old Dan was fading. Her heart still broke when she thought about Greene, but whatever he'd thought about her disappearing, it had happened two days ago and there was nothing she could do about it. She knew that Princess Aurora and Martin would take care of Greene in her absence, so she had to put it out of her mind. Thinking about it was just making her crazy and stopping her from thinking logically. What she had to concentrate on now was Old Dan and this crazy idea he had that they had to escape because "bad people" were looking for them.

Old Dan had been the bedrock of her and David's lives as long as she could remember, and he appeared to be as sane as ever. Against her will, Charla admitted that the only thing she could do right now was to trust him.

At least for a few more days.

The Dark Ones

The next morning, they met some travelers on the road, but Old Dan kept his face hidden beneath the hood of his cloak and insisted that David and Charla do the same.

About mid-morning, the horses were walking along the rocky road when something in the grass nearby scared them, making them rear away from it. When Old Dan got them under control again, one of the horses was limping, so David got out of the wagon to investigate. Lifting the horse's leg, he felt it carefully.

"It feels sound," he reported. "Probably just a sprain."

Old Dan sighed and looked around. There was a rider approaching them from the east, his horse trotting along easily. Old Dan observed him silently for a moment, then pushed his hood back so the man could see his face. As the rider drew near, Old Dan raised his hand to hail the man, who obligingly stopped.

"Good day to you, sir," Old Dan said, but his lack of teeth made it hard for the other man to understand.

Charla leaned forward. "He says good day to you, sir."

The rider nodded and responded, "Good day to you as well!"

Old Dan mumbled and Charla translated. "He asks whether there is a stable nearby where we can get a fresh horse. Ours seems to have gone lame."

The rider turned and pointed back the way he'd come, giving them clear directions to a stable a quarter mile down the road.

After thanking the man for his help, Old Dan directed David to run to the stables and bring back a fresh horse.

David was back within the hour, perched on the back of a horse along with one of the stable boys. They jumped down, David and Charla harnessed the fresh horse to the wagon while the stable boy set off with the limping one toward the stables, and then Old Dan shook up the horses and pulled the wagon back onto the road.

"Did you have any problems at the stables?" Old Dan asked David.

"No, none," David said, then frowned.

"What?" Old Dan asked, a note of alarm in his voice.

"Oh, I'm sure it's nothing… but there was a man there who kept hanging around while I was talking to the stable master. It seemed like he was listening in, so I was careful not to say too much. But it was odd."

"What did he look like?" Old Dan asked.

David shrugged. "Couldn't see. He had the hood of his traveling cloak pulled up so his face was shadowed. But…" He hesitated, then shook his head. "It must've been my imagination."

Old Dan insisted that he explain.

"Well… there was some kind of heat haze or something around the man. It made him hard to look at."

Old Dan frowned and snapped the reins to hasten the horses. "It's not far now. We can make it," he muttered to himself. Charla and David exchanged frowns.

A mile down the road they happened upon an overturned wagon blocking their way. Old Dan fussed under his breath while David got down to talk to the owner of the wagon, who didn't seem at all worried that his cart was blocking the road. He merely stood gazing at it, puffing unconcernedly on a pipe.

David spoke with him a moment, gaining only a few shrugs from the man, who eventually stirred himself to point desultorily toward a faint path that led into the woods.

David returned and reported, "He says that path goes a little way into the woods, but then it turns east and meets back up with the main road just up there." He pointed toward where the road disappeared around a curve.

"Good," Old Dan said in relief. "We can't afford to lose more time." He clicked his tongue, snapped the reins, and they were moving.

It was dark in the woods, almost as dark as dusk. Charla shivered although the air was warm, and Old Dan muttered furiously, trying to reassure himself they had no choice but to follow the path.

They rode about two hundred yards along the path before it turned east.

"It's fine, see?" Charla pointed out to Old Dan. "We're turning east now, so we'll be back on the main road soon."

"I don't like it, no I don't," Old Dan muttered, shaking his head and looking side to side fearfully.

Charla was just opening her mouth to attempt more reassurance when both horses suddenly shied and stopped dead before trying furiously to back in the traces, whinnying shrilly. Charla and David jumped down to grab the harnesses, all the while glancing around to see what had frightened them.

Suddenly the horses stopped whinnying and froze where they stood, their eyes rolling so the whites showed. Charla was relieved for a moment that they had calmed down... but then an intense wave of cold swept over her. Shivering, she looked around and saw Old Dan motionless on the wagon seat, staring into the woods ahead of them.

Charla turned away from the frozen horses and saw *him*.

Leaning against a tree at the edge of the trail was a man, looking quite harmless and average... but there was something odd in the air around him, a sort of dark haze that made his form seem to shimmer and shift. He wore a traveling cloak with the hood pulled up.

"That's him," David hissed. "The man at the stables!"

At that, the man looked up. His face was still shadowed by the hood, but they could just make out a smile on his face. Charla's sense of unease grew, the shivers still shaking her. Glancing around, she saw Old Dan staring wide-eyed at the man.

"Having a hard time with your horses, eh?" the stranger asked, looking back down at the fingernail he was cleaning with a short knife. His voice was a low rasp, but he somehow seemed to be talking directly into Charla's ear, so that she flinched in an effort to get away from it. The man glanced up at her, then flipped his knife into the air, caught it, and tucked it into his belt.

"Yes," Old Dan answered the man curtly, his form rigid, face expressionless.

"Ah, that's a shame, that is," the man replied calmly, walking toward them. Again the soft voice caressed Charla's ear, and the shivers turned into spasms that shook her frame, jerking her hands against the horse's harness.

Reaching up to his hood, the man began to lower it.

Charla's heart began to race, her breaths coming faster and faster. She did not want to see what was under the hood, she did *not*.

But when the hood came down, it revealed an average face, nothing memorable about it… except for that darkness that blurred the man's features, and an odd play of light that seemed to twist and curl along his skin. Charla took one shaking hand off the harness and rubbed her eyes, but it didn't help. Something about the man was definitely *wrong*.

He stopped about ten yards from where Charla stood. "Yes, it's a real shame," he whispered, then raised his nose and *sniffed*.

The horses *screamed* and began rearing frantically again. Charla felt blind panic and turned in terror toward her grandfather, who was already shouting, "To *me*, children!"

As she scrambled to pull herself onto the seat, Charla saw more cloaked men stepping out of the trees around the wagon, men who had the same unnatural darkness around them, the same odd play of light on their skin.

Old Dan was trying to push her and David behind him, while she and David tried in turn to shield Old Dan, but they all froze as the circle of men moved toward the wagon as one. Charla's heart was racing and every instinct in her body screamed at her to *run*, but she couldn't leave her family. She grabbed hold of Old Dan and David and frantically pulled them toward the back of the wagon… but the strange men had already surrounded them.

The man who'd spoken reached out and grabbed Charla, pulling her roughly away from Old Dan and David. As he did so, she saw that the weird play of light wasn't *on* his skin… it was *under* it. There was glowing writing of some kind crawling beneath the dark skin, sliding across his cheeks and into his hairline, across his forehead and down his nose, disappearing under the neck of his cloak.

Bile rose in her throat and her head swam, her vision blurring.

Charla tried to scream as he pulled her across the wagon seat, but the man opened his mouth and sucked at the air between them, stealing her voice. "Delicious," he whispered, gripping her arms, hurting her, as he climbed onto the wagon. Menace flowed off him in waves, overwhelming her, and that horrible shifting, glowing skin filled her vision.

She barely had time for one more fear for Old Dan and David before the panic completely flooded her mind, and she fainted dead away.

Waking Nightmare

Charla's head hung down, the back of her neck stretched almost past endurance, but she didn't have the strength to raise it. She'd originally been standing, but she was too weak now, so her whole weight hung from her arms, which were tied to something above her head.

When she'd finally regained consciousness, she found they'd been taken to a large cave. She couldn't see her grandfather or David, but she knew they were nearby, because she could hear them screaming.

She knew why they were screaming, because soon she was screaming, too. The men who'd taken them were determined to find out where they'd been going, and they had no compunction about using pain to eviscerate the answers from unwilling subjects.

The torture had lasted for hours, continuing at a pain level that was almost unbearable, but not quite. If she passed out, that was no good to the Dark Ones, as she now thought of them.

She could hear them talking in low voices nearby, so she didn't open her eyes. She'd kept her eyes closed as much as possible, except when they pulled at her eyelids so she had no choice but to see what they wanted her to see, which was usually some fresh torture they'd devised for David or Old Dan.

Sometimes Charla almost hated her grandfather as she listened to the agonized sounds of his torture and that of her brother. When it was her turn, all she could do was scream that she didn't know anything about where they were going. Old Dan had never told them what the Dark Ones wanted to know, so she couldn't tell the secret in order to save David, or herself, or Old Dan.

And Old Dan was tougher than she would have believed, because he hadn't broken under the torture. Some part of Charla realized that he must truly believe in whatever secret he was keeping if he wasn't giving up the information to save her and David from torture. But a bigger part of her just hated him. Pain that bad, for that long, makes you forget any other emotion, including love.

Or maybe it didn't make one forget entirely, because neither she nor David told the Dark Ones that only Old Dan knew where they were going, and why.

Charla had babbled freely after just a few minutes of unrelenting pain and listening to her loved ones scream. She'd told the Dark Ones everything that had happened to her in the barn the night she found the box of sand. They'd questioned her closely about the vision she'd had, asking her to describe the village, the snowcapped mountain, the appearance of the old man who had called her "*skaeweer.*" And she hadn't stopped there. She'd babbled on and on, telling them everything about her life she could think of, hoping something, anything might stop the horrible pain.

The only thing she hadn't told them about was Greene, because she was afraid they might kidnap *him*, torture him, to make her talk.

David had told them everything he could think of, too. He was in another part of the cave most of the time, but she could hear his shrieks and frantic words, going on and on about their lives and every moment of their trip since they left Archenland.

Charla told the Dark Ones that her grandfather had said they were leaving Archenland in order to protect those they loved, because "bad people" would be looking for them.

When she said that, the Dark Ones standing around her laughed, and one of them leaned into her face. "So what do you think, *skaeweer*? Are we *bad?*"

As he sneered at her, waiting for an answer, she stared in terror. He was still surrounded by that odd mist that blurred his outline, but this close up she could easily see his skin and the writing that moved under it. The words moved slowly enough across his face and down his neck that she could've read them if they'd been in any language she recognized.

Watching the smooth glide of unknown writing under his skin, Charla felt her stomach begin to churn as terror rose in her mind, overwhelming her body. She gagged and began to vomit as the Dark One stepped back and laughed.

As the torture continued through the night, Charla wept and pleaded, begging the Dark Ones to let them go, or at least kill them and end the suffering.

But they didn't.

They focused most of their torture on Old Dan, seeming to think that hurting him was the way to make Charla and David talk. He babbled, too, like Charla and David, but his speech was so hard to understand while he was being tortured that even Charla and David had no idea what he was saying. But when he could be understood, he was telling the Dark Ones anything to make the men stop the torture… except the one thing that *would*.

Eventually, the Dark Ones went away and Charla, hanging from her bonds, fell into an exhausted sleep.

Deliverance

There was the sound of footsteps, then Charla felt the rasp of a knife cutting through the rope that bound her arms above her head. When the rope parted, she fell to the ground, too weak to hold herself up. Her arms felt like they'd been pulled from their sockets, but the relief of not having her body suspended from them was so great that she wanted to cry. She'd cried too much the previous day, though; there were no tears left.

"Get up, girl," a voice growled. She kept her eyes closed even when he kicked her, because she couldn't stand to see that crawling skin.

He kicked her again, viciously this time, and she tried to stand, but couldn't even make it to her knees. The Dark One growled and grabbed one of her arms, pulling her across the cave floor like a sack of potatoes. The lumps and bumps of the ground and even banging into the rock wall were nothing compared to the torture, though, so Charla didn't care. She just hung from his grasp, banging along, feeling nothing but gratitude for the respite.

After a few minutes, she heard the Dark One talking to another, and she was hefted onto a strong shoulder so that her head and arms bounced against the Dark One's back while he carried her as easily as a child. Then she was dumped on the ground, eyes still closed, and her wounds were bandaged by rough hands. A voice growled about what a waste of time it was and another voice said, "No use to us if they die now, is it?"

Just then Charla heard a sound in the distance. The Dark One bandaging her wrist stopped as the others fell silent. Charla opened her eyes a crack and saw in the light of the lanterns that the Dark Ones were all looking toward the front of the cave.

The sound came again, closer, and Charla realized someone was singing outside the cave. Her eyes flew open and her heart began to pound as she realized this might be a chance to escape, but before she could fully grasp the idea, the Dark One grabbed her arm and jerked her to her feet, pulling her deeper into the cave, where lanterns showed the limp forms of Old Dan and David dangling by their wrists from huge spikes in the stone wall. Charla let out a moan, and the Dark One clamped a hand over her mouth.

"Not a word, girl, or I'll give all of you bloody grins, understand?" he growled, drawing a dagger from his belt and holding it up so the lantern light slid across the shiny metal like the glowing words sliding under his skin.

Charla closed her eyes and fought the nausea down.

The sound of singing outside the cave was growing louder. Charla heard tambourines and voices crying out wordlessly in shrieks and exclamations, and she understood. A Sinti caravan was passing near the cave.

The Sinti were traders, selling items they made or taking payment in goods for the entertainment they brought to rich and poor alike. Most nights around Sinti campfires were filled with singing and dancing. Local villagers often attended the gatherings, which was how Charla had come to know the Sinti.

Their singing had a particularly wild feel to it that couldn't be mistaken for anything else, so Charla knew it was a Sinti caravan approaching the cave. She wasn't sure how to feel about that, though, since some Sinti had an unsavory reputation, but she would happily risk some unsavoriness to be rescued.

But not if it would cost Old Dan and David their lives.

The sounds of singing and music from the caravan, the shrill cries, increased in volume for a few moments until Charla thought they must be inside the cave, then died away abruptly.

A clear voice called out, "Who stands in the darkness of the cave?"

One of the Dark Ones called back, "Be on your way. There is nothing for you here, wanderer." The words were civil enough, but the tone was not.

There was a short silence, then the voice of the Sinti came clearly to Charla. "Why don't you remove your hood, stranger? Let the Sinti be the judge of whether you have something we want."

Charla held her breath. The next few minutes would almost certainly lead to some kind of violence, and there was no telling what the Dark Ones might do to keep their secret. The Sinti were known to be skillful fighters, but Charla was willing to bet they'd never engaged anyone like the Dark Ones.

There was silence, then a sharp cry, and suddenly the sound of metal clashing amid the high, clear yips of the Sinti. Grunts of pain, angry shouts, all combined into sounds that made Charla's heart race. She prayed the Sinti would win the battle, but if they did… what would they do with her family?

The noise went on and on, with the grunts and cries of pain sometimes sounding as if they were right outside the rock wall where the Dark One still stood with his knife to Charla's throat. Charla's eyes were wide with fright as the body of a Dark One fell through the opening beside her.

With a curse, the Dark One holding Charla pushed her to the floor as he leapt into the main part of the cave, yelling as he slashed down with the dagger in his hand. After a stunned moment, Charla forced her weak legs to stand so she could run to David's limp form. She began trying to release him from his bonds, but she couldn't reach the rope holding his wrists far above him.

"Grab my knees and lift me up," David said weakly, surprising her. She looked up and saw his eyes were almost swollen shut, but he was looking at her. She grabbed his knees and used all her remaining strength to raise him enough so he could grab the knotted rope and slide it from the spike. His upper body dropped onto her and they fell to the ground panting for a moment, gathering their reserves, then Charla released David from his ropes and they stumbled to Old Dan.

He was so small, so frail, that Charla could easily lift him on her own, and David made short work of removing the rope from the spike so he and Charla could lower their grandfather to the ground.

As they crouched over Old Dan, the noise in the outer cave began to die away, until they finally heard a fierce, triumphant yelling from many voices. It sounded like the Sinti had won. But did that mean they would be friends to the prisoners?

Charla frantically unknotted the rope still around David's hands, then she and David froze, hoping they would go undiscovered, but the lantern hanging on the rock wall gave them away.

A face peered in at them. It was a Sinti man, his long black hair covered with a colorful scarf, earrings glinting in both ears. "Here!" he called over his shoulder as he walked to where they crouched next to Old Dan.

His face as he looked down at them was hard, his mouth grim. Charla and David stood as one to protect their grandfather, but the Sinti paid them no notice. He suddenly bent and reached out to gently press his fingers against Old Dan's neck.

Charla hissed, "Don't you touch him!" as she pushed him away.

The Sinti man said, "We mean you no harm. Let us care for him."

Surprised, Charla was frozen for a moment, unsure what to do. Two more Sinti appeared, a man and a woman, and helped the first man raise Old Dan to carry him from the cave.

The woman turned to Charla and David. "Come. Mother awaits you."

Charla exchanged a glance with David. She wasn't sure she wanted to know who Mother was, but she and David hesitantly followed the woman.

The bodies of the Dark Ones lay strewn around the main part of the cave. Charla stared at them as she passed. The weird mist that normally surrounded them was gone and… she leaned closer to one to make sure… the terrible glowing writing beneath their skin had disappeared.

But as she approached the bodies of Dark Ones lying at the entrance to the cave, she could see that wasn't completely true. In the daylight, she could see traces of the writing under their skin, but it was no longer glowing or moving.

Her stomach queasy and mind in turmoil, she reluctantly stepped from the cave into the dim light of sunset, where the Sinti awaited her.

Mother Tarni

Charla stepped from the darkness of the cave to see a crowd of people and wagons before her. The faces of the fifty or so Sinti gazing at her were dark, their hair even darker, but brilliantly white smiles gleamed in the light of the setting sun. Golden earrings, bracelets and necklaces gleamed on men and women alike, but the women had their hair caught back in brightly colored scarves, while some of the men wore their long hair bound at the nape with wide metal bands or leather cords.

A hand reached out to help Charla, and she stared at the Sinti man to whom it was attached. He looked like the other men, with his long, dark hair pulled back in a leather thong, but he was taller than them, almost as tall as her betrothed, Greene. Charla's heart skipped a beat as Greene's beloved face drifted into her mind, but she sternly pushed it aside. She couldn't afford to show weakness in front of this stranger.

The man simply smiled and motioned with his hand. "Come, little one. I am Jamison of the Sinti. You are safe."

Charla narrowed her eyes and tried to look fierce, but his smile didn't change. He just waited patiently with hand outstretched. Reluctantly, she took it and let him help her down the steep descent from the cave, his strong hands steadying her when she faltered. Her legs were terribly weak. The torture certainly hadn't done her any good, and the last push to release David and Old Dan from their bonds had exhausted the last of her strength.

She slowly followed along behind the Sinti who were carrying Old Dan to the nearest wagon, where gentle hands handed him up to be received by others. The smiling Sinti man who'd helped her from the cave silently paced alongside her, not hurrying her, only holding her arm securely and keeping her upright when she stumbled over the rough ground.

Charla looked ahead to where brilliantly painted Sinti wagons stretched along the trail. There were about thirty Sinti men, women and children standing beside the wagons, while others remained perched on the wagon seats, their horses calmly cropping grass as they waited.

The wagon into which Old Dan had been handed was the largest and most colorfully decorated. Jamison, the Sinti man holding Charla's arm, led her to it just as a tall woman came out of the wagon.

Jamison murmured, "Mother Tarni would speak with you."

Mother Tarni's hair was long and black like the other Sinti, her eyes deep-set, her mouth firm. The scarf she wore around her head was dark red fringed with large gold beads. Unlike the other Sinti, she had no piercings, but a large necklace of dull metal with enamel carvings covered her entire throat and collarbone above the simple unbleached muslin blouse and full black skirt she wore. Her high black boots were dusty, but the simplicity of her clothing did nothing to hide her innate power.

"Dan is badly hurt," the woman said in a husky voice.

Charla stared. "How do you know….?"

"His name?" the woman finished. "Your grandfather is an old friend. The Sinti aided him many years ago when he was in need."

Charla glanced over at David, who was leaning on a young Sinti man. Her brother looked as puzzled as she was, but Charla didn't have the energy to question the woman.

The Sinti woman nodded. "You must rest. You will be safe with us. Come." She turned to ascend the stairs into the wagon, and Charla wearily allowed the Sinti man to help her up the stairs while David followed.

The interior of the wagon was a surprise. For one thing, it was much larger than it appeared to be outside. Charla had peered into Sinti wagons before, so she knew how efficiently everything was stored inside, but this one went far beyond what she'd seen before.

Immediately inside the door there was a short hallway consisting of deep cabinets on either side and drawers with latches to hold them shut when the wagon was moving.

Just past the cabinets, a large folding wall bed had been lowered, and Old Dan had been placed on it. There were three Sinti standing around the bed, carefully bandaging Old Dan's wounds, spreading a thick herbal paste on the worst ones. A young Sinti woman was holding a cup to the old man's mouth, and he had revived enough to swallow the liquid. The girl saw Charla watching and said, "It is a draught for dreamless sleep, to help him heal."

Charla nodded and looked to the right, where a narrow wall bed hung on chains beside more cabinets and drawers. The Sinti settled her on the bed so they could take care of her wounds, and settled David on a low stool to do the same. Once the healers were done with Old Dan and he was tucked into the large bed, the healers carefully helped David to the bed and finished dressing his wounds there.

Charla continued looking around the wagon as the Sinti worked on her. There was a heavy curtain to her right that extended across the entire width of the wagon. She presumed this must be where Mother Tarni slept. The woman was giving quiet orders to the Sinti, who left the wagon and returned with bowls of cold meat and fruits. From the cabinets, they brought simple cutlery and plates on trays, which they set on the wall beds beside Charla and David. Old Dan was already fast asleep.

One of the Sinti climbed into the wagon with a pitcher of cold water. Silver mugs were produced from one of the deep drawers, and Charla watched in fascination as the Sinti pulled out cunning shelves in the wall, which had deep wells to hold the bowls and mugs and keep them from moving when the wagon was in motion.

Mother Tarni said to Charla, "We must leave this place. We will drive through the night. But first I must ask you… How did they find you?" Mother asked.

Charla asked, "You mean the Dark Ones?"

"The Dark Ones?" Mother Tarni mused. "Yes, that is a good name for them. How did the Dark Ones find you?"

David spoke up, "Ma'am, it was me. I went to a stable to get us a new horse when ours went lame, and one of the… Dark Ones was there. I don't know what drew his attention to me, but he must have followed me."

"The bitter sand," Mother Tarni said.

Frowning, David asked, "The what?"

"The *skaeweer* has recently touched bitter sand. I smell it very faintly on all of you, but the scent is strongest on her."

"Oh," David said, realization in his eyes. He turned to Charla. "That must be why the stranger sniffed the air when he stopped our wagon. He smelled the sand."

Charla was barely listening. As soon as Mother Tarni said there was a scent that the bitter sand had left on her, she'd started worrying that more Dark Ones would trace her by the same means.

Mother read the expression on her face and reassured her.

"The scent is not strong, and would not draw any Dark Ones who weren't already in the vicinity, unless you were in a place of great power such as where the three borders of the northern kingdoms meet."

Excitedly, David turned to Charla. "That's what Grandpop said, too! He said we had to stay away from there!"

Mother Tarni nodded. "Your grandfather is very wise." She turned back to Charla. "We must remove the scent of the bitter sand on you tonight, though. I believe there is a way to use it to draw away any more Dark Ones who might sense its presence."

She motioned to one of the Sinti girls, saying, "Gather items for the *saiwola*," and the girl left the wagon.

"Come," Mother Tarni beckoned Charla, leading her behind the heavy curtain, which concealed a bed covered in pillows and blankets, with larger pillows on the floor. Mother Tarni seated herself on one of the floor pillows and motioned for Charla to do the same.

The Sinti girl reappeared with several small bottles in her arms, which she placed on the floor beside Mother Tarni. The Sinti girl then fetched a large wooden bowl and a small whisk broom made of herbs tied together, and placed these by Mother Tarni as well.

Mother Tarni took each bottle and poured its contents, each a powder of a different color, into the bowl, then whisked them together with the broom. She closed her eyes and raised her face to the ceiling, speaking words in a tongue Charla didn't know. Lowering her face, she opened her eyes and raised the whisk broom to lightly draw it through the air around Charla. Wherever the broom of herbs and powder went, a trail of colored dust followed, until the air was thick with multicolored motes swirling around Charla. Mother Tarni was still crooning in the unknown tongue, and she suddenly stopped painting the air with the broom and raised her face again to the ceiling, her eyes open this time as she called out in a loud voice.

Charla felt an odd tingling sensation on her skin and the air around her seemed to shimmer like sunlight on water… then the sensation and illusion were gone.

"You are fresh and clean as a newborn babe now, child," Mother Tarni said as she rose and handed the bowl of powder and small whisk broom to the girl, saying quietly "Take these to Jamison. I will speak with him soon."

Mother Tarni put out a hand and pulled Charla to her feet. "Now you must rest. You have a long journey ahead of you and must regain your strength."

Charla had so many questions, but as soon as Mother Tarni said "rest," her body felt overwhelmingly weary. Nodding, she stumbled back to her bed and fell into it, barely noticing the gentle hands that pulled the covers over her and lightly touched her forehead in blessing.

Mother Tarni listened intently as Charla related everything that had happened since they'd left Kingham Village, then turned to talk to Old Dan, seeming to have no problem understand his garbled speech.

Watching them, Charla's mind whirled as she tried to understand everything that had happened over the past week. Finally, she shook her head and put the thoughts away, telling herself she'd examine them later. Instead, she turned her gaze to Mother Tarni.

The woman, neither young nor old, sat motionless upon the ornately carved wooden chair, only her eyes moving as she watched Old Dan's face. Her hands were draped gracefully on the arms of the chair, her long legs crossed at the knee. Today she wore a crimson scarf figured with gold embroidery, and her long black hair fell over one shoulder.

The rest of her clothes were simple: an embroidered white blouse with full sleeves pushed up to the elbows, the same long black skirt from the night before, beneath which the toes of her well-worn black boots showed. She again wore the wide, almost barbaric necklace, and her arms could hardly be seen for the gold and silver bangles on them.

But after a quick glance at her clothing, it was her face that caught Charla's attention.

The Sinti queen's skin was dark, almost as black as Old Dan's. She had straight black eyebrows and a finely carved nose with slightly flared nostrils. Her lips were thin, her mouth somewhat small, as were her deep-set eyes, but their clear green color glowed in the sunlight. It was the expression in her eyes that was most compelling, though. They were calm and wise, seemingly untroubled by the encounter with the Dark Ones the previous day.

As Charla watched, the clear green eyes turned to her and the thin lips opened. "*Skaeweer,*" Mother Tarni said.

Charla jumped and glanced at her grandfather, who was watching her intently, as was the Sinti queen. They seemed to be waiting for an answer.

"You…" Charla cleared her throat. "You said that earlier. I don't know what it means."

"You have heard that word before?" the Sinti woman asked.

Charla hesitated, glancing at Old Dan again. He nodded, and she reluctantly said, "Yes, but it was just in the dream."

"The dream?" Mother Tarni's eyebrows rose and a faint look of amusement crossed her face. "Is that what it was?"

Charla didn't know how to answer.

Mother Tarni studied her for a few more long moments, then said, "It was no dream. You have been called. You are the *skaeweer*, the guardian."

Questions bubbled to Charla's lips, but Mother Tarni had already turned back to Old Dan to ask him more about their time with the Dark Ones. Charla glanced away, her eyes drawn unwillingly to the cave where the Dark Ones had kept them captive. She tried to keep her eyes away from the bodies lying there, but she couldn't help but look.

But the bodies were gone.

"Where are the Dark Ones?" she blurted out, interrupting the Sinti queen's conversation.

Mother Tarni glanced at the cave and said, "Jamison has taken the bodies south in order to draw any remaining Dark Ones away."

Any remaining Dark Ones? Charla didn't want to think about that.

Jamison

As Jamison rode along with the five Sinti he'd chosen to accompany him, he thought about the conversation he'd had the evening before with Mother Tarni.

The girl and two men they'd rescued from the cave had been taken to Mother Tarni's wagon for treatment of their wounds, and after a few minutes one of the Sinti women had come out with a bowl of the blessed powders that Mother Tarni used to perform the *saiwola* ceremony. After some time had passed, the Sinti queen had come to find Jamison where he stood holding the bowl by the campfire.

Jamison had turned to her. "Are they well?"

Mother Tarni had shrugged. "Time will tell. We've done what we can. They are weakened by the evil that captured them, but they are resting comfortably now." She paused, then said, "I believe the girl is the *skaeweer*."

Jamison had been shocked. He'd never thought to meet a *skaeweer* in his lifetime.

Mother Tarni had gestured toward the bowl in his hands, where a small broom made of herbs lay. "This is dust of the bitter sand, which was gathered from the girl's clothes during the *saiwola*."

Jamison had nodded slowly. The bitter sand certainly seemed to indicate that the girl was the *skaeweer*.

Mother Tarni had said, "Gather the bodies of the Dark Ones."

Jamison had frowned. "Dark Ones?"

She'd gestured toward the dead bodies in the cave opening. "So named by the *skaeweer*. Take their bodies and ride south with the broom containing the dust of the bitter sand. I sense that there are other Dark Ones, even more powerful. They are most likely on the Southern Road, where their power will be magnified. You must draw them away so the *skaeweer* can retrieve the Eye and take it to safety."

Jamison's face had hardened. "It is time?"

She'd nodded. "The *Grauta Beadu* is near."

Jamison had called five of the Sinti men and women to him. "We ride south within the hour. Gather horses for yourselves, along with a wagon, and provisions for five days."

As the Sinti went to follow his orders, Jamison had made his way to a brightly colored wagon around which some children were playing, their shrill voices and laughter rising in the air.

Smiling, Jamison had walked to a little girl about five years old. Her long dark hair was loose, flowing down her back as she ran with the other children. As she darted past him, Jamison had reached out to sweep her up into his arms.

"Daddy!" she'd squealed, hugging his neck. "Alma was so funny just now! She…"

He'd listened to her with a smile, then hushed her. "I'm going away for a few days."

Her face had fallen. "Why?"

"Mother Tarni commands it."

She'd looked sad, but didn't argue. The Sinti never questioned Mother Tarni's orders.

"When will you be back?"

Jamison had kissed her forehead. "Before you are all grown up… although that is happening so quickly, I might be wrong."

She'd giggled.

Jamison had said, "You'll stay with Sheila while I'm gone."

His daughter's face had immediately lightened. Sheila was a particular favorite.

"Now go play with the other children. My heart stays with you…"

"And mine goes with you," she'd finished the Sinti farewell, her sweet voice making his heart hurt. He'd kissed her again and set her down, then turned away, fighting to keep the pain from his face.

As Jamison had taken his seat on the wagon and the other Sinti had mounted their horses, Mother Tarni had pressed a small bottle into his hand. "Use it wisely," she'd said. Jamison had nodded, and they were off.

Riding along in the wagon the next day, Jamison looked around at the Sinti who'd come with him. The stiff way they moved in their saddles told him their muscles were as tense as his.

They'd been traveling deep in the forest all morning, trying to get as far south as they could without traveling the Southern Road, but now they could see it ahead of them through the trees. The time had come.

Jamison halted the wagon.

"Unwrap the bodies and open the silver box with the broom of herbs."

They obeyed, carefully removing Mother Tarni's blankets from the dead bodies before opening the silver box, which they placed in the midst of the bodies. A light dust flowed from the box, drifting in the faint breeze.

Jamison instructed, "We must stay on the Southern Road long enough for the scent of the bodies and the bitter sand to reach the Dark Ones north of us. When we leave the road, they must be near enough to follow the scent."

The faces around him were grim. They knew that if the Dark Ones were that near, there was a good chance they'd be close enough to attack the party of Sintis. If Mother Tarni was right that the Dark Ones they'd be drawing south were more powerful than the ones they'd fought in order to rescue the *skaeweer*, they would be hard put to fight their way free.

But Jamison had chosen his group wisely. They were all seasoned fighters, sober-minded and careful, but willing to risk their lives for the mission Mother Tarni had set them.

So they squared their shoulders and sharpened their focus, following the wagon onto the Southern Road without hesitating.

Becoming Sinti

When Charla finally raised her head from the hearty bowl of stew she'd been given along with a hunk of buttered bread, she was surprised to see that while she ate, the Sinti had been reloading everything into the wagons. Only Mother Tarni's chair and the one Old Dan sat on remained. Some of the Sinti began throwing dirt on the fire as she watched.

David had finished his bowl of soup as well, but Old Dan had barely started on his, so intent had he been on talking to the Sinti queen.

Mother Tarni stood up. "I will leave you to finish your soup, old friend. I have things to attend to." She motioned and the girl who'd awakened Charla that morning came over. "Sheila will assist you with new clothing," Mother Tarni said to Charla. "You must look like a Sinti if you wish to remain safe."

Charla looked hesitantly at the girl, who was attired in the Sinti costume of full-sleeved loose blouse, long skirt and scarf, but hers was the most colorful outfit Charla had seen yet, the blue shirt and red skirt contrasting with a scarf of mingled green and pink.

Even the woman's boots had been painted with colorful flowers. Over one arm she carried some folded cloth.

Sheila smiled and held out the folded cloth. "My brother is fetching clothes for your grandfather and brother, but you will be the most beautifully arrayed of the three, I assure you!" She smiled at Charla, a twinkle in her eye, and pulled her back toward Mother Tarni's wagon.

When Sheila finally pronounced Charla ready to face the Sintis, Charla was laughing and flushed. Sheila had helped her take a very welcomed and thorough bath in the curtained area of Mother Tarni's wagon, and then treated Charla a bit like a doll. She'd worked the small buttons on the front of a full-sleeved blouse into their loops with practiced fingers, then unfolded a green dress, which she tugged down over the blouse. The bodice of the dress was covered in colorful embroidery in a design of flowers and vines, and a matching belt encircled Charla's waist.

Sheila surveyed Charla critically. "You need…" she murmured, then began tugging some of the bangles off her arms and pushing them onto Charla's, while Charla laughed and protested that she didn't need any jewelry, but she sobered up when Sheila said simply, "You must pass as Sinti now, my friend. Let me do this for you."

Charla subsided, and dutifully admired herself in Mother Tarni's burnished brass mirror when Sheila pronounced her ready. Charla liked bright colors, and the clothes certainly were beautiful. She expressed her deep appreciation to Sheila, who beamed and pulled her out of the wagon to rejoin the Sinti.

The Sinti set off within the hour, the wagons pulling out in a tidy caravan, with Mother Tarni's wagon in the middle of the others. Old Dan, grinning and sporting a colorful Sinti scarf on his head, rode with the Sinti Queen on a spacious padded seat tucked under the deep overhang at the front of the wagon. In front of them was a simple wooden seat upon which rode two muscular Sinti men, one holding the reins of the horses, the other's head turning slowly side to side to survey the woods around them.

Since they were still recovering from their wounds, Charla and David also rode in the wagons, but most of the Sinti were either on horseback or walking alongside the caravan, singing and playing instruments as was their wont.

As dusk fell, the Sinti drove their wagons off the road onto a well-worn path that led to a large clearing, and began to make camp.

The camp had settled into a drowsy sort of quiet. Supper had been eaten and dishes were being washed with much laughter and cheerful chatter. Charla and David sat silent, watching the Sinti as they moved about the camp.

Also sitting silently was Mother Tarni, but the Sinti queen was staring into the distance rather than watching the hustle and bustle around her. The fingers of one hand tapped out a slow rhythm on the arm of her elaborately carved chair. As the last dishes were dried and put away, the Sinti began to return to the fire in groups of three or four and talk quietly. One older man, his graying dark hair caught back in a thick band of silver, came to sit at Mother Tarni's feet with his guitar. He gazed at her tapping fingers for a moment, then began to pluck a similar rhythm on his guitar, eventually adding in chords and rills. He began humming and then singing in a low voice as a young man sat down next to him with a tambourine, which he tapped lightly against his leg as he softly sang harmony.

Mother Tarni seemed oblivious, but when the music started her fingers became still.

Two Sinti men came out of Mother Tarni's wagon carrying Old Dan between them. The old man had spent the afternoon in bed at the Sinti queen's command. "You must regain your strength while you can," she'd said, her tone brooking no argument. "It will be needed soon." Old Dan had meekly obeyed, eating the soup and hearty bread Charla and David brought him for the midday meal and supper, along with a precious orange for dessert.

But now, Mother had decreed that the old man should join her at the Sinti fire.

As the Sinti men set him carefully down in the chair beside Mother's throne, the old man grinned toothlessly at her and mumbled his thanks for her hospitality. Mother smiled in acknowledgment and said, "But that is not the most important thing we have to discuss, friend. We must talk about the Dark Ones."

"You said you could protect us from them," Charla blurted.

"As much as anyone can protect you, I can," Mother returned calmly.

"How did you defeat them the other day?" David asked, leaning forward intently.

"By the power of Oynos," Mother said.

Charla and David exchanged glances. Oynos? Charla frowned, wondering if Mother Tarni was having them on. Or worse, was she not completely sane? It wasn't the first time she'd talked about Oynos as if he were a real person, someone working in their daily affairs. People prayed to Oynos and worshipped him at temples all over Eoroe. But he was a sort of invisible fatherly presence, rather than a power that could stop men like the Dark Ones.

And yet, the Sinti had done so.

Charla turned her attention back to the conversation at the campfire. Mother Tarni was questioning Old Dan. "Tell me, friend, how you came to be in Vallenland. Are you going to Mount Ciel?"

Old Dan nodded.

"What did you say?" Charla demanded.

Mother Tarni and Old Dan ignored her. Charla felt a rush of emotion, made up of the terror, the uncertainty, the grief she'd felt since they left Archenland. Without thinking, she said loudly, "I just hope we're going home soon since I was supposed to be married by now!"

Everyone turned to stare at her, making Charla flush, and then scowl because she had every right to be upset!

"What's this?" Mother Tarni asked Old Dan. "The *skaeweer* was to be married?"

Old Dan nodded a bit sheepishly and confessed that he'd completely forgotten to tell Charla's betrothed that they were leaving.

"Ah," Mother Tarni said, and compassion slipped into her eyes. Charla felt tears blur her own eyes, all the emotions she'd been stuffing down rushing to the surface.

Mother Tarni motioned for one of the Sinti, the young man with the tambourine, to come closer and said to him, "Ethan, you will go to Kingham Village in Archenland to tell Charla's betrothed..." She paused and looked at Charla.

Surprised and suddenly hopeful, Charla choked back a sob and said, "Greene! His name is Timothy Greene. He's one of King Richard's guards."

Mother Tarni smiled at the pride in her voice and continued, "Tell Greene that Charla and her family are safe, and we will escort them back to Kingham Village when their journey is complete."

The young man turned away to do as she commanded, and Charla humbly gave her thanks to the Sinti queen, who nodded in reply and turned back to Old Dan.

Charla rubbed her hand over her eyes, ashamed to be crying, but so relieved that at least Greene would know that she hadn't run out on him. Of course, that had been a week ago now, a week during which Greene must have been frantic with worry. Would he ever forgive her? Would he understand she'd had no choice?

It was too unbearable to think about, so she forced herself to concentrate on Greene getting the message that she was safe. For now, she'd choose to believe that he would welcome her with open arms when they finally returned, instead of being furious with her.

Mother Tarni was talking to Old Dan again. "We must get you to Mount Ciel, friend. Why did you not use the northern route?"

"I planned to, but it was blocked with rocks too heavy for my grandson to move."

Mother nodded. "So you chose to go through Vallenland, hoping that staying off the main road would afford you more protection... but instead it led you to the Dark Ones," she surmised.

Old Dan nodded with a sigh.

Mother Tarni studied him a moment, then smiled. "But that is enough talk. Now is the time for the Sinti to celebrate our new friends!" She motioned and the man next to her began to play a lively tune on the guitar, while some girls with tambourines stood up and began to dance, whirling in circles around the fire as the tambourines rang in the still night air. Other women and men joined the dance, while others raised their voices in song.

Late that night, when the Sinti camp was quieting down, Mother Tarni walked back to her wagon with Charla's family. A couple of the strong Sinti men carried Old Dan inside and then returned to the bottom of the wagon stairs to stand guard. Mother Tarni closed the door and pulled heavy curtains over the small windows.

Charla, Old Dan and David seated themselves on their beds, sinking into the feather mattresses with a sigh. It had been a long day… a long week.

Mother Tarni surveyed their weary faces a moment and said, "There are some things that are too important to risk other ears hearing, so we will not speak of them until we reach our destination."

"Mount Ciel?" Charla breathed.

"Yes," Mother answered, then held up one hand as Charla started to ask another question. "You want to know many things," Mother said. "All will be answered in time, but it must be in Oynos' time, not ours. You must be patient." She repeated firmly, "We will not speak of important things until we reach the mountain."

Charla sighed but Old Dan gave Mother Tarni his sweet, toothless smile and wished the Sinti queen a good night.

Mother Tarni disappeared behind the curtains around her bed, and the evening was ended.

An Unexpected Message

Aurora was in her chambers at the castle, talking with Martin for the fiftieth time about where Charla might be, when a maid knocked on the door and entered, saying, "Princess Aurora, the king asks that you attend him in the weapons room."

Raising her eyebrows, Aurora followed the maid from the room, her husband close behind her.

They entered the weapons room to see an unexpected sight. King Richard, in his fine clothing, a heavy crown on his head, was talking with a rather wild-looking young man. The boy's long black hair was caught in a clasp at the nape of his neck. He had earrings in both ears, and heavy silver rings on his fingers. His simple shirt of muslin had the sleeves rolled up to bare his impressively muscled forearms, and dusty black boots were pulled over his dark pants.

Martin breathed in her ear, "*Sinti*," and Aurora nodded. The wandering traders were known for their musical talents and had entertained Aurora and her family at Kingham Castle before. She didn't recognize this young man, though.

The Sinti boy turned his head as they came in and Aurora saw a serious face and long, slanted eyes of a clear green color.

King Richard said, "Aurora, allow me to introduce Ethan of the Sinti. Ethan, this is my daughter Aurora and her husband Phillip Martin."

The boy gave them a casual nod, which they returned without taking insult. The Sinti respected no authority outside their own leaders.

King Richard continued, "Ethan is one of the Vallenland Sinti."

Aurora raised her eyebrows. That's why she didn't recognize him. Sinti tribes could be found in all the kingdoms of Bryten, but they rarely spent time in kingdoms other than their own.

The king said, "Tell Aurora what you told me."

Ethan said, "Mother Tarni sent me to find a man named Greene."

Aurora frowned. She'd heard of the Sinti queen, but why would she be interested in Greene? She glanced at Martin, but he looked as puzzled as she.

The Sinti boy continued, "I am to give him a message."

Aurora gasped, "Is it about Charla?"

Ethan stared at her a moment, then said, "I can tell you no more."

"It's about Charla! It has to be!" Aurora said, hoping he'd somehow acknowledge she was right, but he just stared at her.

Aurora turned back to her father. "I know you said Greene and Jacobson are to remain completely incognito, but couldn't we find some way to get this message to Greene?"

Her father slowly shook his head. "I'm sorry, darling, but I have no idea where they are, and we can't spare anyone to look for them."

Aurora nodded, but looked at Martin, her eyes pleading with him to find a solution. His eyes thoughtful, he turned to King Richard.

"The Sinti go where they want with no interference from the rulers of a country. Could we use their network to get a message to Greene?"

King Richard pondered a moment, then turned to Ethan. "It's very important that no knows Greene works for me while he's in Arlesland. Would you be willing to try to find him there?"

The boy shrugged. "It doesn't matter whether he is here, or there. I am charged to give him this message."

Aurora's eyes lit up and she started to speak, but her father waved her to silence and cautioned Ethan, "If the message *is* about Charla, Greene must not receive the message until he has finished his mission."

Aurora protested. "But, Father, he needs to know Charla is alright!"

Her father was adamant. "He *needs* to not get himself or Jacobson killed. If the message *is* about Charla, and he gets it before he finishes his mission, he will be distracted at the very least."

"But what if the message is that Charla is grievously wounded?" *Or dead*, Aurora wanted to add but couldn't bring herself to say the words.

King Richard shook his head. "Mother Tarni would've sent the message to me instead of Greene if it were a matter of life or death."

Aurora fumed inwardly. She wanted to know what the message was, and she wanted Greene to know immediately, too!

The Sinti boy was watching her, and seemed to read her expression easily. "Your concern for your friends does you honor, Princess. But Oynos is in charge of all things. Have faith."

Aurora frowned. Leaving everything up to God wasn't something she was entirely comfortable with, if there was some action she could take to help things along.

Ethan said to King Richard, "How will I find your man Greene if he is passing as an Arleslander?"

Aurora laughed. "Well, he's much taller than most men, for one thing, and so is the other Guard he's traveling with, Jacobson. So look for two very tall men. Greene has wavy brown hair, blue eyes, and a dimple in one cheek…"

Her voice trailed away as she saw the grins on her father and Martin's faces. "Oh, stop it! I only know all that because of the time I spent…" Her eyes grew wide and she ran from the room, returning a few minutes later with a paper clutched in her hand.

"There!" she said, handing the paper to Ethan. "That's Greene!"

Martin leaned sideways to look at the picture, then rolled his eyes at Aurora, grinning as he sat back in his chair. "I thought you got rid of those," he teased.

She flushed. "Well, it took me a very long time to get that perspective right…" she hedged.

Martin gave a shout of laughter and pulled her to him for a hug. "Whatever you say, monkey," he said, kissing her hand.

Ethan was studying the picture. "It is a good drawing. You have much talent," he said.

King Richard reached for the picture and surveyed it critically. The young man in the sketch was seated cross-legged on the ground, with a squirrel nibbling on an acorn in his hand. He wore a guard uniform and his hair was tousled, the dimple in one cheek giving his grin an extra layer of charm. His eyes were warm, his affection for the artist apparent.

"Ah, yes," her father said with a grin. "The infamous art lessons!" Aurora flushed again and firmly took the paper from her father, who chuckled.

Handing the paper back to Ethan, she said, "Take this with you to show the Arlesland Sinti, and then you can burn it!" she said, making a face at her husband.

Martin burst into laughter.

The Old Folks

After leaving the wagon in which they'd been smuggled out of the village, Greene and Jacobson made their way back to the main road. There was a steady stream of people heading south, so they easily slipped in among them.

Unfortunately, walking alongside them didn't make the people more inclined to talk. Greene and Jacobson attempted to start conversations with several Arleslanders, but the people just looked at them askance and kept walking. Then they tried walking near large groups, trying to overhear some of their conversation.

What they heard was talk about Uriah conscripting young men to join his army. Many of the boys were doing everything they could to evade the king's command. Opinion was divided amongst the travelers as to whether that was understandable, or whether the young men should risk their lives for the common good.

The best bit of information they managed to overhear was that Uriah was building the army up to strike against the wicked northern kingdoms, who'd had their feet firmly planted on the throats of the southern kingdoms for decades. "Aye, King Uriah now, he knows what's what with those northerners," insisted one burly man. "They think we're dirt on their shoes, but Uriah will show 'em! Then the riches will flow into Arlesland, you'll see! It's hard now, but our valiant king will smash them and take what's rightfully ours!"

It was as his friends cheered on the speaker that one of them happened to spot Greene and Jacobson skulking behind the group and yell, "What're you lookin' at, you two? Better keep your eyes on the road and your ears to yourself!" He shook a fist at them, and Greene and Jacobson wisely dropped their eyes and slowed their pace.

Nothing much happened other than that for their first hour on the road, but then they heard a voice calling out ahead of them. Puzzled, they scanned the road, but the people ahead of them continued walking, none of them seeming to hear the noise.

The sound of the voice got louder as they walked on, until finally they spotted an old man sitting on a fallen log beside the road. He was calling, "Please, sir! Have pity on an old man! Only a few hours of your time would I take! Please, help me if you can!"

Slowing, Greene and Jacobson looked at the people around them, but the travelers going both north and south passed by the old man, ignoring his pleas. Greene and Jacobson exchanged a glance, weighing the cost of following their conscience against the need to blend in.

Jacobson muttered, "We have to help him."

Greene hesitated, then nodded. "Follow my lead." He made his way through the steady stream of people to where the old man sat.

The man had a ruff of pure white hair ringing his freckled head, below which were rheumy eyes and sunken cheeks. He continued to call out in his wavering voice until he spotted Greene and Jacobson angling toward him, then the old eyes lit up and his pleas gained power.

"Oh, sirs! If you could help me, I'm sure you would gain favor in our valiant king's eyes! It would take but a few moments of your time and you would earn my deepest thanks!"

Greene laughed derisively. "What need have we of your thanks, old man? Why are you bothering everyone with your whining, and how would it benefit us?"

The man's face fell for a moment, then he rallied. "No coin have I to give you, kind traveler! But a warm meal and comfortable bed for you and your friend, those I offer you freely!"

Greene laughed again. "What tasks must we undertake to earn your dubious generosity?"

"Oh, kind traveler! The recent storm dislodged some shingles from my roof, but as you can see, I've injured myself and can no longer climb a ladder! All I ask, kind sirs, is that you nail some boards over the hole. It would take no more than an hour of your time, I assure you!"

Greene glanced down at the clumsy bandage on the man's foot before scoffing, "An hour? More like three, or I miss my guess! But you're lucky, old man! My friend and I lost our money gambling last night, so we're in need of a place to stay and a meal. We are at your service, sir!" He gave a mocking bow, as did Jacobson.

The old man stumbled to his feet, leaning heavily on a cane as he dragged his injured foot up and gingerly put his weight on it. "Oh, thank you! You'll be twice-blessed young men for your generosity! I assure you, the work I need done will be only the tiniest inconvenience to men such as yourselves, so strong and healthy as you are!" As he said it, he scanned them up and down, his eyes noting their muscles.

Greene said hastily, "Stop your talking, old man! We don't have all day! Lead on!"

The old man immediately turned and began hobbling along an overgrown path. "Only a little way, good sirs! Only a little way, I assure you."

As they watched him lurch along, dragging his poor injured foot, Greene glanced at Jacobson and saw the same pained look on his friend's face as he was sure was on his own. Greene glanced over his shoulder to make sure they were out of sight of the main road, then he motioned to Jacobson and they moved up beside the old man, scooping him up to rest on their linked arms, his arms around their necks.

Greene said cheerfully, "Too slow, old man! Time is money! Or in this case, time is *food*!"

The old man chuckled and relaxed against them, his body going limp as his benefactors strode along on their long legs. "Yes, yes, as you say, friend. No time to waste on these old legs! Hurry on to the main event!"

They made their way through the forest for several minutes until they passed over a hill and saw a small clearing before them. A modest cabin was nearest the path, with a small field of vegetables stretched out behind it and a few scrawny chickens pecking in the dirt near the narrow lean-to. A dirty old dog raised his head from the shade beneath the porch and began to bark in a rusty voice, his tail thumping in the dirt. His barks brought an old woman to the door of the cabin, where she stood wiping her hands on her apron.

"Mother!" called the old man as Greene and Jacobson put him down. "Friends are here!"

The sight of the old woman beaming at them, of the old man hobbling up the steps to her, touched Greene's heart so he couldn't keep up the pretense of unconcern. When the old man introduced himself as Theo Jones and proudly introduced "Mother" as "Eliza, my sweet wife of seventy years," Greene took her small, soft hand in his and gently shook it.

"It's an honor, ma'am," he said sincerely. "My name is Timmy."

"And I'm Johnny. We're happy to help in any way needed," Jacobson said as he shook hands in turn.

The two old faces beamed at them a moment, then Mr. Jones hobbled back down the stairs and around to the back of the house, where a ladder rested.

Greene and Jacobson insisted that Mr. Jones direct their efforts from the comfort of a milking stool they found in the lean-to. He wanted to hold the ladder while the men carried planks and tools up it to repair the roof, but they managed to convince him they could handle it themselves.

While they worked, sweating in the afternoon sunshine, Mr. Jones kept up a steady stream of conversation, sometimes raising his voice to ask a question of Mrs. Jones, whereupon would come an unintelligible answer from inside the house, which invariably brought a response of "Yes, yes, just as you say, Mother!"

When Mr. Jones finally paused to draw breath, Greene seized the moment to ask the talkative man a question. "This is our first visit to Arlesland, so we don't know much about King Uriah. What kind of ruler is he?"

The old man hesitated, then said, "Well, now, Mother and I, we keep to ourselves, we do, and we don't have much to do with the king, so I can't say much about that. But what I can tell you all about is my grandchildren! Oh, what scamps they are!" And the old man didn't give Greene a chance to interrupt again.

Greene and Jacobson did a much more thorough job of repairing the roof than Mr. Jones expected them to, earning his fervent thanks in the process. Once back on the ground, they looked around at the pile of wood that needed cutting, the decrepit chicken house, the rows of bean canes that were listing heavily to one side or another, and the unsteady porch support.

Ignoring Mr. Jones's objections and the ones Mrs. Jones added when he called Mother to lend her voice to his, Greene and Jacobson got to work on the most urgent tasks, and had made good inroads on the repairs when Mrs. Jones called them inside for supper.

Greene and Jacobson washed up at the outside pump and left their dusty boots beside the back door, then walked into a house full of good smells. The house was one big room, with a small sleeping alcove hidden behind a draped curtain.

Mrs. Jones had ears of corn and beans from the small garden, tomatoes from the vines by the front porch, and cool water from the well. A large loaf of bread was ready to be cut, with the knife and a small bowl of butter laying ready by Mr. Jones's place.

Mrs. Jones clucked around them until Greene and Jacobson were settled at the table, even going so far as to tuck napkins into the necks of their shirts, patting them on the shoulder as she did so. Greene and Jacobson exchanged grins, then quickly bowed their heads as Mr. Jones began to pray.

"Most gracious Oynos, we are thankful for this bounty you have set before us, and we offer up a special thanks for the blessing you have sent us in the form of these fine young men. Guide them in all their endeavors, and watch over them in their travels."

"Amen," they all murmured, and Mrs. Jones began clucking again as she urged large portions of everything on her guests.

"Now, Timmy and Johnny, tell us all about yourselves." Mr. Jones said.

Greene took a moment to wipe his mouth with his napkin while shooting a glance at Jacobson. "Well, sir, we're traveling from Bagginsland to Reimsland." He left out the usual story that they had relatives in Reimsland, because he just couldn't lie to this sweet old couple any more than he had to.

Fortunately, Mr. Jones was quite willing to leave it at that. "Ah, Bagginsland! We know it well, don't we, Mother?"

Mrs. Jones was smiling and nodding. "Yes, indeed! Father was born there, you know," she confided to Jacobson. "I met him when I went north to try to find work, and we ended up raising a family there."

"Yes, yes," Mr. Jones agreed. "Thirty years we had there, thirty very happy years." He sighed.

At Greene's inquiring look, Mrs. Jones said, "My parents were doing poorly, you see. None of my brothers or sisters were willing to take on the task of taking care of them, so Father and I decided it was up to us. It was hard to leave behind our friends and our children, but they were grown up with families of their own." She played with her fork a moment, pushing beans around on her plate. "I didn't want to come back to Arlesland," she said softly, looking from Greene to Jacobson. "It's not a… happy place." She shrugged, looking toward her husband.

He sighed. "We've struggled to fit in here. At first we were busy taking care of Mother and Father Higgins, but once they passed on… We tried to make friends in the community, but…"

Mrs. Jones took up the tale. "But they resented me for living in a northern kingdom for all those years, and they resented Father for being a native of Bagginsland. They wanted nothing to do with us."

"And, I have to say," Mr. Jones confided, "I'm glad we keep to ourselves nowadays. Things have gone from bad to worse these last few years since Uriah took over from his father. The old king was bad, but Uriah…" He shook his head.

Greene hated to pump the old couple for information, but he couldn't pass up the opportunity when they seemed so willing to confide. He couldn't ask them about Uriah's plans for war, but there were other insights they might offer.

"We've heard that Uriah wasn't always as… paranoid he is now. Were you here when he was young?"

"Oh, yes," Mrs. Jones said. "We moved back when he was maybe… ten or eleven?"

Mr. Jones nodded. "Yes, about that time. He grew into a fine young man."

Mrs. Jones nodded. "He was different than his father. Quieter, bookish, you know. We'd see him standing by his father when they visited the villages. His father would be harsh, ordering us to work harder to pay our taxes to him, but when Uriah spoke up, he praised us for our hard work and encouraged us to do our best and help each other when needed. Usually his father would cut him off when he started in on that, but we could tell he was a thoughtful young man. But then…"

Mr. Jones nodded. "Uriah changed drastically."

Greene leaned forward in his chair. "We heard he was deeply affected by the death of one of his friends?"

Mr. Jones answered, "Not just a friend, but one of his guards, a young man he'd grown up with. I think that not only was Uriah affected by his friend's death, but by how close he'd come to death himself. If one of his guards could be killed… I think it must have worked on his mind. It's the only thing that explains his behavior."

Mrs. Jones was nodding in agreement.

Greene saw an opening. "So… his paranoia… do you think it extends to the northern kingdoms? Could he think he's in danger from them?"

Mr. Jones said, "Oh yes! He's made that very clear in the past few years. One reason he's become so popular is because he's managed to make the northern kingdoms the scapegoat for all of

Arlesland's woes. The failing crops, the droughts, the starvation so many of our people face… it's all due to some vast conspiracy from the north. And the people are desperate for someone to blame, so they believe it!"

Mrs. Jones interjected, "The one thing Uriah didn't lose over the years is his charm. He doesn't bother with it most of the time, but when he turns it on… he makes you believe the only thing he cares about is you, that you're the most important thing in his life, that he'll do anything to protect you, so of course *he* isn't responsible for what's happening to Arlesland. He claims he tries so hard to make the kingdom prosper, but he can't do much because the northerners are determined to keep us down."

Greene asked, "And do you think his hatred of the northern kingdoms could lead to war?"

Mr. Jones nodded somberly. "There are rumors that he's preparing for war. He's been recruiting young men for his army…"

"But they don't want to go," Mrs. Jones said. "Rumor is he keeps his troops as starved as the rest of us, sending them like lambs to the slaughter. Why would Uriah spend money feeding men who are just going to die? The men are desperate not to go into his army, not least because they'd leave behind families to starve without the men to work the farms. Uriah's good at working his charm, but even his charm can't overcome that."

She studied Greene and Jacobson for a moment. "How long do you plan to stay in Arlesland?"

Greene fumbled for an answer that wouldn't be a lie. "We're not in any hurry. Thought we'd just wander along, taking our time."

Mrs. Jones was shaking her head. "I wouldn't recommend that, young man."

"Get you through and out as soon as possible, I would, yes indeed," Mr. Jones nodded.

"Why? Are we in danger because we're not from here?" Greene asked.

Mr. Jones answered, "No… it's more that *everyone* here is in danger."

Mrs. Jones nodded uneasily. "There's some kind of… feeling that's been slowly taking over Arlesland. It's been growing worse since Uriah came to power. His paranoia seems to feed it, and it spreads like a disease. Most of the people in the towns and villages have caught it. They're suspicious and greedy, cruel and selfish. Those of us out here in the country, the ones who keep to ourselves, we've done better, but even *our* neighbors have grown fearful and distrustful. I think Father and I have done better because we had all those years in Bagginsland when we didn't have to worry about surviving like the people here did."

Mr. Jones agreed. "It's a bad place, a fearful place. It's not healthy for you to be here, especially traveling through the towns and villages as you will be. This place… it works on your mind in the worst way."

Greene and Jacobson exchanged a glance. There was no way they could avoid the villages and complete their mission. They had to be where the people were so they could gauge what was happening.

Mr. Jones regarded them a moment, then said, "Maybe it will help you understand what I mean if I tell you more about Uriah."

Greene and Jacobson nodded, trying not to look too eager.

"Uriah has a twist in him, something that makes him pure evil at times. Sometimes his mask slips completely and he shows that side of himself publicly, but more often it comes out in the worst kind of deviousness. He has many nobles who frequent his court, of course, and many who claim they're his close friends, but I don't think they're very smart to do so. Uriah has a habit of killing his close friends, you see.

"The worst part is that, although he may react with anger at first, call them out publicly, then he'll suddenly act as if they're bosom pals again, throwing banquets for them and such. But at some point in the future, maybe many years down the road, that person will disappear or have an 'accident.' Even worse, Uriah might decide to make a spectacle of them. And those spectacles…" Mr. Jones gave a sudden shiver. "You don't want to know what he does. Most kings would have their enemies thrown in jail or publicly beaten, but there have been terrible rumors that Uriah gives them poison and makes his whole court watch them die a horrible death. But even that's the easy way out! The other things he does… well, they're not fit for a decent person to talk about. Disgusting and vile." Mr. Jones shook his head, shivering again.

"I think," said Mrs. Jones, "the most disgusting part is that after watching the traitor die, Uriah makes a public proclamation about how he wanted to be a friend to the man who betrayed him, but the man's actions drove him to treat him so. And by the end of the speech, if you can believe it, he has the public eating out of his hand again and actively seeking his approbation. It's a twisted, horrible thing, and makes me fear for the whole kingdom when Uriah has them believing his actions are justified. You can be convinced to kill *anyone*, if you think like that."

They were all silent for a moment, then Mr. Jones said, "Well, let's not talk about that anymore! Surely there is something uplifting we could discuss instead."

Mrs. Jones gave a sigh and nodded. "Indeed! Let me read you the latest letter from our youngest daughter, all about the antics her little boy has been getting into!"

As she bustled off and Mr. Jones stared thoughtfully into the fire, Greene and Jacobson exchanged a glance. They'd heard more than they'd bargained for, and now they absolutely did *not* want to draw King Uriah's attention.

As the talk and the fire dwindled down, Greene glanced around the room. There was no loft, and as far as he could tell there was only one bed in the curtained alcove. Maybe he and Jacobson were going to sleep in the lean-to?

"Now, young gentlemen, I promised you a good meal and a comfortable bed for the night!" Mr. Jones rocked to his feet, wobbling a moment as he found his balance, and made his way toward the curtained alcove. Puzzled, Greene and Jacobson followed him, and saw him proudly gesturing to the bed behind it. "Your feet may hang off a bit," he said, eyeing their length, "but I can assure you it is mighty comfortable. Our oldest son built it, and our daughters stuffed the mattress." The old man was proud as he motioned them to come into the alcove.

Jacobson asked hesitantly, "Where will you and Mrs. Jones sleep?"

Mrs. Jones called from behind them, "Don't you worry! We have plenty of blankets and we'll be very comfortable tonight!"

They peered out from the curtain and saw the old woman gingerly bending over to place several quilts on the floor. As they watched, dumbfounded, she hobbled over to pull cushions from the chairs to use as pillows.

"No," Jacobson said firmly as Greene shook his head. "You are not giving us your bed."

Mrs. Jones began to soothe them, with Mr. Jones adding his assurances that they would be just fine, but Greene and Jacobson were adamant.

Greene said, "We are absolutely *not* taking your bed. You are very sweet to want to give it to us, but that excellent meal and your company is more than enough payment for the work we did."

Mrs. Jones's hands fluttered in agitation and Mr. Jones began to remonstrate with them, but Greene and Jacobson were firm. The old folks protested a little more, but finally gave in.

"You remind me of my sons," Mr. Jones said quietly. "Such good boys you are. I know your parents are proud."

The old couple allowed themselves to be banished to their comfortable bed, and after a while, their lantern went out. The only light came from the guttering fire.

Greene and Jacobson were silent in the dark, thinking over all they'd learned, and eventually felt sleep overtake them.

The next morning, Greene and Jacobson were up before Mr. and Mrs. Jones. They carried logs in to build up the fire, gathered eggs from the chickens, and milked the cow they found wandering around the yard with her calf. By the time the old folks appeared from the sleeping alcove, their guests had set the table and Jacobson was frying eggs while Greene sliced bread.

"Oh!" came the cries as the old people looked around at everything, their mouths and eyes wide in astonishment. Tears sprang to Mrs. Jones' eyes as she thanked them for such an unexpected gift. "Someone cooking breakfast for me…"

"And doing chores for *me*," her husband interjected.

"It's just the most wonderful thing!" Mrs. Jones finished. "Such a blessing! It's just the thing our own children would do for us if they were here!"

After they'd seated themselves and Mr. Jones had asked the blessing, Greene asked, "Have you considered going back to Bagginsland now that Mrs. Jones' parents are gone?"

The Joneses exchanged glances. Father said hesitantly, "We would certainly love to. We've stayed this long because we feel so sorry for our neighbors. They are hard-headed and believe Uriah's lies… but they're so pitiful. Some of them are our age, but they've worked so hard all their lives that they're just worn out. They fuss and fight with their families, so some of them don't have anyone else to depend on."

"We've been looking after them when we can, taking them some of the food we grow," Mother said. "Father is still able to get around pretty well. He can't swing an ax as well as he used to, but he can cut up the smaller branches that blow off the trees and things like that, and so far that's sustained us. It's getting harder for us to move around the garden, bending to pull weeds and such, so we *have* been thinking more and more about moving back north. We'd need help to do that, though, and we hate to bother our children. They're so busy with their own lives. So, as long as we're needed here and can help, we might as well stay. We're far enough off the road that no one bothers us much."

Greene and Jacobson nodded, but Greene knew that Jacobson, like himself, was trying to work out how they could help the old couple get north, while still completing their mission.

Greene and Jacobson got the Joneses into the best shape they could, spending the morning cutting logs into kindling, and even visiting the Jones' closest neighbor, a cantankerous old woman who merely grunted when they showed up to do the same for her.

They brought in produce from the garden and stored it in the cold cellar. They gathered apples, and found some small pears from a stunted tree growing in the shade of the large pines out back.

They even re-wrapped the clumsy bandage on Mr. Jones' hurt foot. "My arthritis is so bad, it's hard for me to wrap it well," Mrs. Jones said, embarrassed about the job she'd done.

"And I can't even reach down that far!" Mr. Jones laughed.

As he tucked the end of the bandage neatly in, Jacobson said, "It's no problem at all. We've enjoyed our visit with you, and we're happy to do whatever we can before we leave."

They ate a hearty lunch with the Joneses, and Mrs. Jones packed them enough food for two good meals, then they filled their water bags with clear water from the well, hugged the old couple goodbye, and reluctantly set off on their way.

"Think they'll be alright?" Jacobson asked as they turned to give one more wave to the couple receding into the distance.

"Not if Uriah goes to war," Greene said grimly.

"We could stop back by here on our way home," Jacobson suggested.

Greene nodded. "If we come back this way, and have time. If not… maybe we can get word to their children in Bagginsland."

Satisfied, Jacobson strode beside him with renewed energy, but Greene still worried.

"I see you, Sinti!"

Jamison and the Sinti had placed the box of bitter sand among the bodies of the Dark Ones and were now riding along the Southern Road. Knowing that they were deliberately drawing evil beings of great power toward them had silenced the Sinti tendency toward songs and laughter. The faces beneath their colorful scarves were serious, heads turning side to side as their horses trotted along the dusty road.

Jamison, driving the wagon, had his attention suddenly drawn from the road when he felt the small bottle inside his jacket growing warm. It was the bottle Mother Tarni had given him, the one she'd urged him to use with caution. He immediately shook up the reins of the horses pulling the wagon, and they broke into a swift trot.

The bottle became uncomfortably warm against his shirt just as Jamison spotted the Reimsland border ahead. He felt a surge of relief. Drawing the Dark Ones out of the northern kingdoms was key to Mother Tarni's plan, so crossing the Reimsland border was imperative.

The Sinti stopped long enough to throw Mother Tarni's blankets loosely over the bodies of the Dark Ones before they reached the border gate. The bored Reimsland guards waved them through without the wagon even slowing down. Around a curve in the road, Jamison turned the wagon off the road and bumped along the uneven ground into the forest. He pulled up the horses and leapt from the wagon as some of the Sinti dismounted to remove the horses from the harness and saddle one for Jamison to ride.

The silver box containing the bitter sand still lay open among the bodies of the Dark Ones. Jamison grabbed it and slammed it shut, then leapt onto the horse and tucked the box safely into the saddlebag. The other Sinti shook up their reins, swiftly following Jamison as he fled into the woods, leaving the wagon of dead bodies behind.

The bottle in his pocket was burning Jamison's skin now.

They raced through the forest, the horses swerving around boulders and leaping over fallen trees.

Jamison felt the skin of his chest blistering from the heat of the bottle.

They're too close. Even the Golden Grain won't help if they follow us all the way to the border.

With the thought, he pulled up his horse and waved the other Sinti past him, calling "Make for the Bagginsland border!" as he turned to go back the way he'd come. The Sinti didn't argue, just lay flat along their horses' necks and rode like the wind.

As Jamison rode back toward the wagon they'd left behind, the pain of his blistering skin became unbearable. He reached into his pocket with his gloved hand and pulled out the bottle, which was still uncomfortably warm even through the leather.

The wagon of dead bodies was in sight now and for a moment Jamison was confused. There was no one around it.

But then he saw them.

Or, more accurately, *felt* them.

A miasma flowed off them, hitting him like a rock wall, as they rode into sight. Jamison felt his body begin to shake with unreasoning terror, and gritted his teeth to keep them from chattering. The control that Sinti learned from an early age enabled him to remain where he was, but he couldn't master the instinctive reaction of his body.

There were five Dark Ones riding hard through the trees, the hooves of their horses flowing over the ground as if they barely touched it. They wore streaming dark cloaks, the hoods shading their faces like night on a grave.

The Dark Ones halted at sight of the wagon, pulling their steaming horses up to circle and stamp around it as the hooded heads swiveled to keep the dead bodies within in view.

Jamison, shielded from their sight by a wide tree, stayed as still as he could. His horse had frozen when the Dark Ones rode into view and now it trembled beneath him, deep waves of fear sweeping through its muscles.

He couldn't see the faces under the dark hoods, but somehow he thought they were *sniffing* the air around the wagon.

Jamison heard a low murmur of voices. The Dark Ones made as if to dismount and Jamison flexed his muscles and tightened the reins, ready to escape as soon as they were off their horses… but then one of the hoods turned sharply toward him, and the others froze.

Sounding as if it were right beside him, a soft voice whispered in his ear.

"I see you, *Sinti.*"

Jamison tried to make his hands pull the reins, make his thighs squeeze the sides of his horse, make any move at all to get away. But fear flooded his body and he couldn't move the tiniest muscle.

It was the pain in his hand that finally broke the spell. The bottle had grown red hot and was blistering his palm, steam rising from the leather glove. As the pain grew, it overwhelmed even his fear of the Dark One, and Jamison began to pray.

His teeth were gritted so hard he couldn't speak the words, but they filled his mind.

O blessed Oynos, I do beseech you, save this your servant from the power of the Dark Ones. O blessed Oynos, I do beseech you, save this your servant from the power of the Dark Ones. O blessed Oynos…

His frozen muscles unclenched and his mind screamed *"Ride!"*

Jamison jerked his reins to the side just as he brought up the hand holding the bottle of Golden Grain and threw it toward the Dark Ones.

As his horse screamed and wheeled to flee, Jamison saw the bottle turning slowly in the air, almost floating, until it suddenly smashed on the ground.

The explosion of golden grain hid the Dark Ones, the wagon, everything from Jamison's view, and he heard the Dark Ones screaming in rage.

Jamison's horse was in headlong flight by then. He made no effort to get it under control, merely glad to be moving away from the horrible fear and dread surrounding the Dark Ones. The Golden Grain would disorient the Dark Ones, make it hard for them to follow his trail, but that was no reason not to fly like the wind away from them.

The horse ran, sweat streaming from it like water, until it finally stopped from pure exhaustion. Jamison had no idea where they were, but as he began to look around for a stream where his spent horse could refresh itself, he heard a soft call.

"Jamison!"

The other Sinti were running toward him from a thick glade of trees to his left. Their eyes wide, they came to support him as he dismounted onto shaky legs.

They wanted to know what had happened, but Jamison would only say, "I was delivered by Oynos."

The Sinti nodded somberly, placing their hands palm-to-palm and touching them to their foreheads in reverence. "The grace of Oynos," they murmured.

"The grace of Oynos," Jamison repeated, then his legs gave way as he fainted.

Bother Me No More

A servant opened the door of Uriah's chamber and bowed to the king, who was waiting impatiently for his valet to finish arraying him in splendor (which in Uriah's case consisted of black breeches and a plain black doublet, with a thin crown on his dark hair).

The servant murmured, "This just arrived by pigeon, Your Majesty."

Uriah snatched the small tube, pulled out the note curled inside, and dropped the tube on the floor, where the servant discreetly retrieved it. The king's golden eyes narrowed as he read the missive.

Have you acquired the sword? Although broken, it is still a symbol of my family's power. If you bring it to me, I can assure you of my support. Otherwise, you must work much, much harder.

Remember all I've taught you. Bide your time, wait to exact revenge on those you suspect of rebellion. They may yet help in your plans to conquer the northern kingdoms. Continue pressing your people to show their dedication through sacrifice.

Find the sword. Prove that you can create a true fighting force. Until then, bother me no more.
  -R-

Uriah growled low in his throat. "Bother me no more"! As if she weren't the one who'd contacted *him*, asking if he was ready to invade the northern kingdoms!

Under his annoyance, though, there was a thread of fear. Was he wise to align himself with the queen of Sutherne? She was powerful, no doubt. But would she really allow him to rule Bryten as she'd claimed, or would she snatch the prize from him?

Since he'd first met her, the power she held had grown from one small kingdom on the southern continent to encompass the entirety of Sutherne. Her assurance in her power and her disdain for him had grown at an equal rate, so now she treated him rather like an insect on the sole of her boot: necessary to attend to, but only in order to remove it permanently.

Scowling, Uriah read the note again. That blasted sword! She'd first told him about it months ago, demanding it as part of their bargain. How was he supposed to find a broken sword in a kingdom full of them? According to her, the sword wasn't broken in half, as most were, though, rather having a crack along the length of it.

Throwing the note in the fire, Uriah picked up another letter, one he'd received the day before from King Albert of Reimsland, his only ally. He had convinced Albert to join him in the attack on the northern kingdoms after hinting that he had the support of the queen of Sutherne.

Have you solved the problem of recruits for our army? My people are starving just as yours are. I must tell you, your advice years ago to force my people to give me every extra bit of food along with all their valuables seems to have been a very ill-sighted goal now that they're starving. It doesn't seem to have worked well for you, either, judging by the men you've sent to our new training barracks.

Uriah ground his teeth at the insult. King Albert had come to Uriah many years ago, trying to determine how he commanded such a fanatically loyal populace. Uriah had enjoyed stringing the other king along without revealing his methods, until the day he realized they could combine resources.

Uriah flung Albert's note on the fire as well and strode from the room. Today was his usual day to inspect the granaries.

Climbing the steps to the balcony at the top of the first storage building, where he could overlook the full barrels his subjects had sent, he listened vaguely to the report of the recorder of the granaries.

The scowl faded from Uriah's face as a thought struck him. How stupid he was. The answer to one of his problems was simple: His soldiers should be the only well-fed citizens in Arlesland. He wouldn't have any problems getting volunteers then, he'd wager.

Leaving the granary recorder in mid-sentence, Uriah practically ran back to his chambers. Striding to his desk, he sat down and set quill to paper.

Greetings, Albert. I know how to create our army.

As he finished the letter and gave it to a servant, his captain of the guards entered the room.

"Your Majesty, there is a soldier here to see you…"

Uriah cut him off, waving an impatient hand. "You know I have no time for petty complaints!"

The captain bowed in acknowledgment. "Yes, Your Majesty. But he has knowledge of the sword you seek."

Uriah's eyes lit up. "Bring him!"

The captain leaned into the corridor and waved someone forward. Uriah critically surveyed the man who hesitantly entered and bowed low before him. He wasn't a young soldier, but Uriah didn't recognize him.

"Where are you stationed?"

"At the prison castle, if it please Your Majesty!"

Uriah frowned. He hadn't visited the southern prison in years, not since… He pulled his attention back to the present.

"My captain says you have knowledge of a sword."

"Yes, Your Majesty!" The soldier looked at him with glowing eyes, as if thrilled to offer this gift to his king.

Uriah waved for him to continue.

"Your Majesty, it happened many years ago. I was at the house of one of the other soldiers, and there on his table was this sword. Cracked right down the middle it was, just like the one you're seeking. I laughed and asked why he kept such a thing, and he said it had belonged to his father."

Uriah's eyes narrowed. "You saw the sword with your own eyes?"

The soldier nodded.

Trying to hide his excitement, Uriah asked, "What is the name of the man?"

The soldier told him.

Fighting Dens

After leaving the Joneses, Greene and Jacobson continued going south. They had enough food from Mrs. Jones to last for two days if they ate sparingly, and it was early enough in their trip that they could afford to miss a meal or two, but they anticipated that the mission would last at least two weeks, possibly three, so making money was imperative.

"We could get work on a farm," Jacobson suggested.

Greene pondered the idea. His instinct was to stick to the villages, despite what the Joneses had advised. Jacobson was against it.

"They might be on the watch for us in the villages," he pointed out. "I'm sure those soldiers from the last village aren't too happy we evaded them."

Greene agreed. "But are they angry enough to waste resources on finding us? I say we make our way to the next village and judge the reception we get from the guards at the gate. If any villages have gotten word to be on the lookout for us, it'll be the ones in this area. I don't think it would be smart to avoid villages the whole time we're here."

Jacobson reluctantly agreed.

As on the previous day, there were other travelers on the road, but they weren't interested in making conversation. Greene did manage to get one man to give them a tip on making money, though. When Greene mentioned they were looking for short-term work as they made their way toward Reimsland, the man looked him and Jacobson up and down and grunted, "Might try the fighting dens. There's one in every village. Men like you could make some good money there."

Jacobson seemed puzzled. When he and Greene were alone again, he asked, "What's a fighting den?"

Greene looked at him in surprise, then remembered that the only thing similar to a fighting den where they lived in Kingham Village was the stable yard where some of the men liked to gather for good-natured fights, the kind where you helped your opponent up after you knocked him down and laughed about it afterward at the local tavern.

Greene, however, had grown up in Fairham Village, the most violent village in Archenland, where there was a *real* fighting den. And he knew something about the Arlesland fighting dens, too, because his father had fought in them during his travels as a young man.

"A fighting den is... not a nice place," he finally said. Glancing at Jacobson, he admitted, "But we can make some money, if we're smart." He gave a sudden grin. "And it's a great way to work off some energy!" After a minute, he added, "And anger."

Jacobson frowned and didn't reply.

They had no problems getting into the next village. The bored guard barely glanced at them as they shuffled through with the other travelers who were bunched up at the gate. Finding a quiet alley, they pulled out the food that Mrs. Jones had packed for them that morning and ate it along with some of the purloined vegetables they still had from the first village. Then they carefully counted out some of the precious coins Jacobson still had and made their way to the local tavern.

Sipping mugs of small beer, Greene and Jacobson watched the villagers around them, who hunched over their food and talked in low voices.

Jacobson said in a low voice, "At least we're starting to look like we might fit in."

Greene met his eyes and grinned. As King's Guards, they kept their hair neatly trimmed and were usually clean shaven, but four days on the road had made both a bit shaggy. They'd washed up at the Jones' farm, but as soon as they left they'd rubbed some dirt onto their hands and faces to look rougher.

Greene smiled to himself at the thought of what Charla would say if she saw him, but then the pain of her leaving hit him and he firmly put thoughts of her out of his mind.

Think about her when you're done with the mission. That's all you can do.

The men a couple of feet away were throwing coins on their table and getting to their feet. One of them clearly said, "…fight starts in a few minutes. Supposed to be some good ones tonight."

His companion grunted and said, "Hope you brought plenty of money, if you have any left from last night."

The first man said, "Ha! I might just back a winner tonight!"

The other man laughed. "Fat chance. Never have, never will."

Greene and Jacobson threw their own coins on the table and followed them out.

Jacobson managed to keep his jaw from dropping when they walked into the fighting den, but Greene saw how wide his friend's eyes were as he looked around warily. Greene felt his own jaw clenching as his stomach started to roil.

Greene fought against the panic, but he couldn't dredge up any other feeling except despair. Everything about this place reminded him of his father. The smells of sweat and blood, the raw voices urging violence … it felt like home.

His da had dragged him to a fighting den when he was only ten years old. The young Greene had been horrified at the rage that permeated the air, a rage even greater than when his father was in the grip of his demons at home. Watching his father pummel a man into a bloody mess that night, Greene had unexpectedly found himself grateful. At least his father never unleashed that level of violence on his family.

Greene's father had been trained in dirty fighting techniques in dens like this one, and his strength made him a formidable opponent. He'd never lost a fight as far as Greene knew, and he'd almost killed a few men. Witnessing one of those fights, Greene had been terrified, especially when it took five grown man to pull his father off the other man. What if his father lost control with his family like that?

It was one reason Greene had finally left home. He worried about leaving his mother and sisters, but he'd realized that he was the one who truly enraged his father, the only one with a chance of challenging him. His mother was adept at calming his father, and his sisters followed her lead, but his father's rage was worse, much worse, when Greene, with his strong body and unyielding mind, was around.

Now Greene was right back in his worst nightmare. He didn't want to be here, didn't want to do the things he'd seen his father do in the dens back home.

Jacobson, watching him closely, saw his distress and pulled on Greene's arm to get his attention. Jacobson had grown up with a father full of rage, too, and he and Greene knew they were taking a risk putting themselves into such a situation, but they'd talked it over carefully earlier that day.

"Remember the plan," Jacobson cautioned Greene.

Greene's jaw unclenched and he took a deep breath.

"I'll go first," Jacobson continued.

At that, Greene relaxed and almost smiled. Their plan was to fall back on their tried-and-true approach of bringing humor to intense situations, so he knew he'd enjoy watching Jacobson put on a show.

They watched several fights first. The same men fought over and over, picking different opponents each time, so Greene and Jacobson were able to study them and learn their weaknesses. The men were all much thinner than Greene and Jacobson, but their bodies were covered in lean muscle and they moved well, pummeling each other with powerful fists and vicious kicks.

After each fight, the winner took a third of the money that was bet on the fight. The best fighters soon had wads of cash carefully buttoned into the inside pockets of their pants, which were the only thing they wore in the ring except their boots.

Finally, Jacobson stepped up when the ringmaster called for a new opponent. The man in the ring was one of the larger fighters and had knocked his other opponents down quickly, barely giving them a chance to defend themselves.

As Jacobson walked forward, the crowd parted in surprise, looking up at the stranger and whispering among themselves about his chances of winning. A flurry of betting took place, and Greene was pleased to see that a decent amount of money flowed toward the man recording the bets.

Jacobson was divesting himself of his jacket and shirt, handing them to Greene to hold. The crowd was surveying Greene now as well, whispering about whether he'd follow his friend into the ring. Greene tried to keep a slightly dumb look on his face. He didn't want to give the game away.

Jacobson ambled into the ring, long limbs loose and gangly as he looked around with an innocent grin on his face. His shorter opponent sized him up a minute, then attacked.

Jacobson let himself get pummeled a bit until blood was flowing from a few cuts on his face, then swung his arm around awkwardly and managed to whack the man's head so he went reeling to the edge of the ring. He fell against the spectators, who yelled and thrust him back toward Jacobson. The man shook his head and came back swinging.

Jacobson let him make contact and fell back, his arms and legs windmilling as he tried to keep his balance. Greene snorted a laugh, then caught himself and dropped his head, shaking it in apparent dismay at his friend's clumsiness. Jacobson picked himself up off the floor and swung again, this time managing to catch his opponent under the chin and send him crashing to the floor.

The man wallowed around in the dirt for a moment, then came to his hands and knees, scowling up at Jacobson. Concern on his face, Jacobson reached down to help him up, but the man yelled an obscenity and slapped his hand away. Jacobson shrugged, making Greene laugh inwardly, and waited for the man to regain his feet.

Greene wished he'd bet on Jacobson himself, because he could predict exactly when Jacobson would deliver the knockout blow.

Jacobson watched the man sway and shake his head, obviously exhausted, and Jacobson's face puckered. The man stumbled toward him and punched at his head, and Jacobson awkwardly punched his opponent's stomach and then delivered an uppercut that landed with enough strength to send the man flying backward to land on the floor, where he lay still among the settling dust.

The crowd stared a moment, waiting for the man to get up, but the fight master counted down the seconds and declared Jacobson the winner. The majority of the crowd was disgusted and responded with boos, but a few lucky men grinned as they were awarded their winnings. Jacobson was all humility as he accepted his cash in turn and kept murmuring what a lucky surprise it was, until he seemed to catch himself and said loudly, "But of course I knew I'd win in the end." The crowd surveyed him with narrowed eyes, trying to judge how good he really was.

Greene had thoroughly enjoyed Jacobson's performance, and was feeling calmer as he in turn hesitantly stepped forward to join a fight. As he handed his shirt and jacket to Jacobson, his friend loudly told him not to worry. "Just do the best you can!" he said, clapping Greene on the shoulder in support.

But the crowd noticed that Jacobson didn't lay any money down on his friend, so they once again bet a hefty amount on Greene's opponent, although a few intrepid individuals put their money on the stranger.

Greene followed Jacobson's example of uncoordinated awkwardness and managed to somehow win his own fight. The crowd didn't boo him, though, instead staring at him and Jacobson, with a few encouraging them to fight some more. Greene and

Jacobson humbly resisted their efforts for a few fights and then let themselves be persuaded.

They won their second fights as well, and seemed to be gaining confidence, so when they stepped up for their third fights, the majority of the money was on them for the first time. They ended those fights a little more quickly, and proudly accepted the additional money they'd earned as the favorites in the fight. Even though they hadn't earned the favorite's money in the first two fights, they'd still made out well due to the unusually high amount of money placed on their opponents and, most importantly, they'd managed to enjoy the fights instead of giving into the darkness that hovered within the fighting den.

A few of the men who'd won large amounts of money backing them insisted on taking them out for a drink afterward, and one of the men insisted that they sleep in his barn that night instead of spending some of their precious winnings on a room at the inn. Of course, he did charge them almost as much as they would've spent at an inn for the privilege, but they were happy to do so as it meant they got to talk to him a bit on the ride to his farm.

Lying comfortably on piles of hay in the barn that night, Greene and Jacobson talked in low voices about what they'd learned. The men, believing Greene and Jacobson were citizens of Reimsland, had talked openly in front of them about Uriah.

"What was he saying right before we left the tavern?" Jacobson asked. He'd gone to the bar to settle his and Greene's bill and had come back to hear the tail end of the conversation.

"He was talking about Uriah conscripting local boys into his military. He's promising them three meals a day, *and* he's offering to give their families one good meal a day in honor of their sacrifice, so everyone is encouraging them to join."

Jacobson frowned. "So Uriah found a bribe that works. Did they say how many have signed up?"

Greene said, "There have been thirty from this village alone."

Jacobson whistled. It wasn't a very big village, so thirty was an impressive number. Another thought struck him. "But if Uriah is taking the healthy boys, who is left to work the farms and give him the extra food he's demanding?"

Greene said, "The older men, women and children."

Jacobson said, "And what happens when those boys die in the attempt against the northern kingdoms and their families are starving because Uriah is using all the food for his dying troops?"

Greene said, "Yeah. Very short-term planning on Uriah's part, and his people don't see the flaw in his argument, either."

Jacobson said, "They're probably so desperate for food they'll do anything to get it now, instead of worrying about later."

From Bad to Worse

Jacobson had been jubilant over their success in the first fighting den, and Greene had been cautiously relieved, too. Now they had a way to make money, and being in that environment didn't seem to have done them any harm.

But Greene was worried about the long-term effect of the fighting dens. Jacobson's home life had been as bad as Greene's, with both fathers beating their spouses and children, but Jacobson had managed to hold onto a basic sense of optimism that Greene struggled with.

Greene had grown up in a village settled by one family, whose descendants had inherited a streak of uncontrollable anger, so Greene had been immersed in a culture of rage since the day he was born. Maybe that was the difference?

Whatever the reason, Greene was afraid of the effect the fighting dens might have on him in particular. The night before, when he'd been knocking those men around, especially during the third fight when he didn't have to pretend to be so clumsy, he'd felt a small stirring of rage, that powerful feeling that threatened to destroy everything he held dear. He couldn't see another reliable way to make money in the villages and towns, though.

Greene tried not to worry, tried to believe he was strong enough to hold onto the man he wanted to be, the man Charla had loved.

But he saw a hint of the darkness waiting for him, the edge of an abyss over which he was terrified to fall.

A few nights later, they finally learned a new piece of information for their mission: a rumor that Uriah was being backed by a power out of Sutherne, the southern continent. Greene remembered Princess Morgana comparing Arlesland to Sutherne, remembered the rumors he'd heard over the years about it. But how could there be a power in Sutherne strong enough to pose a threat to the northern kingdoms of Bryten? The only rulers in Sutherne were over small kingdoms (almost tribes rather than kingdoms) that warred among themselves.

He and Jacobson talked it over that night. They'd tried some casual questions on the man they'd overheard talking, but he'd just stared at them menacingly, and the new gambling friends who took them out for drinks after their nightly fights hadn't seemed to know anything about Sutherne.

As Jacobson snored beside him, Greene tried to focus on the new piece of information and what it might mean in Uriah's play for power over the northern kingdoms.

But all he could think about was the fights he'd won that night. He'd had that feeling again, the sick anticipation, the power when his opponent lay bloody in the dirt. He'd noticed Jacobson looking at him strangely afterward.

But what bothered him most wasn't Jacobson's reaction; it was the thought of Charla's. Had she ever looked at him like that without him knowing? She'd been concerned enough to leave, and it had to be because she was scared he would lose control around her. She'd never seen him in a fit of rage, but she and Princess Aurora were good friends. He knew Aurora and Charla had talked about the time when he'd almost killed a man while protecting the princess. Aurora would've discussed it with the best intentions, just to make

Charla aware of Greene's temptations, and he was sure she'd painted him in the best light possible, but something had put doubts in Charla's heart.

And now, he was afraid Charla's instinct was right, that his control was only skin-deep. Greene wondered if this was the way it had all started with his father. Would his enjoyment of hurting someone grow until he couldn't control it, either?

Worrying about it, agonizing over it, started Greene on a spiral into a darkness he couldn't control.

The next night, Greene almost ruined his and Jacobson's money-making scheme. His first fight completely lacked the lightheartedness of the previous nights. Instead of turning the fight into a series of pratfalls, he merely avoided his opponent's punches until he was bored, and then punched him hard enough that the man was unconscious before his head bounced off the hard-packed dirt.

Jacobson pulled Greene out of the fighting den as soon as he'd collected his winnings. Jacobson wanted to go straight up the room they'd already reserved at the inn, but Greene insisted on going to the tavern to see if they could find out any more about Uriah's connection to Sutherne.

Jacobson's eyebrows rose when Greene, instead of ordering his usual tankard of small beer, ordered a strong drink and tossed it off, immediately signaling the barkeep for another one.

Greene saw Jacobson's look and scowled. "What, you think I don't deserve it? I'm tired of fighting, tired of this place." His scowl took in the tavern but Jacobson knew he meant Arlesland itself. He tossed the second drink off as quickly as the first one, then put the glass down with a thump on the table and put his head in his hands. "I'm just so tired," he muttered.

Jacobson wanted to be sympathetic, wanted to reassure him and give him the strength to continue, but Arlesland was getting to him, too. The seething anger of the fighting dens, the faces of the exhausted village women, the children who were too weak from hunger to even play. The sneers aimed in his and Greene's direction, and the overheard whispers of how they must be from the northern kingdoms that were responsible for all of Arlesland's problems… it weighed heavy on Jacobson's spirit.

Actually, he wasn't sure why he and Greene were still getting dirty looks from the Arleslanders, because as far as he could tell, they looked a lot like the locals now, other than their height.

They could afford food and a room in an inn each night now, but the quantity of food wasn't what they were used to, so he and Greene were stripped-down versions of themselves. Their muscles were still hard, but they were more stringy than powerful. They hadn't bothered to shave or even wash their faces or hands since they'd left the Jones farm, except when they were so dirty they could no longer stand it. Being too clean definitely marked them as foreigners, though, so they avoided it as much as possible.

The only benefit Jacobson could find in Arlesland was that the alcohol was cheap, but that came with its own problems, as Greene was thoroughly demonstrating.

Greene managed to down another glass of liquor before Jacobson could convince him to leave the tavern, but he was asleep as soon as he fell into bed, which at least gave Jacobson the chance to worry in peace.

The Reimsland Sinti

The rocky cliffs of the Bagginsland border kept Jamison's group from leaving Reimsland after their run-in with the Dark Ones, but they camped against the cliffs to afford themselves as much protection as they could. Jamison knew that smashing the Golden Grain of Oynos across their path so far away should keep the Dark Ones from picking up their trail, but the confrontation had drained him so that he felt the need to be close to the northern border. The two southern kingdoms, Reimsland and Arlesland, had a darkness to them that hadn't yet infected the three northern kingdoms. The Sinti, with their strong faith in Oynos, were able to bear it better than most, but tonight they were glad to have at their backs a land that was dedicated to goodness, to following Oynos.

When they broke their fast the next morning, Jamison felt like himself again. He and the other Sinti discussed whether they should return north to meet up with Mother Tarni and their families, or continue farther into Reimsland.

Jamison wanted to head home to Vallenland, where his young daughter awaited his return, but his priority must be in service of the Sinti tribes as a whole, and he knew what that meant.

"We should warn the Reimsland Sinti about the Dark Ones," Jamison acknowledged. "We don't know what effect the calling of the *skaeweer* may have, and Reimsland and Arlesland are particularly susceptible to dark influences."

Jamison's group loaded up their horses and headed southeast, coming upon the Reimsland Sinti in the late afternoon.

They spent that evening trading news with their Reimsland brethren about their respective kingdoms, and pondering what the advent of the *skaeweer* and the Dark Ones boded for the future. Jamison and the leader of the Reimsland Sinti spent the late hours of the night closed up in the leader's wagon, discussing the looming possibility of the *Grauta Beadu*, the Great Battle that was foretold in Sinti lore.

"Mother Tarni says it is at hand?" the Reimsland Sinti leader asked somberly.

Jamison said, "You should plan to come north when the signs are clear. We will prepare a place for you."

The other man nodded, his eyes on the ground. "It will be hard to leave this land," he said, looking up at Jamison. "It is a harsh land, no doubt," he said, mouth twisting in regret. "But… it is home." He shrugged. "The Sinti are better off than the commoners, because we bow to no one. King Albert has no jurisdiction over us. We come and go as we please and make our own laws. So… it will be hard to leave our home."

Jamison nodded and gripped his shoulder in commiseration. "We will help you make a new home," he promised the man.

A knock came on the door of the wagon and one of the Reimsland Sinti entered. "Jamison, one of your Vallenland brothers has arrived."

Surprised, Jamison went with him. The camp was quiet, most of the Reimsland Sinti having been in bed for hours, but the Vallenland Sinti stood in a small knot by the campfire, talking to a man Jamison easily recognized.

"Ethan!" he called in a low voice. "Did Mother Tarni send you?"

Ethan gripped his arm in greeting and said, "Yes, but not to you. She sent me to seek a man who I'm told is in Arlesland."

Confused, Jamison motioned him to have a seat by the fire. "Tell me," he said as the other Vallenland Sinti seated themselves.

Ethan quickly relayed the mission Mother Tarni had given him to find Timothy Greene, and how it had led him to King Richard of Archenland, and then onward to Arlesland. He showed them the sketch of Greene, and repeated King Richard's admonition that Greene not hear the message until his mission was complete.

Jamison turned to the other Vallenland Sinti, "Ethan's mission from Mother Tarni leads him to Arlesland. I will cross the border with him tomorrow to complete this task. Will you go with us? Mother Tarni has not laid this burden on you. You are free to return home if you desire."

The other Sinti immediately assented to travel to Arlesland. Jamison thought sadly that his reunion with his daughter would be further delayed, then put the thought from his mind. Oynos had caused their paths to cross with Ethan's, so they must help him.

The next afternoon, they reached the Arlesland border.

Jamison had heard many rumors about King Uriah's harsh treatment of his subjects, so he was intrigued when he saw how muscular the border guards were. When Jamison commented on it to the Reimsland Sinti who had accompanied them, they murmured that Uriah always made sure the upper levels of his guards were well-fed, and now there were rumors he was doing the same for his foot soldiers.

"They say he's preparing for war with the northern kingdoms."

Jamison wasn't surprised. Mother Tarni had been expecting such a development for long years now, but he hated the poverty and despair that war would be bound to cause Uriah's subjects… especially if they were already going hungry to fatten up Uriah's military.

Jamison's group bid farewell to the Reimsland Sinti and crossed into Arlesland, hoping to find Greene soon so they could return to their families.

Mount Ciel

Mother Tarni's caravan left the cave behind and began traveling east. Two days later, Old Dan told Charla they should reach their destination that day. Mother Tarni's wagon was usually in the middle of the Sinti caravan, where it could best be protected, but that day the Sinti queen moved her wagon to the front of the caravan and placed Charla and David on the front seat beside the driver. Mother Tarni again sat with Old Dan on the cushioned seat under the deep overhang of the roof.

Charla watched as the green forest gave way to barren land, the trees replaced with the steep sides of a canyon. Eventually, the wagon halted. One of the Sinti men came forward to help Old Dan down and join David in carrying the old man forward.

At Mother Tarni's instructions, Charla went ahead of them, walking hesitantly among the scattered rocks and sand of the shady canyon. After a few moments, she walked around a curve in the canyon to find nothing but a sheer cliff of stone rising hundreds of feet into the air. She turned as David and the Sinti man carrying Old Dan appeared behind her.

"There's no way through!" she exclaimed.

"There is for you, child," Old Dan said. He looked behind him as Mother Tarni appeared carrying a dagger. She approached Charla.

"Hold out your hand, *skaeweer*," she said.

Feeling a bit frightened, Charla obeyed.

Mother Tarni brought the knife blade swiftly across Charla's palm in a shallow cut, making blood well up. She said, "Make the offering, child," and motioned toward the blank stone wall.

"Offering?" Charla had no idea what she was supposed to do, but they were all looking at her like she should, so she hesitantly walked over to the stone wall and held out her hand as if she were offering… something!

The blood dripped off her hand and sizzled on the hot sand, creating a large cloud of steam that rose as high as the cliff before her. She smelled the same bitter scent as the sand in her dream and opened her mouth to exclaim, but as she inhaled she began to cough. She waved her bloody hand to disperse the cloud before her… and saw a wide passage through the rock where none had been before.

She gasped and looked back to see a similar look of shock on David's face, but her grandfather was smiling in satisfaction. Mother Tarni and the Sintis merely gazed at the pathway as if it were normal for solid rock to disappear.

Charla turned back to face the passage and moved slowly forward, the rest of the group following. Reaching the end of the canyon, she was momentarily dazzled by the sun, which beat down in tangible waves of heat. She threw up one arm to shade her eyes and moved aside so the rest of the party could come through.

As her eyes adjusted, she saw yellow sand stretching in front of her until it ended at…

The base of a snow-capped mountain.

Charla gasped and looked to the left. There were the trees and the sun-baked village, just as in her dream… her *vision*.

She turned with a gaping mouth to see Mother Tarni gazing at the huge mountain. She caught Charla's eye and said, "Mount Ciel," gesturing toward it.

Old Dan was grinning as he looked about him.

"Home," he said, tears in his eyes. "We are home, children."

The Sword

King Uriah was sitting at his desk in the morning sun, finishing a letter to one of his former soldiers.

… Out of appreciation for your many years of service to both my father and me, I have asked rather than demanding, but my patience is at an end. I am assured that you have the sword, so continuing to pretend you do not will lead to grave consequences. Do not test me.

Uriah scrawled his initials, sealed the letter with wax and the imprint of his signet ring, and handed it to his servant. "Tell the captain to ride within the hour."

His captain of the guards requested an audience with him that afternoon.

"Well?" Uriah demanded.

"He still insists he has no knowledge of the sword, Your Majesty," the captain answered.

"Do you believe him?"

"No, Majesty."

Uriah grabbed a vase from the table next to his armchair, sweeping it up to hurl it at the wall in one smooth motion. How *dare* the man defy him? Through his seething rage, a tiny voice within asked if it might be better to forebear punishing the man. Perhaps *she* wouldn't like it? Perhaps it would be better to torture the information out of the man?

But the voice was quickly stifled. *He* was the king; *he* was the one being insulted. *She* was the one who'd taught him to have no mercy. No matter how much she wanted the sword, he would be damned before he'd let one of his subjects get the better of him. Especially one who had been sworn to his service.

He scowled. Uriah knew his subjects well, knew they would please him if they could, especially a former soldier. He knew it was extremely unlikely this man had the sword, so it was safe to vent his rage and impotence on the man. He'd just have to convince *her* of that if she chastised him.

She hadn't said she wouldn't help him if he *didn't* find the sword for her; she'd merely said her support would be assured if he *did*.

He looked up at his captain, his eyes narrowed in rage. "*Kill him. Kill them all.*"

Fire!

The next morning Greene awoke frowning and biting Jacobson's head off for every little remark. Jacobson put up with it for a while, pity warring with annoyance in his heart, then announced it was time for them to get away from the villages for a while. Greene immediately began a furious protest.

For the past three days, they'd been heading west toward King Uriah's castle. Greene was sure they would overhear something about Uriah's plans the closer they got to the castle, but Jacobson was convinced that the reception they'd been receiving from the locals was rapidly deteriorating. The village they were currently in was only a few miles from the castle, and the people seemed to be more tight-lipped here than in the villages farther away, and Jacobson found their malevolent stares hard to ignore.

As Greene continued to argue for staying on the road they were on, Jacobson simply picked up both their packs and set off in the direction he wanted to go. Greene stared after him for a moment and then followed, muttering to himself.

That night, Jacobson insisted that they camp out rather than going to a village. He hoped that if they could keep to themselves for a few days, Greene would regain his equilibrium and they could continue with the mission. If not, Jacobson was contemplating cutting their time in Arlesland short. He knew how important the mission was, but no one had expected that the despair that seeped through the very air of Arlesland would have such an effect on Greene and himself. Captain Anderson would just have to find other guards to continue the mission if he and Greene hadn't gathered enough information.

Watching his friend as they trudged along that night, Jacobson decided Greene's mood was deteriorating so quickly because his defenses were low after Charla's defection, but Jacobson had to admit he was having a hard time keeping focused on their goal himself.

He, like Greene, desperately wanted to go home.

Getting away from the villages didn't have the soothing effect Jacobson had hoped for. The next day, he caught Greene attempting to buy liquor from one of the other travelers when they stopped at a stable to refill their water skins. When he angrily confronted him, Greene took a swing at him. Jacobson drew back in shock, but when Greene furiously leaned in and yelled at him, Jacobson's blood boiled and he shouted back. Greene took another swing at his head and this time Jacobson ducked and tackled Greene.

The men who'd bet on them in the fighting dens would've been shocked to discover just how viciously the buffoons could fight when they really meant it. The travelers standing around the stable yard stared for a moment, mouths agape, and then money began furiously changing hands as they cheered on the men who were punching each other bloody.

Martin's prediction to Captain Anderson about Jacobson was quickly proven true: When pressed, Jacobson was a much better fighter than anyone had realized. He wore Greene out with a series of blows that knocked Greene to the ground, where he sat wobbling around, shaking his head.

Jacobson, fury still raging through him, felt a stab of satisfaction as he bent over catching his breath. Greene looked utterly defeated, as he should after his rotten behavior for the past two days, and Jacobson reveled in the power he'd felt as he'd put the jerk in his place.

Standing up, he strode over to the well and yanked a bucket of water away from the man holding it. Leaving the man open-mouthed, Jacobson walked back to where Greene was trying to stand up, and dumped the bucket over his head, watching silently as Greene spluttered and shook the water from his hair.

Feeling calmer, his naturally sunny disposition beginning to reassert itself, Jacobson took the bucket back to the well, let it down and drew it up full, returned it to the man with a muttered, "Sorry," then strode back to Greene and offered him a hand.

Greene regarded it for a moment, then begrudgingly grasped it. Jacobson pulled him up, immediately letting go, and turned without a word to continue down the road. After a moment, he heard Greene following him.

Greene was feeling put-upon and sullen when he and Jacobson bedded down that night in an abandoned barn surrounded by trees. After unpacking their food for a silent meal, Jacobson had ignored Greene and gone about the business of making his pallet for the night.

One of the walls of the barn had fallen down so the wind whipped through almost as badly as if they'd been outside, but Greene was grateful for the flimsy wall of the stall he had chosen because it gave him the illusion of locking Jacobson and the rest of the world out.

He'd never been so exhausted emotionally. Nothing his father had ever done, none of the beatings he'd given Greene, had ever compared to the mental anguish he was in now. Mostly he was still furious with Jacobson for thwarting him today, for taking a detour that guaranteed they couldn't find the information they need to complete their mission.

But a small part of him was horrified at how he'd attacked Jacobson, how he'd lost control with his friend. He knew he'd been losing command over himself for the past week in more than one way, and now he had proof he was on the verge of becoming a person he desperately didn't want to be.

The worst thought, the one that was torturing him now, was what Charla would think if she could see him now. How she would shrink away from his touch with fear in her eyes.

She'd been right to leave him, and she'd never come back. He'd never be loved so completely ever again. He'd never deserve it, no matter how hard he tried. Life would never be good again, *he* would never be good again.

The terrible thoughts beat uncontrollably through his mind until hot tears fell from his staring eyes, his throat working as he tried not to cry out his anguish.

It overwhelmed him until, finally, he fell into a restless sleep.

Smoke.

The smell drifted into Greene's mind, making its way into the nightmare he was having. But eventually the nightmare broke and he woke up fully aware that something nearby was burning. He immediately jumped to his feet, striding quickly to where he could see Jacobson standing in the door of the barn, peering into the night.

The fear he felt drove their fight from his mind. "What is it?" Greene asked. "What's burning?"

Jacobson merely pointed at a red glow beyond the trees and started running, with Greene right behind him.

As they burst from the small copse, the red glow became leaping flames that had almost entirely overtaken a farmhouse several hundred yards away. The glow from the fire lit up the area around the house for quite a ways, and far in the distance Greene noticed men on horseback riding furiously away from the house.

Off to the right was a large barn. Jacobson's arm swept out and he shouted, "Look!"

Turning his head, Greene saw a girl running from the barn toward the house as if the hounds of Heol were at her feet.

"She's not stopping," Jacobson said and flattened his stride to intercept the flying figure, with Greene right behind him. Jacobson caught up to her first, reaching out to grab the slight figure around the waist just as she made a leap for an open window.

"You wanna die?" he yelled above the roar and crackle of the flames.

"Let me go!" she screamed, pushing and kicking at him. "Let me go! I have to save them!"

Uh oh. Greene grabbed the girl's shoulders, wrenching her back from pummeling Jacobson and yelled, "Save who? Who is in there?"

"My family!" she screamed. "Ma, Pa, my brothers, and the little ones." Her face crumpled and she sobbed, but doubled her efforts to free herself, her fists flailing wildly at Jacobson.

Greene released her and ran to the water trough at the back of the house. He jumped in, dunking himself completely, then scrambled out, clothes and hair soaking, and ran for the open window the girl had been aiming for. He jumped headfirst and landed inside, rolling as he came up. His clothes began sizzling and the heat of the blaze made him sure his skin was going to suffer, wet or not.

Coughing from the smoke, Greene dropped to the floor and began to quick-crawl around the room. He located a bed fairly quickly and yanked the sheets completely off it, bundling them around the small, still forms that had dropped to the floor with it, and staggered upright long enough to run back to the window and drop his bundle into Jacobson's waiting arms. Jacobson handed the bundle to the girl and ran for the water trough so he could join Greene inside the house.

Greene was quick-crawling into the next room, where he could hear some faint cries. They stopped as he got closer, so he tried to shout, hoping to hear enough of a response to guide him to them. The smoke choked him, though, and turned his shout into an uncontrollable cough. As he collapsed sideways, trying to breathe, he bumped against a hard surface and knew that he'd found another bed.

Yanking the covers off this time wasn't as easy. The bodies on the bed were larger, not large enough to be adults, but too heavy for Greene, who was struggling to breathe, to pull them off. He staggered to his feet, lungs heaving against his attempt to hold his breath, and focused all his might on bundling the forms in the sheets and stumbling with them toward where he thought the window was.

Jacobson's hands suddenly grabbed his waist and almost threw him toward the window. As Greene fell against the frame, trying to pull the bundled forms with him while heaving for breath, Jacobson pushed them closer to the window and set off deeper into the house.

The sobbing girl outside helped Greene get the bundled forms out the window and started dragging them away from the house, straining against their weight.

Greene took as deep a breath as his burnt lungs would handle, and crouched over, knowing this was the last foray he'd be able to make into the inferno. He lurched away from the window just as a weak scream came from inside the house, followed by the sound of crashing. Greene's heart lurched. The roof was caving in.

Adrenaline flooded his body and he surged into the dark, his lungs frantically trying to overcome his attempt to hold his breath.

He stumbled around, arms waving wildly as he bent over as close to the ground as he could get in a crouch, trying to find another doorway to reach the farthest bedroom. Just as his hands found the searing doorframe, a body was flung against him. He grabbed it and lurched back the way he'd come, dragging the limp form to the window and tipping it out. His eyes were streaming from the smoke, but he could see the girl grab the body and heave it away.

Greene took a second for one more breath, trying to ignore the searing pain in his lungs, and turned to find Jacobson. There were shouts coming from deeper in the house, and Greene shut his eyes and ran toward them as fast as he could, feeling the skin on his ears crisping from the heat.

Two forms appeared in the smoke, one being dragged by the other. Greene grabbed the limp one and added his muscles to Jacobson's as they stumbled toward the window and pushed the body out through the flames now ringing the window. Before Greene could do anything, he felt himself being tipped out the window, too, and as he hit the ground he felt Jacobson land on top of him.

Gagging and coughing, the two men rolled away from each other and tried to catch their breath, but the screams and sobs of the girl near them soon brought them staggering to their knees.

The girl was crouched on the ground, holding in her lap the head of the last victim they'd brought from the burning house. She was screaming, "Pa! Pa!" Looking beyond her, Greene saw small bodies sprawled on the sheets they'd been wrapped in, their limbs crumpled and lifeless. He felt sick to his stomach and looked around for the other adult they'd brought out. It had been a woman's screams he'd heard, and he saw her body just behind where the girl knelt sobbing. The woman was lifeless, but as Greene turned his eyes back to the weeping girl, he saw the eyes of the man in her arms flutter open.

The man was horribly burned and had a deep gash in his chest, ribs showing through the burned flesh. He was fighting for breath, trying to say something. As Greene crawled toward them, he heard the man gasp, "sword," and then his head rolled to the side as his body went flaccid.

Clutching him to her, the girl raised her head and wailed, the pain in her voice making Greene shiver in the heat of the burning house.

Jacobson staggered over to the water trough, where he threw water on his face and scrubbed soot from his stinging eyes. He filled the bucket and brought it over to Greene, who splashed his eyes, then Jacobson took the bucket and gently began to wash the face of the dead woman, tidying her hair as he carefully wiped the soot away, then pulling her nightgown down and arranging her arms and legs neatly.

Greene watched him for a moment, wondering why he was doing it, then realized that when the girl finally let go of her father's body, she would be further traumatized to see her family's bodies strewn around like smoking garbage. Wearily, Greene got to his feet and went to help.

By the time the girl's wails had quieted to sobs and her rocking of her father's body had stopped, Jacobson and Greene had sponged off the faces of the girl's family as best they could, then carefully arranged them on the sheets, with the mother in the middle and the children's bodies snuggled up next to her. Except for the mother's burned clothing and hair, they might have almost been sleeping. The children had succumbed to the smoke before the bedclothes had started burning, so they were unmarked by fire, their small faces peaceful in their final sleep.

After they'd escaped, Greene and Jacobson had thrown water from the trough into the house through the window, but it was obvious from the first couple of buckets that it was pointless. The water saved the area around the window and the floor just inside it, but everything else continued to burn.

The girl had insisted that they help her carry her family into the barn and they'd done it without arguing. Silent tears had rolled down her face as she looked at them, but she hadn't fought Greene and Jacobson when they'd gently pulled a sheet over the pale faces and urged her to lie down on the hay in the barn.

Before she'd sobbed herself into an exhausted sleep, they'd asked her if the men who'd torched the house were likely to come back. She'd merely shaken her head, tears flowing, and turned her back to them.

Greene knew he and Jacobson would have to bury the bodies, but they were exhausted and he was sure the girl would want to say goodbye to her family, so they decided to wait until morning to do it.

After they'd gotten the girl settled, Greene and Jacobson took stock of the animals in the barn. Although there were several stalls, all they found was one mare with a colt that looked only a few days old. The mare was panicked, circling the stall around and around her colt, whinnying at the smell of fire. Jacobson opened the stall and drove her into the paddock, where there were already three other horses shivering at the far end, nostrils quivering at the terrifying smell of smoke. Some sheep were also circling in agitation in their pen behind the barn, but they calmed down when Greene and Jacobson shut the barn door and blocked out much of the noise and smell.

A few sleepy chickens raised their heads from under their wings when Greene and Jacobson glanced into their hutch, but most of them seemed unfazed by the upset, and the goats they found in another pen seemed oblivious, too.

Greene and Jacobson dropped the bars over the barn doors, dressed the burns on each other's arms as best they could, then fell onto the hay and into a deep, dreamless sleep.

Elaria

Greene and Jacobson awakened the next morning to the sound of the heavy bars across the barn doors being lifted and slid back, then the light in the barn grew brighter. Trying to ignore the pain of their burnt arms and faces, they pulled on their boots and made their way outside.

The girl, her back turned resolutely to the burnt house, was gathering eggs from the henhouse while the clucking chickens pecked at grain around her feet.

She turned and Greene saw how ravaged her face was. She hadn't bothered to wash the soot off her face and hands the night before, and her short, dark hair was standing on end. Her body drooped with grief.

The girl said wearily, darting a glance up at them. "I don't have much to offer you but eggs for breakfast."

"We have food," Jacobson said, and trotted back through the trees to get their satchels.

As Jacobson laid out some flatbread, the girl said, "My name is Elaria."

As Greene introduced them in turn, Jacobson gave her one of his sweet smiles and went to get some water from the well outside the barn. After they'd eaten, Elaria dipped a cup of water from the bucket, then took Greene's arm and began to soak the bandages off. She winced at the sight of the bubbling skin on his hands and arms, pondered a moment, and went hesitantly toward the house.

Greene and Jacobson watched as she began to rummage in a small garden plot on the other side of the house, returning with her arms full of herbs and, surprisingly, a bit of fresh, dripping honeycomb with a few bees still attached.

She poured water on their wounds to soak the bandages off, then crushed some of the plant leaves into the cup, using a smooth rock as a pestle to pound the fibers and release the juices. Soon she had a thick green paste into which she dripped some of the honey. She turned to Greene and surveyed his bubbling skin, then dipped her fingers into the cup and began smearing the mixture onto his arms and hands.

The relief was immediate. A feeling of coolness spread over the bubbling skin and the pain receded to a dull ache. Sighing in relief, Greene said, "Thank you. That feels wonderful."

She turned to Jacobson, who sighed, too, when she spread the healing mixture on his burns. "How did you learn to make that?" he asked.

Elaria scooped up a small amount of the green mixture, spreading it lightly across the burns on Greene's head. "My mother is… was a healer." Her breathing hitched, but after a moment she was able to go on. "I'm sorry about your hair," she said.

Trying not to mind too much, Greene reached up and touched the crisp ends that were all that remained of the wavy mass that Charla had so loved.

Jacobson and Elaria were talking as she wound strips of clean cloth from her petticoat around his arms and hands, as well as his head.

"It was the king's men," she was saying. "My father offended the king's men and they returned to burn down the house." There was bitterness in her voice. "It was only pure luck that I wasn't in the house, too. Pa wanted me to stay with a mare that foaled two nights ago. She hasn't been eating well and Pa was worried she wouldn't produce enough milk for the foal. But she's fine. I should've gone back to the house. Maybe I could've stopped them from burning it." She turned her face away but Greene could see how she screwed her eyes up to keep from crying.

"You probably would've died, too," Jacobson said, reaching out with his bandaged hand to squeeze her shoulder. "Now you can keep their memories alive. As long as you live, they do, too."

Elaria shook her head. "I wish I were dead, too," she said dully. "Being dead wouldn't be so painful."

As Elaria finished her breakfast, Greene asked, "Do you have family or neighbors you can stay with?"

Elaria shook her head. "No family. If I stay with neighbors, word might get back to the king's men. I'd rather they think we all died."

"Do you think they might try to kill you, too?" Jacobson asked.

Elaria shrugged. "They might. Pa told me the king wanted something Pa didn't have. The king is crazy enough to think I might know where it is."

"What was he looking for?" Greene asked.

Elaria shrugged again.

In the end, Elaria agreed to come with them. Her eyes were wary, but she seemed to realize she'd be safer with them.

"We'd better disguise you, though." Jacobson surveyed her hair, which was cut in jagged clumps, as if she'd tried to cut it herself.

Elaria flushed and mumbled, "I don't like long hair. It gets in the way."

Greene merely said, "That will make you easier to disguise if we get you some different clothes. A boy traveling with two men wouldn't raise eyebrows like a girl would."

Jacobson was sniffing at his clothing, which was covered in soot and had holes all over it from the fire. "Do you think we could take the time to wash our clothes? People will remember us if we show up reeking of smoke."

Elaria surveyed the holes in their clothing and said, "I've got something better," and ran off to the end of the barn. She came back with her arms full of clothing. "My da's work clothes," she said breathlessly, her eyes determinedly dry.

Elaria's father's legs were shorter than Greene and Jacobson's, so the hem of his pants left a lot of bare ankle, which thankfully didn't show once they put their boots back on. His work shirts, although threadbare, were plenty big and hung off their shoulders enough that the sleeves covered most of the bandages on their arms, although the ones on their hands and heads still showed. Elaria had a solution for that, too: worn leather gloves for their hands, and floppy hats for their heads.

Greene and Jacobson surveyed themselves. If they'd hoped to look unremarkable, they certainly achieved it with the ragged clothes. Certainly no one would think they were from one of the prosperous northern kingdoms now!

Elaria had disappeared to the back of the barn again, and after several minutes she came out wearing some clothing she'd found back there. "My oldest brother's," she mumbled, picking at the shirt. She'd wound some kind of tight cloth around her chest, so that even her slight curves had disappeared, and the loose breeches concealed her small waist and wider hips. She swung a light cloak over it all, and disappeared into her new identity.

When Greene and Jacobson asked Elaria where she'd like them to bury her family, Elaria hesitated for a long moment, going to survey the sad forms under the sheet. Finally, she said, "I think Pa would think it's more important for me to be safe, so… I think we'd better leave them for the neighbors to find." She choked back a sob.

Greene thought it over. He wanted to suggest something, but it was an appalling proposal. She saw his hesitancy and said, "What are you thinking?"

"I hate to suggest this, but it would make it look like you died in the fire rather than escaping, which would keep you much safer…" He paused and she motioned for him to go on. "We could arrange your family so it looks they just barely managed to escape the fire themselves. Then the assumption would be that you weren't able to get out. I doubt anyone would bother searching for your body."

Elaria turned to stare at her family under the sheet again, tears flowing freely. She finally nodded and tried to speak around the knot in her throat. "Nothing can hurt them now. I know Ma and Da would want me to be safe. I can't bear to disturb their bodies, though, so I'd be grateful if you'd take care of it."

Jacobson gripped her shoulder for a moment, then he and Greene began the horrible task while Elaria went as far from the house as she could.

Greene and Jacobson undid all the kindnesses they'd done for the small family the night before. They smudged their faces with soot and sprawled their bodies, loosely wrapped in the sheets, near the window as if they'd been flung out and lay as they'd landed, then arranged Elaria's beloved Pa just inside the window, as if he'd managed to get his family out, but had succumbed before escaping himself.

They surveyed the scene and saw nothing to indicate they'd been there, then went back to the barn and removed all signs of their presence as well. Elaria came in as they were finishing, her eyes and nose red. She didn't make reference to their task, but she remained silent as they began talking about what they should take with them.

They decided to lock the mare and her colt back into a stall and leave them behind for the neighbors. There were four horses loose in the paddock, so they agreed to take one for each of them to ride, and another to sell. They could knock down one end of the paddock to make it look like the horses escaped.

Greene and Jacobson still had their fighting money, so they insisted that Elaria should keep whatever money was made from the sale of the horse.

"We'll let you know if we need the money for food, but the horse is yours, so you should get all the money when you sell it," Greene said. Before she could argue, he changed the subject. "I think you need a new name, since you're passing as a boy. How about Eli?"

Elaria nodded, and soon they were on their way.

They rode the horses hard that day, trying to get as far away from the farm as they could. They were riding west again, but the road they took circled to the south of Uriah's castle, so Jacobson hoped that would be enough to keep the bad miasma of the king from affecting Greene.

Greene had been quiet while they rode, keeping his thoughts to himself. Jacobson was glad the other man hadn't had any outbursts in front of Elaria, and hoped he'd passed through the worst of whatever was eating at him.

That afternoon, before it got dark, they found a clearing and built a fire to cook their supper. When dusk settled into darkness, they lit a lantern, partially closed the light guard on it, and doused the fire.

Greene and Jacobson were sitting at their ease against their satchels, watching the horses cropping grass nearby, while Elaria rearranged her pack. She'd hurriedly grabbed some things from the barn that morning, and now she laid them all out and began to repack them.

Done, she folded the top over the satchel, then picked up a belt laying next to her. She buckled it on, and slid daggers into the sheaths on each side.

Jacobson spoke up. "Nice knives. Can I see one?"

Elaria slid one out of the belt, flipped it around in her hand, and flung it across the fire to land quivering, expertly implanted, in the dirt a foot from Jacobson's leg.

Jacobson huffed out a laugh and picked up the dagger, weighing the balance.

Greene said, "Looks like you'd be good in a knife fight."

Elaria shrugged her shoulders, staring at the ground in front of her. "Never been in one. Pa liked knives and so did I, so he taught me to handle them."

Greene's eyes drifted to her horse, where a hilt rose from the scabbard on the saddle. "What about that sword?"

Elaria didn't raise her head. "It's broken. The only reason I brought it is because it's the only thing, besides the knives, that Pa gave me." Her mouth twisted.

There was silence for a moment, which Jacobson broke when he stood up and walked the dagger back to Elaria. "You probably don't want *me* throwing this. No telling where it would land," he said.

Elaria's lips curved in an almost-smile as she took the knife.

"You think he's joking," Greene said wryly. "But he's not. The only way he'd land that knife next to your leg is if he were aiming for that tree," he said, pointing several yards away.

That garnered the first real smile they'd seen from their new companion.

Old Dan's Story

Mother Tarni's caravan had made its way into the valley of Mount Ciel and spread out in a circle close to the empty village. The Sintis had unpacked their cooking things and were preparing a meal, chattering and laughing as usual.

Mother Tarni had assured Charla that the opening in the rock would close behind them when the last wagon was through. "There will be no trace of our presence beyond the entrance. That is how your family has kept this place safe from the dark forces for hundreds of years," the Sinti queen explained.

Some of the Sinti, along with Charla and David, had carefully approached the village when they'd first come through the pass. There had been no signs of occupation: no people, no smoke from cooking fires, and when they reached the far side of the village, they saw why.

There was row upon row of sandy graves there, maybe fifty in all, each marked with a simple round stone at the head. At the far end of the row of graves, the body of an old man, the same man Charla had seen address her as *skaeweer* in the vision, lay wrapped in a colorful blanket. His face was peaceful, the searing heat of the desert already mummifying his body.

The Sinti surveyed the graves and the body of the old man, then softly murmured "Blessed Oynos, receive your faithful servants," pressing their hands palm-to-palm and touching them against their foreheads.

One of the Sinti women turned to Charla and David. "They made a brave stand against the dark forces that descended on them, and were successful. They will be richly rewarded by Oynos."

Charla asked hesitantly, "Did the old man bury all of them?"

The Sinti woman nodded. "They would have protected him with their last breath, given their lives for him, because he was the only one with the power to weaken the Dark Ones so the others could defeat them. They were successful, and he sent them onward to Oynos before giving himself to God as well. His time was over."

Charla asked, "The Dark Ones attacked the village?"

The woman gestured to something on the other side of the line of graves, where a trail led toward the mountain. Charla walked over to look and saw cloaked bodies, fallen where they'd died. The lines under the skin were very faint, but she could see them.

"But how did they get through the canyon?" Charla asked, fearful that the protection around the canyon wasn't as strong as Mother Tarni claimed.

"That is a question for Mother Tarni," was the calm reply.

When Charla and David returned wide-eyed to their grandfather to report what they'd seen, Old Dan told them to wait until after the meal to discuss it. "Patience," he cautioned. "You will know all soon."

Finally, the meal was over, dishes washed, the Sinti were sprawled around the fire with their musical instruments, plucking them quietly, and Old Dan was seated comfortably in his usual chair by Mother Tarni. Charla and Dan were sitting on the ground before him, their patience becoming impatient.

Mother Tarni turned to Charla. "You have a question for me."

"How were the Dark Ones able to breach the canyon?"

Mother Tarni nodded. "A good question indeed. My guess is that no one of your blood had left or entered the canyon in many years, which lessened the power of the protections put in place here. When the people of the village shed their blood during the attack, the protection was once more renewed."

Old Dan was nodding. "Your time was near, child," he said to Charla. "It was necessary for the protection to wane, for those here to give their lives, in order for the call to go out to you."

Charla's eyes were wide. "But that's horrible! They had to die so I would have a vision? Why was it so important?"

Old Dan said softly, "It was Oynos' will. They gave their lives gladly. They knew this day was coming." He saw Charla's frustration. "You will understand when I tell you our story." He glanced at Mother Tarni, who nodded

Old Dan cleared his throat and began.

"Hundreds of years ago, there was a great cataclysm across the continents of Eoroe, a great war between good and evil. The details are lost to time, but what we do know is that one of our great ancestors was entrusted with a valuable jewel. This was not *just* a jewel, though. It was key to the survival of mankind.

This is how it all came about.

Our great ancestor, Josias, was just a man, no one of great importance, but Oynos loved his pure heart. One night Josias was awakened by Oynos, and opened his eyes to see a great blue jewel hanging in midair before him. There was no light in the room, but the jewel glowed as if lit from within. Josias had never seen anything so beautiful.

'Josias,' came the voice of Oynos, 'I am entrusting you with the Eye of the Unseen World. You must keep it safe until it is called for. But be wary; if the dark forces capture it, they will strive to turn it to their will. You must protect it with your life, and teach your children to do the same. From this day forward, only someone of your blood will be called *skaeweer*, guardian of the Eye. You must take your family and flee to the place I have prepared for you, where you will spend the rest of your days guarding the Eye. One day I will call one of your descendants to bring the Eye from its hiding place to fulfill its destiny, but until then, you must protect it in the home I have prepared for you.'

Josias awakened his wife and children, and they packed up all their household, setting off to follow God's will.

They traveled for days, until they came upon a thick grove of trees with a stream running through it, and behind the grove, a huge mountain.

As they stood gazing in wonder, the ground suddenly rumbled, and mighty cliffs rose from the earth, forming a great canyon as massive boulders rolled down to shut off the valley around the mountain.

Filled with the spirit of Oynos, Josias declared, 'This is Mount Ciel, the mountain that reaches to Heaven. It will be our home from this day forward. No one who is not of my blood will find this place, and we will guard the Eye of Oynos here for the rest of our days.'

Josias put his hands on the shoulders of his young daughter and son. 'Children, Oynos has decreed that I will be *skaeweer*, the guardian, who shall bear the burden of the Eye. When the time comes for me to journey home to Oynos, one of you will take the joy and burden of *skaeweer*. Until that time, you must build a life here in the valley of Mount Ciel, while I spend the rest of my days on the mountain, where the Eye will be safest.'

Josias' family was saddened by this, and begged him with much weeping not to leave them. 'It is a command from Oynos,' he said, holding them close so they could not see the tears falling from his eyes. 'This task is a great honor for our family. We must not refuse it.'

His family could not control their tears, but they helped him pack a small bag of provisions for the climb. 'Oynos will provide what I need when I reach the top,' he assured them, hefting the bag over his shoulder and touching the hidden pocket in his shirt where the Eye rested.

He set off up the steep mountain, forging a path where none had gone before. His family watched from the valley until it was too dark to make out his form, then they went to bed weeping. When they awoke, they were startled to see snow on the peak of the mountain. Josias' wife wisely said, 'Oynos has made Mount Ciel impossible for anyone but the *skaeweer* to summit, and even the *skaeweer* must prove themselves worthy.'

After many days, Josias' family resigned themselves to their loss, and turned their thoughts to their new life. They built huts near the stream and firepits in the sand, sowed seeds for food, and built pens for livestock.

Josias' family grew. When his son and daughter were of marriageable age, they went back into the world to find mates and bring them back to Mount Ciel. Thus Josias' family increased for hundreds of years. Most of them left Mount Ciel to make lives in the outside world, but there were always a few families who stayed. Soon their huts filled the sand around Mount Ciel.

One day a widow named Amiet was called to be the *skaeweer*. She packed her things and began the arduous climb up Mount Ciel. None of the previous *skaeweers* had been seen after they made the climb, so the parting with her family was bitter. Amiet was proud to take on the task of *skaeweer*, but sad to leave behind her father and children.

One night after Amiet ascended, her young daughter had a dream, a vision from Oynos. In it, she was like a bird, soaring through the air, the wind lofting her higher and higher. She saw her mother Amiet at the top of Mount Ciel, the Eye safely held in her hands. But as the daughter-bird wheeled around the peak of the mountain, an ill wind of darkness blew from the south and descended upon the village far below. The darkness swirled around the huts and trees, and settled into the sand, poisoning it.

As the daughter-bird watched, she heard her mother Amiet calling her.

'Daughter! Tell my father to take you and your brother and leave the village! A day is coming when the village will be attacked by the forces of Heol, and we must have people of our blood safely hidden away from here. When you leave, take with you some of the poisoned sand. One day, you will be called as *skaeweer* when my time is done. The poisoned sand will lead you back to Mount Ciel when the time is come. Hurry!'

The daughter-bird closed her wings and dove for the village that was now trapped in the poisoned sand. The ground rushed nearer and nearer… and suddenly she was back in her bed. She rushed to her grandfather, who was surprised and fearful when she told him all she had seen. But he lit a lamp and went from his hut to rouse the elders of the village, who agreed that he and his grandchildren must set out that very night. The weeping of the village was terrible that night, because they loved the man and his grandchildren, and because they realized a great evil was approaching.

The grandfather and children journeyed through the canyon and into a kingdom where Oynos was revered, and made a new home in a quiet village, where they lived peacefully for many years."

Old Dan paused in his story and smiled at his grandchildren. "I can tell you this story because *I* am Amiet's father, and *you* are Amiet's daughter and son."

Charla's head was whirling. She finally managed to get her mouth unstuck. "*I*… am Amiet's daughter? *I* was the daughter-bird?"

"Yes, granddaughter. You were the one who brought the vision from Oynos and set us on a different path than the one we expected."

Charla shook her head and stared at David, who looked as shocked as she felt. "But… I don't remember anything about that! When I saw the village and mountain in my vision weeks ago, none of it looked familiar! Nothing looks familiar *now!*"

Old Dan said, "Oynos was protecting you. He caused you to forget, so you would not pine for the life you left behind. I was not so blessed, and it is bittersweet to be back now, when all my family lies dead." He looked toward the village, where the silent graves lay. There was quiet for a moment as his grandchildren tried to take in what he had told them of their family.

"Were the villagers… our *family*… defending the base of the mountain when they were killed?" Charla asked. "Were the Dark Ones trying to scale it to take the Eye?"

Old Dan nodded. "That would be my guess, child, and our family succeeded in holding back the Dark Ones."

"How can you be sure?" Charla asked.

"Because the world still stands," he answered simply.

Charla and David were silent, overwhelmed by everything Old Dan had told them, trying to understand their lives in light of this new knowledge. Their grandfather watched them, waiting.

"So… does that mean our mother… Amiet… is still alive?" Charla finally said.

David's head came up, a painful hope in his eyes.

Old Dan smiled. "Yes, child. Your mother Amiet still lives at the top of Mount Ciel, still guards the Eye of Oynos."

"And… can we see her?" Charla's question was hesitant, remembering that none of the *skaeweer*s had ever been seen after they climbed Mount Ciel.

"Yes, child," Old Dan answered. As Charla and David took deep breaths, smiles breaking on their faces, questions on their lips, the old man cautioned. "But the *skaeweer* cannot return to the village. We must go to her." And he looked to the north, where Mount Ciel loomed thousands of feet in the air, its sheer sides and snowy heights mocking them.

David's mouth fell open. "We have to climb the mountain?"

Old Dan chuckled. "Yes. But Oynos will be with us."

Charla didn't think too much of that (it seemed like Oynos had put their family through an awful lot of pain over the years), but another thought had occurred to her. "So… in my vision, the village elder called me '*skaeweer*.' But you said my mother is *skaeweer*? Can there be two at once?"

Old Dan shook his head sadly. "No, granddaughter. If you have been called, it is because your mother's time is almost ended."

Charla felt tears start to her eyes. "She's dying?"

"Yes, child." His voice was very gentle as he reached down to put his hands on her and David's shoulders. "But you will get to spend a short time with her. And one day you will see her again, when Oynos calls you home, too." He smiled at them. "Now, children," Old Dan said, "It is time for bed. We have a big day tomorrow."

"Why? What's happening tomorrow?" Charla asked.

Old Dan turned to look up at the mountain. "We go to see your mother."

Mouths agape, Charla and David followed his gaze.

"Tomorrow?" Charla managed to squeak, appalled. Their wounds from the torture of the Dark Ones had been healed by the Sinti medicine, but she was still getting used to the feeling of being safe. She certainly wasn't ready to climb a mountain that was meant to make her prove her worthiness as *skaeweer*, a position she didn't even want.

Old Dan chuckled. "All will be well, child. Trust in Oynos."

Eli to the Rescue

The next morning, Greene and Jacobson set out early with their new companion, heading for a good-sized town a few miles down the road, where they could try to sell the extra horse. They arrived in the late morning, but the horse market didn't open until the afternoon. Their stomachs were rumbling, so they located the local tavern and ordered a simple but filling meal. Greene ordered small beer, which made Jacobson a little uneasy, but there wasn't much alcohol in it, so he didn't protest.

They ate in silence, Elaria because she preferred it and Greene and Jacobson because they were listening to the talk around them.

"…Sutherne…" The almost-whisper caught Greene's ear. He casually adjusted his chair so it was closer to the man who'd spoken.

"…brother Billy says she's got some kind of army that can't be beaten, and now Uriah's training up an army like it!"

Greene slid his leg under the table and kicked Jacobson's boot to get his attention.

The man's companion scoffed. "An unbeatable army? I'm not saying it's not possible in Sutherne, because I've heard plenty of rumors about what's going on down there and I'd believe most anything at this point… But I'll never believe that Uriah can do the same here. Not if he's using local boys, and as far as I know, that's all he's got."

"Yeah, but he's feeding them all that extra food we're giving him…"

"But he's still working with farm boys! Rumor has it that *she* recruits, or more likely kidnaps, her men when they're just boys. They've got years of experience that ours don't have. Are you sure she's on our side? I'd hate to have her as an enemy, I tell you that."

"Billy was cleaning up at the castle and he found a half-burned note from her in one of the fireplaces. It said she would help Uriah defeat the northern kingdoms if he could prove he was worthy."

His friend was silent as he finished his beer.

Greene and Jacobson stared at each other. Who was *she?*

When they were done with their meal, they retrieved the extra horse from the stable where they'd paid a lad to watch their horses, and set off for the market.

The horse brought less than Elaria thought it should and just about what Greene expected. It was a good amount of money that should take care of her needs for several months, until she could find a position as a servant somewhere. Jacobson cautioned her in a low voice to hide the money, so she stuck it in the inside pocket of her breeches and carefully buttoned the flap, then adjusted her knife belt over it for an additional layer of safety.

As they made their way back toward the stables, Jacobson and Elaria were in front of Greene, who had an uneasy feeling. He glanced around twice, looking for the source of his unease, but saw nothing. His trepidation resolved itself, though, when a man jumped out of an alleyway as Elaria passed, and dragged her into it.

As Greene and Jacobson leapt after her, a couple of burly men jumped out and pounded them furiously with their fists. Greene and Jacobson ignored the pain in their burned arms and hands and fought back grimly, trying to keep Elaria in sight as she was dragged away from them. The odds against them increased, however, as more men poured from the alleyway. Eventually Greene was struggling against multiple men while Jacobson did the same.

Elaria was being held by just one man, but he'd pulled her arms behind her back so she could do nothing, either.

Greene thought that if he could just distract the man holding her, Elaria might be able to reach her daggers and somehow fight her way out of it. But as he made a move toward her, he felt the razor edge of a knife against his throat.

"Ah ah ah, naughty boy," a man purred in his ear. "Not so fast. Not at all, really," drawled the man. "Unless you want a bloody smile for you *and* your friends."

From the corner of his eye, Greene saw Jacobson's sudden stillness and realized he must have a knife to his throat as well. He stared at Elaria across the way from him, her eyes wide with fear.

He had to give her the chance to get free. No matter what it cost.

And, a snide voice inside his head said, *busting these guys up will feel so good.*

A brief vision of Charla's face, eyes wide with fear, flashed in his mind, but he ignored it and pushed forward against the knife.

Seeing him, Jacobson yelled and surged forward as well. Shock immobilized the men holding them long enough for Greene and Jacobson to break away from the knives.

As Greene pulled his arms free, he saw the horror on Elaria's face harden into fury as she wrenched one of her own arms free and reached for her dagger. Then it was chaos around Greene as he and Jacobson fought for their lives, adrenaline surging in their bodies so they didn't notice the pain of their burns or the cuts on their necks from the knives.

Greene heard screams of pain behind him, where Elaria stood, but it wasn't until the man who was trying to choke him suddenly fell backward that he realized Elaria was the one *causing* the screams. He stared down at the man, who had the hilt of a dagger protruding from his throat, and looked up in time to see Elaria slash at the throat of the man punching Jacobson in the face. As the blood spilled, Elaria bent to retrieve her second dagger and slashed her way through their attackers like a whirlwind.

Feeling a surge of energy, Greene pulled his own dagger and did some damage, too, until their attackers turned and ran for the alley entrance.

Hyranstrene and Uriah

Afraid the thieves might return with reinforcements, and sure that either way the story about two men and a boy who knew how to handle themselves in a fight would soon spread in the town, Greene and Jacobson decided it would be best to remove themselves from the vicinity. Accordingly, they retrieved their horses from the stables and made for the main road.

They rode the horses hard for a couple of miles, after which they felt fairly sure they'd left any pursuers behind. They left the main road and made their way through the woods to a small stream, where the horses gratefully drank water and began cropping grass while their riders bandaged their new wounds and sprawled along the bank to partake of food from their packs.

After resting a couple of hours, they mounted again and set off at a slow pace through the trees, riding parallel to the road. When the bright daylight lessened to dusk, they began to look for a good place to camp for the night and eventually found a small hillock with a shallow depression in the ground behind it, perfect for blocking the light of a campfire from the road.

The only bad thing about the protected area was its small size, which meant they had to put their pallets close together. Elaria seemed more comfortable with them since the fight, though, and made no protest when Jacobson put her pallet between his and Greene's, where she would be better protected from any attack.

They settled the horses for the night, cooked a small meal, and sat around the fire, each thinking their own thoughts.

Elaria spoke. "You risked your lives for me today." It was as much a question as a statement.

Jacobson nodded and smiled gently. "Yes. But we're used to fighting so there was a better-than-good chance that we'd make it out without too much damage." He said it jokingly, not wanting to make a big deal of it.

Greene didn't say anything. He couldn't pretend his only motive had been to save Elaria, although that certainly had factored into it. He'd again felt an overwhelming sense of power during the fight, and although part of him had been horrified by it, mostly he'd reveled in it.

Elaria turned to him. "But… they had knives to your throats. You could have been killed. You really could've."

Greene shrugged.

She went on, "You saved my life the night my family was killed, too, and you risked your lives to bring them out of the fire."

Jacobson said, "We'll protect you any way we can. You have our word."

Elaria frowned. "But… why? I have no connection with you. I just met you. There's no reason for you to help me."

Greene and Jacobson glanced at each other and Jacobson said, "Things seem to be… different here in Arlesland, but we were raised to look out for each other. Granted, we might not risk our lives for *everyone*, but… you've been through a lot lately. You've lost all your family, anyone who might take care of you, so we'll protect you if we can. You're free to go whenever you want, of course, but as long as you travel with us, we'll take care of you.

"And don't forget," he said in a lighter tone, "you saved us as well. That was quite a bit of fighting you did with those knives of yours!"

Greene agreed. "I don't really think we did that much to help you… we just gave you a chance to help yourself."

Elaria was shaking her head. "No. I couldn't have escaped without you."

"Well," Greene shrugged, "I don't guess it really matters. We got out of there relatively unscathed… although all that grabbing and punching didn't do our arms and hands any good." He forced a laugh.

Exclaiming, Elaria reached into her pack to pull out some of the green paste. She removed their bandages to reveal skin that was still horribly burned, but no longer covered in angry blisters. When she spread the fresh paste over the burns, the men sighed in relief.

As Elaria rewrapped Jacobson's bandages, she said hesitantly, "I'm very grateful for what you've done for me. If there's any way I can ever repay you, I'll be glad to." She glanced between them, then spoke slowly. "I didn't tell you why the king's men burned down our house."

Greene said, "You told us King Uriah wanted something your pa didn't have, and his soldiers torched the house out of spite."

She nodded, turning to look at the broken sword where it lay beside the satchel she was using for a pillow. After a moment, she hesitantly drew the sword from its scabbard, and tilted it so the light played upon the blade.

Greene and Jacobson could see the crack in the blade that Elaria had alluded to before, the one that made the sword unusable. It was a shame because the blade seemed to be well-made, the dull metal attesting that it was a weapon rather than a ceremonial sword.

Greene leaned forward and Elaria handed it to him. Surprised, he said, "It's lighter than I expected!" as he hefted it in his hands. The blade was wide and sturdy, and the hilt, wrapped in leather to give it a better grip, was solid and filled the width of his hand.

He offered it to Jacobson, who rose to his feet as he took it. "It's lightweight because it's perfectly balanced," Jacobson commented, hefting the sword in turn. "The wrist doesn't have to work as hard to hold up the blade." He raised the sword above his head and slashed down with it, turning to thrust and block an imaginary opponent, then he brought it back to the campfire, dropping to one knee to peer at the sword in the flickering flames.

"What kind of metal is it?" he finally asked, raising his head to look at Elaria.

She shrugged. "I don't know."

Greene asked, "Is *this* what Uriah was looking for?"

Elaria hesitantly nodded.

Surprised, Jacobson asked, "Why did he want a broken sword?"

"My pa used to work for Uriah, as a guard in his prison castle. One night a fellow guard came to Pa's house with a message, and the guard saw the sword laying on a table. Even though it's broken, Pa used to take it out and clean it, make sure it wasn't rusty or anything. The other guard was intrigued by the broken blade and asked Pa why he kept it. Pa explained that it had belonged to his father, and he kept it for sentimental reasons."

Elaria took a deep breath. "Then, about a year or so ago, one of Uriah's men showed up at our house, saying King Uriah was looking for a broken sword and that one of his men had told him about Pa's."

Greene asked, "Did the men say why Uriah was seeking a broken sword?"

Elaria shook her head. "We don't expect the king's actions to make sense, really. Wanting a broken sword is all one piece of Uriah's personality."

"What did your Pa tell Uriah's men?" Jacobson asked.

"He lied and said he finally had melted the sword down because it was useless."

"Did the men believe him?" Greene asked.

"I don't think so," Elaria said. "They went away, but came back a couple more times, more insistent each time." Her breath hitched, but she continued. "They came back the day of the fire. I heard them arguing with Pa, but they finally left. I think… I think Uriah knew Pa was lying to him, and he wanted to punish him."

"So he killed your whole family because your father wouldn't give him what he wanted?"

Elaria nodded, her face crumpling in sorrow.

"Why are you telling us about the sword?" Greene asked.

She studied him and Jacobson. "Because I trust you. And if anything happens to me, I want you to take the sword. My pa died for it, my whole family died for it. King Uriah *cannot* have what Pa tried to save."

Greene stared at her a moment, his mind working furiously, then looked at Jacobson, who looked stunned. Greene knew he must be thinking the same thing: Should they take on this responsibility for a useless sword? If they took it back to Archenland and Uriah found out they had it, it might be another reason for him to attack the northern kingdoms.

But if they managed to get it safely out of Arlesland, maybe it could be a bargaining chip for the northern kingdoms if they were attacked.

Playing for time, Greene asked, "What's the sword called?"

Elaria paused a moment, then said, "Strene."

Greene said, "That means 'strength,' right?"

Elaria nodded. Then she said, "Its full name is Hyranstrene."

Greene frowned and glanced at Jacobson, whose eyebrows were raised. "*Hyran*? I'm not familiar with that word."

Elaria said, staring down at the sword, "It means 'here'…'Here lies strength.'"

"Ah," Greene said, but Jacobson looked confused.

Elaria reached for the sword and sheathed it carefully, laying it beside her pallet where it couldn't be taken without her knowledge.

Greene said, "Elaria… you said earlier that you'd help us if you could."

She nodded.

"Well… you know we came from Bagginsland…" Greene said a quick prayer that he was making the right decision. Uriah had killed her family, so it seemed like a safe bet, and the faster they finished the mission, the better.

"Yes?"

"We were sent to find out as much as we can about a rumor that Uriah is planning an attack on the northern kingdoms," he said.

She just stared at him, and his heart sank.

Uriah's Love

Elaria was thinking furiously, wondering how much she could trust these men. They were asking her to betray the king, a man whose vindictiveness she had good reason to fear.

Greene seemed to realize he'd asked too much of her, and modified his question. "Did your father ever talk about what Uriah was like as a military leader? We've heard stories that he wasn't always as cruel as he is now."

Elaria shifted her gaze to the fire. She was tired, exhausted really. The grief, the violent events of the past two days were catching up to her.

She wasn't used to confiding in anyone outside her family, but maybe it was time to trust someone. Greene and Jacobson had done nothing to make her distrust them. They'd done exactly the opposite.

She stirred, kicking one of the logs so that it fell and burst into sparks. Her father hadn't talked about the king much, but there was one conversation he'd had with her mother on several occasions.

"I've heard he loved a woman once, and it was her death that drove him mad."

Greene's eyebrows rose as he glanced at Jacobson. That was a completely new story. "A woman? We'd heard he went crazy after the death of a good friend…"

Elaria glanced at them from the corner of her eye, then shook her head slightly.

They waited, and finally she spoke.

"I know the story you're talking about. Ma and Pa used to argue about it." She was silent a moment, struggling against a lifetime of keeping secrets. But she was tired, so tired.

She sighed. "Like I said earlier, Pa was a guard at the king's prison castle down south, and he'd heard about the guard who died while protecting Prince Uriah. The guard had grown up with Uriah and been his closest friend. Pa said back then Prince Uriah was kind, and always had a nice word for the guards whenever his father sent him to check on the prisoners. They'd liked the prince, but after Uriah's guard was killed, everything changed.

"But my ma…" Elaria cleared her throat. "Before she and Pa married, Ma was maid to a doctor. That's where she learned about herbs and such. The doctor took care of the prisoners that the old king kept at the southern castle, kept them alive in case the king wanted to question them.

"Ma heard the doctor talking to his wife late one night, after he'd been called to the castle urgently. The doctor said Uriah had a woman, a gentlewoman, in one of the rooms at the castle. She was sick, and the doctor was called to help her, but he wasn't sure he could. He said the woman was dying, and it was pitiful to see the way King Uriah sat by her bedside and begged her to live. But later on the woman died anyway, and Ma thought *that* was what caused Uriah to change so drastically."

Greene and Jacobson were stunned. They'd never heard anything like this before about Uriah. Could he possibly have loved someone so much that her death turned him into the vengeful man who was tearing his country apart? Or was the story just Elaria's mother's romantic notion?

Elaria said, "Ma and Pa didn't meet until after that, so they weren't sure who died first, the woman or the guard. Ma could usually change Pa to her way of thinking, but not about that. Ma was convinced it was the woman's death that drove Uriah mad, and Pa was convinced it was his friend's death." She shrugged. "Maybe it was both."

Greene and Jacobson just stared at Elaria, trying to wrap their heads around the idea of Uriah losing his mind over love for a woman. After a few minutes, Elaria said she was ready for bed, and soon the fire had been quenched and their campsite was dark and quiet.

Greene stayed awake long after Elaria and Jacobson slept, staring up at the stars. He was thinking about the woman Uriah had loved.

He knew how it felt to have love snatched away from him, a love deeper than he'd ever imagined he'd feel. He knew the fear and pain… and he'd also come to know the rage that came along with the loss. Thinking about Uriah, about his father, about the travesty bitterness and rage had made of their lives, Greene forced himself to look deep in his heart.

Grief did terrible things to people. Just look at Princess Aurora and Martin, at how their love turned into bitter grief years ago and changed them into completely different people.

If Charla was gone from his life forever, would rage and bitterness overwhelm him until he became as hateful as Uriah?

Greene had to admit Charla's loss had brought him to a very dark place. Only the need to pull his punches, to control his attacks in the fighting dens, kept him sane. He'd been turning to drink to dampen his rage, but he knew deep down it was doing nothing of the sort. It was just numbing his feelings so he didn't care what he was doing, how he was hurting other people.

The rage inside him, the rage he'd inherited from his murderous father, was boiling again, exacerbated by the atmosphere of Arlesland, the deep despair of its people, and Greene wasn't sure he'd be able to control it this time.

That thought was so painful, so devastating, that Greene made a fatal mistake. As he lay looking up at the stars, he decided to put it out of his mind completely because he couldn't stand looking into that abyss. He thought he was protecting himself, but instead he was walking straight toward the path both his father and Uriah had taken long ago.

Poison of the Spirit

Uriah and Albert stood on the parapet, looking down on the training field where their men beat each other bloody and unconscious, some screaming as they tried to stand and fight on broken legs, or lift swords with fractured arms.

It was a lovely sight. These men were *tough!*

"It's working much better than the old program," Albert rumbled in his bass voice.

"It had better," Uriah growled in return. "Those men I sent after Prince John of Vallenland last month were useless. Boastful and lazy, the lot of them, and too stupid to kill John as soon as they captured him. Instead they tortured him long enough for a rescue party to arrive!" Uriah spat the last sentence, his fury still hot months later.

"That was regrettable," Albert sighed, polite commiseration in his voice, but Uriah knew the other king hadn't lost any sleep over the debacle. Albert had cautioned Uriah at the time that wasting the soldiers on a paltry revenge mission was foolish, and he'd been right.

"Almost as regrettable as your incorruptible son," Uriah said scathingly. Albert's son Bertie, who'd been determined to be the kind and noble ruler his father most definitely was *not*, had been making strides in taking over the kingdom during the king's recent convalescence after a serious illness. When King Albert found out, his fury brought him raging back from death's door to retake his power.

Albert scowled. "I took care of it; did what was necessary."

"Was it necessary to use that *particular* poison?" Uriah asked politely. Uriah had heard that the cleanup of Prince Bertie's bodily fluids after his gruesome death had necessitated changing not only the sheets of his bed and the mattress, but the rug underneath. Only a severe breakdown of the body caused that kind of mess.

"Possibly not, but I thought my son deserved a better ending than your father." King Albert smiled, knowing Uriah's poisoning of his father had gone less than smoothly. At least Bertie's end had been quick, if violent.

Uriah scowled and changed the subject. "Tell me of the new training."

Albert smiled. "Basically, we tear out their old selves by the root and replant them with poison."

Uriah laughed nastily. "A most excellent plan. Tell me more."

"We start with boys who've been abused and neglected all their lives (plenty of those to go around!), and then we use every trick we know to tear them down. We starve them and deny them access to a latrine, wake them at all hours of the night or don't allow them any sleep at all, keep them isolated from each other to keep friendships from forming.

"We assign two guards to every new class of troops, which usually includes twenty boys or men. One guard is harsh and demanding, never giving them any kind of encouragement. The other guard seems to be the same, but after the first two weeks, the second guard begins to sneak them extra water or food."

"Ah. Building rapport with them," Uriah said.

"Building *trust*," Albert corrected. "Much more important." He continued, "Most significantly, the guards divide the class in half, so that for one half of the group, Guard A is the good guard, while for the other half it's Guard B. So you have Guard A building trust with half the men while Guard B builds trust with the rest."

Uriah nodded slowly. "Then you can turn them against each other."

Albert smiled. "Just so. When we put them in the training ring, some of them are reluctant to give their all in a fight. The guard they trust encourages them to do so, saying it's the only way they'll survive, and that the men they're fighting are out to kill them anyway."

"And they all obey?" Uriah asked.

"No. But the ones who don't obey end up dead, which is a great incentive to the others." Albert laughed. "The ones who survive... they're willing to do just about anything as long as it means they get approbation from their superiors. The only positive interaction they have is with those superiors, so they'll do anything for them, even beat the other men bloody and try to continue fighting with broken limbs. Commoners are so easy to manipulate," he laughed, and Uriah smirked.

Uriah knew all about that. The training program started with the emotional manipulation he and Albert had been practicing on their citizens for years, and took it ten steps farther.

He surveyed the bloody fighters beneath him and smiled. He had his army, one even *she* would be proud of.

The Climb Begins

On the morning they were to scale Mount Ciel, Charla woke up feeling nervous after a restless night. She and David had tried to reason with Old Dan, convince him that there was no way he could possibly make the climb with them, but he was adamant. When they asked him how in the world he would do it, he simply answered, "With the strength of Oynos," and smiled at their frustration.

So now here they were, dressed in many layers of warm clothes. The Sinti, who carried all sorts of wares with them, had loaned them heavy pants and thick socks, fur-lined gloves and coats, and sturdy hobnail boots. They wore fur-lined hats and heavy scarves wrapped around their faces. Old Dan was wrapped up in so many layers that he looked like a shapeless lump as he was carried by two of the Sinti to the foot of the mountain.

Charla sighed. She had no idea what he was planning to do, but she couldn't see any way around the fact that it was going to place a terrible burden on her and David to get Old Dan up the mountain, never mind themselves.

But Mother Tarni had seen nothing wrong in Old Dan's adamant desire to make the climb, and she'd simply responded

"Oynos will provide" when Charla demanded to know how it could possibly work.

With a sigh, Charla motioned for David to follow her to Old Dan, and they readied their arms to take his weight from the Sintis. The old man shook his head, though, and said with a smile, "That won't be necessary."

They heard a stir behind them and turned to see Mother Tarni approaching with a small wooden box in her hands.

Puzzled, Charla and David stepped aside as the Sinti queen walked to Old Dan. She paused and said in a clear voice, "May the Strength of Oynos fill you," then opened the box and removed a small brown fruit similar to a date. Old Dan took the fruit, put it to his mouth and took a small bite.

There was silence for a moment while Dan chewed and swallowed. Charla was just getting ready to ask what was going on when Old Dan slipped down from the arms supporting him and took a shaky step.

Charla felt her mouth drop open and saw in her peripheral vision that David's had done the same. As they watched in disbelief, Old Dan's shaky steps firmed and by the fourth step he was walking upright with straight legs and the vigor of a man half his age.

Raising his arms and grinning with delight, he said, "Come now, children! There's no time to waste!" and turned to begin the climb.

Mother Tarni surveyed Charla and Dan, who couldn't seem to move. "You should not be surprised at anything you see on this mountain," she said quietly. "There is much that you do not understand, and trying to make things fit what you believe to be possible will not serve you well here. Now, follow your grandfather. Even with the Strength of Oynos, he will need you on this trip. The Sinti will be here when you return." And with that, she turned back toward the village, leaving Charla and David staring after her in shock.

As they slowly turned to face the mountain again, they saw Old Dan's head pop up from behind a rock a hundred yards up the slope. "Well? Come on! No time to waste!" His head disappeared. Charla and David exchanged a long look, and slowly followed.

After a few hours, Charla and David had gotten over their amazement at Old Dan's transformation, and had started feeling a bit of resentment. He moved like a much younger man, and certainly had more stamina than either of them. He led the way up the mountain, stopping to wait when they struggled, nagging them to keep up.

When they finally stopped for the night in a shallow cave, Old Dan still seemed to be full of energy, humming as he used a flint to spark the dry brush that filled the cave, giving them some much needed warmth. Movement kept them warm as long as they were climbing, but when they stopped, the wind that skirled around the mountain started plucking at their clothes, finding the tiny gaps between layers, and running cold fingers along their skin.

Charla shivered and wondered how much colder it would be as they approached the snowpack that covered most of the mountain. She was glad that they had more warm layers in the bags each of them carried across their backs. The bags were also where the Sinti had packed as many strips of dried meat as they could carry, along with two waterskins each.

"When you reach the snowpack," Mother Tarni had said, "you'll be able to replenish your water. But use it sparingly until then."

Dan urged them to drink up now, though, saying they'd need to keep up their strength. "We should reach the snowpack at the end of the day tomorrow," he estimated, smiling encouragingly at them.

Charla tried to smile back, but even her face muscles were tired. She and David barely managed to curl up at the back of the cave with their packs under their heads before they fell into a dreamless sleep.

They did reach the snowpack the next afternoon. When they could see the snow lying on the rocks about ten feet above them, Old Dan stopped and sorted through his bag, pulling out an ax and a long rope.

"When we reach the snow," he said, "we'll tie ourselves together with this long rope. The hobnails on your boots will provide traction, but there will be steep places where you may slip. I'll use my ax to chip into the ice and hold us in place if needed. Don't worry; as long as you stay roped to me, you won't fall."

Charla and David exchanged horrified glances. Old Dan was going to be their anchor, possibly holding all their weight with his thin arms? That didn't sound like a good idea.

But an hour later, they were both glad Old Dan was the one in front. His inexhaustible energy and enhanced strength was the only thing that had gotten them through the steeper areas of ice. Their legs and arms were so weary they could barely pull themselves up, even with the help of the hobnail boots, which had helped more than Charla could believe.

But even the boots couldn't have gotten her up the last few sections. Old Dan had done that himself through sheer willpower. He would chop his ax into the ice above and haul himself up, the rope around his chest pulling David up with him, and the rope around David's chest pulling up Charla. They had both tried to carry their own weight, but Charla was sure most of the effort had come from Dan. It was an unbelievable feat, and Charla began to wonder how the Strength of Oynos fruit would affect her or David.

They slept deeply in a cleft in the icy mountain that night, their bellies full of dried meat but still feeling empty. Old Dan had been smart enough to bring some of the tinder from the cave the night before with them, so they had a small fire, but they all knew they wouldn't be as lucky the next night.

Charla went to sleep wondering how long they would be expected to keep up this pace. How much longer to the top of the mountain?

The next afternoon there was no talk when they stopped for the night. Snow had fallen on them for the last few hours and they were so cold they could hardly move. Fortunately, the outer layer of the clothes the Sintis had given them was also waterproof, so only the scarves over their faces became drenched and frozen, but the cold still went bone-deep.

There was no cleft in the rock to sleep in that night, no tinder to kindle into a bit of warmth. Instead, they lay down on the path on a somewhat flat spot, with Old Dan in the middle and Charla and

David curled next to him. Old Dan pulled a waterproof cloth from his pack and completely covered the three of them, including their heads, so that the combined warmth of their breath filled the space under the cloth and kept them from freezing that night.

The climb the next day was pure misery. The cold had taken on extra menace in the form of a fierce wind that tried to knock them off the snowy path. Even worse, Old Dan's energy seemed to be fading, even though every morning he took another small nibble of the Strength of Oynos fruit Mother Tarni had given him. That morning, as he put the fruit back in his pack, Charla had seen that there was only a tiny bit left, possibly enough for two more small bites.

"How much longer until we reach the top?" she'd asked him numbly, her lips so cold they could barely move behind her frozen scarf.

"We'll make it," he'd said stoutly, turning to start up the pathway before she could protest that he hadn't answered her question.

But that night, he wasn't so sanguine. She had gotten so used to his energy the past few days that she was shocked when they stopped for the night and she saw that he once more looked like a shrunken old man.

Old Dan saw the shock on her face and patted her hand, smiling. "Don't worry, granddaughter. When you see your mother, it will all be worth it. Oynos will not fail us." He kissed her on the forehead and went to rummage for anything they might use to make a fire.

The only thing Charla could feel glad about was that they had managed to find a cave, a real, honest to goodness cave that went far enough back into the mountain that they were able to completely escape the howling wind outside, although it was still terribly cold.

Old Dan and David found a dry fungus growing on the cave walls that they managed to spark into a fire that was just enough to warm their hands and faces, and begin to thaw their frozen feet. Old Dan put some snow into their lightweight metal mugs, set them in the middle of the small fire, and they drank the resulting hot water, feeling warm inside for the first time in three days.

As Charla sat drowsing before the fire, cherishing the heat of the mug in her hands, she saw Old Dan pull out the Strength of Oynos. He studied the tiny remainder for a moment, then closed his eyes and bowed his head over it. Was he praying? His lips weren't moving and he seemed almost to be sleeping… then he raised his head and put the precious bit of fruit back into his pack.

He called Charla and David to get their packs and dump everything out on the ground. "We need to consolidate everything into one pack that we can take turns carrying, to conserve our energy."

Charla and David nodded wearily, barely able to move their arms to unpack.

They stared at the meager supplies. All that was left was the precious waterproof cloth Dan had used to trap their warmth the night before, a few strips of dried meat, the mugs, the flint they used to spark their fires, Old Dan's ax and rope, and the waterskins.

As they stared at the meager supplies, Charla whispered, "We only have enough for one more day. Will we make it, Grandpop?"

He patted her hand. "Yes, child. Have faith."

When they finished packing the bag, Old Dan pulled them both close, spread the waterproof cloth over them, and they fell into a deep sleep as the air under the cloth grew warm.

Peace and Rage

The morning after Elaria told Jacobson and Greene about Uriah's lady love, Jacobson and Elaria joked around while making breakfast and packing their bags. Greene merely scowled at them as he saddled his horse.

Jacobson was worried about more than Greene's bad attitude. They didn't have much money left in their bags, and he didn't want to touch the money Elaria had gotten from her horse. He pondered the problem as they rode into the next town at midday.

"We're getting low on money," he said in an undertone to Greene as he pulled up alongside him. "I don't want to use Elaria's money, but I don't know what else to do."

Greene turned a scowl on him. "Are you stupid? We'll just do a couple of fights."

Jacobson said hesitantly, "Greene… I don't think that's a good idea. You haven't been yourself lately. Let's talk about it with Elaria. Maybe she'll have an idea."

Greene stared at him coldly. "You've always been a fool, Jacobson. Just shut up and let's get on with it." He pulled his horse up with a jerk at the stable, flung the lead and a coin to the stable lad, and strode off toward an alley where some men were congregating.

Jacobson hesitated, glancing at the confused Elaria, then dismounted. As she slid down beside him, he said, "The fastest way for us to make some money is in the fighting dens."

Elaria's eyes widened and she started to say, "No! We can use..." but Jacobson interrupted her.

"We may have to do that, but let me and Greene do this today. I don't want you in there, though. You stay here and watch the horses, and we'll be back in a couple of hours."

"Are you crazy?" she said. "I'm going with you!"

As he began to remonstrate, she said, "Look, either I go with you now, or I follow you later."

Sighing, Jacobson gave in.

"Help me with this," Elaria said, pulling some kind of harness out of her saddlebag. She began to wiggle her arms through it until it was settled on her back so she could buckle the straps across her chest. Then she unbuckled the sword from her saddle and handed it to Jacobson, turning her back to him. When he just stood there with the sword in his hand, she turned her head and said impatiently, "Put it in the harness so I can take it with me."

"Take it with you?" Jacobson repeated. Why did she want to bring a broken sword?

"I'm not leaving it here," she said meaningfully.

Jacobson seriously doubted Uriah's men would stumble upon the sword if it were left unguarded, but it was her business, so he did as she asked, and a minute later they were striding toward the alley down which Greene had disappeared.

As they followed the groups of men converging on one particular door, Jacobson tried to prepare her for the fighting den. "It really smells. And it's dark. And the men are..." He couldn't finish that sentence. "Just keep really close to me, alright?" He just hoped Greene had the good sense to stick to the plan today, instead of taking his opponent out with one punch like he had the last time.

"One good thing," Jacobson leaned over to murmur in Elaria's ear, "is that our bandaged heads will make us look even more incompetent than usual." He grinned at her.

Elaria was puzzled by his remark as she followed Jacobson into the fighting den. Incompetent? He and Greene were excellent fighters, so what was he talking about?

Her nose twitched as she was surrounded by the yelling men. Elaria was used to the smell of people who'd been working hard on the farm in the sun. It wasn't necessarily a pleasant smell, but at least it was produced by honest work. But this stench was made of rage and despair.

The men pressed hard against her on every side as she and Jacobson made their way through the crowd. None of them took any notice of her, dressed as she was in her brother's clothes.

Finally, they came to a large room where the shouting and curses overwhelmed her senses. Elaria stuck her fingers in her ears and tried to breath shallowly through her nose, to take in as little of the foul air as she could. She almost ran into Jacobson's back as he paused to look around, then made his way to where Greene stared narrow-eyed at the men bashing their way to oblivion.

The look on Greene's face scared her. She hadn't talked to him much since the night he'd tried to save her family, but his fearlessness in jumping into the fire for people he didn't know had impressed her deeply. She'd forgiven his scowls and silences in the days following, always remembering the way he'd risked his life. His bravery when they'd been set upon by the thieves had earned him even deeper approbation from her.

He'd been harder to like than Jacobson, but Elaria was used to being around men who were hard to like. Arlesland wasn't a happy place.

But the look on Greene's face now was the look of an animal stalking its prey. Every muscle was still, only his eyes moving, nostrils flaring as if scenting meat.

Jacobson murmured something in Greene's ear. Greene made no sign of acknowledgment for a moment, then gave a sharp nod.

As the fight ended, Greene started to move toward the ring, but Jacobson pushed him back and ambled forward himself, a slightly stupid grin on his face.

The next few minutes were very confusing for Elaria. She'd seen Jacobson and Greene fight the men in the alley. She knew how good they were, how unflinching. But Jacobson was nothing but clumsy now. He stumbled and flailed, somehow managing to land a few blows, and then trip his opponent so the man sprawled forward straight into Jacobson's fist. The surprised grin on Jacobson's face as he was declared the winner brought mostly boos from the backers of his opponent, with a few cheers from those who'd been bored enough to put some money on him.

Elaria glanced up at Greene to see what he'd made of Jacobson's display and was surprised to see a faint smile on his face. His eyes were no longer narrowed, and his shoulders had lost some of their tension.

As Jacobson rejoined them, Greene congratulated him and watched another fight, then started to move toward the ring himself. Elaria was startled to see the same self-deprecating grin on his face as the one Jacobson had sported during his fight and watched with interest as he displayed the same clumsy fighting style, with a similarly surprising knockout at the end.

He rejoined them clutching his fistful of prize money and shouted over the yells of the crowd, "I guess today is our lucky day!" Jacobson happily agreed and clapped him on the shoulder.

When the two men stepped forward for their next fight, Elaria saw several men pointing at them as they placed their bets with the fight master, and the money Greene and Jacobson clutched afterward was significantly larger, as were their grins.

Elaria, glad to finally see a smile on Greene's face, was beaming along with them when they returned from their third fights with the largest haul yet. As Greene and Jacobson started to make their way to the exit door, several men tried to get them to stay, but they yelled "Don't want to press our luck!" and kept going.

One man followed them out the door and offered to treat them to some liquid refreshment. Over the beer, the man tried to find out more about them, but Greene and Jacobson were vague, not saying much more than that they were headed west on their way to Reimsland. The man tried to convince them to stay one more day so he could bet on them for the next fight, but they said, "Nah, we don't like to stay more than one day in a town. We'll be moving on in the morning."

By the time Greene fell into bed that night, the small satisfaction (possibly even happiness) that he'd felt during his and Jacobson's fights was long gone. He was again frustrated and angry that he was stuck in this awful kingdom, and a feeling had been growing on him all day that, wherever Charla was, she needed him desperately. Her need, his inability to help her, all culminated in a rage he was barely able to control.

When he finally drifted into a fractured sleep, his fears coalesced into a terrible dream where Charla was crying out his name, sobbing in anguish, begging him to come to her. In the dream, Greene kept trying to reach her and couldn't. She was lost in a fog. He caught glimpses, but could never see her clearly.

Grief

Charla woke stiff, every muscle in her body aching. Someone was calling her name. Befuddled, she thought for a moment it was still night, then realized the waterproof cloth was still over her head. She pulled it off and saw dim light seeping into the cave.

Blinking, she heard her name again.

"Charla!"

David stepped into view, tension in his body.

"What?" Charla threw the cloth off and unsteadily got to her feet, her body protesting.

"He's gone! I woke up and he was gone so I thought he'd gone outside, but he's not there!" David was babbling, turning frantically from side to side, as if looking for something.

"What? What are you talking about? Who…?" She looked around, realizing for the first time that Old Dan hadn't been huddled under the cloth with her. "Grandpop? He's *gone?*" Her voice rose on the last word, fear making her blood run cold.

She and David rushed to the mouth of the cave, peering into the swirling snow and calling for the old man, but the wind snatched their words away. Glad more than ever for her hobnail boots, Charla carefully stepped into the brilliantly white world that was so beautiful to look at and so treacherous to enter. Without speaking, David went left to look down the trail they'd climbed the day before, and Charla began to climb the trail on the right. There were no tracks in the snow, which made Charla fear Old Dan had left hours before, and the snow had already covered his tracks.

She'd only been looking for a few minutes when she heard a frantic shout behind her. She made her way back as quickly as she could and found David tugging at something on the ground, something half buried in snow.

"Grandpop!" she screamed, slipping on the ice in her haste.

But it was too late, much too late.

Old Dan's shrunken body was very much in evidence when they managed to brush the snow off, because the old man had removed all but his small clothes. His body was frozen stiff, the beloved smile on his face. His arms were outstretched, as if he'd been reaching for something when he breathed his last.

Charla wanted to cry, but the air was so cold that her tears froze immediately. She made horrible moaning, keening cries until David pulled her to her feet, away from the body, and back into the cave. There they found Old Dan's clothes, the neatly folded layers he'd left for them to use after his death.

Then the tears did flow, albeit slowly because Charla and David were so dehydrated. Charla collapsed into David's arms and the two of them wept, huddled there beside the clothes of the man who had sacrificed his last bit of warmth for them.

The terror of the past week had kept Charla from thinking about Greene very much, mostly because thinking about him made everything so much worse, but now he was *all* Charla could think about as she tried to escape her grief.

"Greene, Greene!" she sobbed, the deep cry of a child seeking solace.

When Charla and David finally came to their senses late that afternoon, they realized that Old Dan hadn't just left the clothes for them. He'd also left the last bit of the Strength of Oynos.

"He meant for us to go on," David told Charla, who was arguing that they should go back down the accursed mountain. "We have to, or he will have died in vain."

But Charla couldn't bear it. Old Dan had been her rock for so long, and now she didn't have the strength, the willpower, to go on without him.

David held her and rocked her, and eventually she slept.

In the morning, she was calm. She felt dead inside, but she had accepted her grandfather's death, the sacrifice he'd made for them.

David was right. They had to go on.

When David awakened, she started another small fire and heated water in their mugs, then divided out the remaining strips of dried meat. They ate in silence, then divided up the clothes Old Dan had left them. David slung the almost empty bag across his back, and they walked to the cave opening. Charla took the Strength of Oynos out of Old Dan's handkerchief, weak tears blurring her eyes as she did, and pulled it into two small pieces. She gave one to David, and put the other in her mouth.

It was chewy, like the date it resembled, with a stringy outside and soft sweetness inside. But the taste was different than anything she'd had before. It tasted like…

Sunlight on a stream, a warm breeze in the trees, the flutter of butterfly wings on her skin. It tasted like joy and hope.

Charla felt the energy rising in her, like someone had opened the top of her head and poured in a full measure. She'd never felt so capable, so strong.

She grinned at David, who grinned back. They didn't say a word, just walked into the glistening world outside and began to climb like they were scaling a gentle hill.

When night fell, they were still climbing. Their unnatural energy had worn off a few hours earlier, but it had been replaced with a stamina that made them feel they could continue climbing all night. And so they did.

On and on they went, while the moon rose in the sky, so close they could almost touch it. They paused a few times, looking far down the mountain to where they could see lanterns shining in the village below.

But no… it was much too far away to see the lanterns, surely? Charla rubbed her eyes, but the lights were still there.

When dawn came, the lightening sky showed they were almost to the top. Charla wondered what they would find. At her lowest point, which had come the night her grandfather sacrificed himself, she had doubted everything about their mission. She'd doubted her grandfather's sanity, doubted her mother was at the top of the mountain, or, if she was there, doubted she would still be alive.

And most of all, she'd doubted the existence of the Eye. She'd even doubted the existence of Oynos.

But once they'd tasted the Strength of Oynos, she no longer had any doubts. She fully believed they would find her mother and the Eye, and that she and David would safely make it back down the mountain.

As the sun broke in the east, Charla and David paused, listening. There was a sound on the wind, like singing. They looked up at the top of the mountain above them and saw a swirl of snow there, like someone had thrown it into the sky to whirl in the wind. As they watched, it went on and on, swirling and dipping to fall on the mountain.

Puzzled, Charla thought it seemed as if that was where the snow was originating, rather than falling from the sky. After a moment, she shook her head and nudged David to keep going.

Finally they were at the top. It wasn't a peak, though. Instead, they stood on a flat spot in front of a huge rock with a cleft in it. Charla was flooded with a feeling that there was something beyond that cleft… something for which she'd been waiting her whole life.

They stopped to catch their breath, then clasped hands, grinning at each other. This was it! They were about to meet their mother!

They stepped into the cleft…

… and into another world.

Fighting Within and Without

Elaria woke up that morning with the usual ache in her chest for her dead family, but also hope that the day with Greene and Jacobson would be full of the same smiles that the successful fights yesterday had brought. Her hope was dashed at breakfast when she saw a scowl even worse than usual on Greene's face. Jacobson talked to Greene, suggesting that they turn south again since the road they were on was now taking them closer to King Uriah's castle. But Greene stubbornly shook his head, insisting they had to stay on the road that led to more villages, rather than detouring into the country.

Elaria hoped they would make it through the day without tempers boiling over, and they almost did. The men had barely spoken to each other all day when they rode into the next town at mid-afternoon. They had a meal, then Greene got up without a word and headed for the fighting den. Jacobson silently followed, but paused before entering the den to try to convince Elaria to go back to the inn to wait for them. She stubbornly shook her head and followed him in, reaching over her back to make sure her sword was safely strapped on.

She was prepared this time for the show of incompetence that Greene and Jacobson put on. Last night, by the end of the fights Greene had been grinning broadly, but after each fight this time the scowl quickly returned to his face. By his third fight, he made no pretense of awkwardness, just walked into the ring and knocked the guy out with one furious blow, leaving the crowd gaping in silence.

He grabbed his money and pushed his way out of the den, Jacobson and Elaria trailing in his wake. By the time they followed him into the tavern, he was knocking back a strong drink, with his hand raised for another.

They ate supper in silence until a couple of men approached them, settling in the chairs near their table. One of the men leaned over to Greene and said, "I saw that last fight of yours. Looks like you might know what to do with those big fists of yours after all." He smirked at Greene, but the smile slid off his face when Greene met his eyes with a stare that made Elaria's blood run cold.

Jacobson spoke up, drawing the man's attention to himself. "Maybe we do, maybe we don't. What business is it of yours?"

The man gladly turned to him after another uneasy glance at Greene. "Well, see, it's just that King Uriah has put out a call for fighting men. He's paying a nice bonus to anyone who joins, along with three good meals a day."

Jacobson shrugged. "We're not from here. Just making our way through to Reimsland is all."

The man grinned. "Well, that's no problem, since King Albert of Reimsland is working with Uriah, see? They've built a new training facility on the border between Arlesland and Reimsland, and they're sending troops from both kingdoms there."

Jacobson glanced at Greene, who had looked up at this news. Jacobson said casually, "Oh, yeah? What's it all about, then?"

The man shrugged, but his companion leaned forward and said quietly, "War against the northern kingdoms is what I hear."

The other man shoved him and snarled, "You don't ought to be talking about the king's plans like that." He glanced uneasily at Greene and Jacobson.

The second man scoffed. "Aww, what are you worrying about? They may not be from here, but it's obvious they're no northerners! You don't see that much anger up north." He stared at Greene in admiration.

Greene didn't say a word, but the quality of his silence suddenly took on a menace that made Elaria's hair rise on her arms. The other men seemed oblivious as Greene shoved back his chair and headed for the bar. Jacobson's eyes followed him and he brusquely told the men they weren't interested, waving them away as they tried to argue.

Elaria watched unhappily as Jacobson went to the bar and said something in Greene's ear, at which Greene hunched his shoulders and turned his back on Jacobson as he downed yet another glass of liquor. Jacobson slammed his hand down on the bar and came scowling back to the table where Elaria sat, throwing down some coins and motioning for her to follow him upstairs to their rooms.

She was glad to lock the door behind her, glad to climb into bed and pull the covers over her head, glad to try to forget the stressful day… but she couldn't fall asleep. As she lay there, eyes wide in the dark, she heard heavy footsteps stumble to the room next door, then a rumble of voices raised in anger. She pulled her pillow over her head, but she couldn't shut out the sharp words. Finally there was silence, and finally she slept.

Tracking Greene and Jacobson

Jamison's group, now traveling with the Arlesland Sinti tribe, first found word of Greene and Jacobson at a tavern south of the Bagginsland-Arlesland gate. The tavern owner said there had been a couple of strangers there about a week ago.

"Jumped some of my regular customers they did, out of the blue, for no good reason!" he said righteously.

Jamison pulled out the sketch of Greene and the tavern owner nodded emphatically. "Yep! That's one of 'em alright! You can ask Missy over there. They started the fight because of her, claiming my regular customers were harassing her, but I'd never put up with such behavior. She weren't in no danger. Right, Missy?" he said, scowling at her.

The girl nodded without looking up from her work. When Jamison and Ethan tried to talk to her, telling her that the men they were searching for were thieves, she wouldn't answer while the tavern owner was standing there listening, but when he walked to the back of the building to get some more liquor, she gave a frightened glance at the picture of Greene and her eyes softened.

Scowling at Jamison, she said fiercely, "I don't believe they would steal anything! They were good men and they helped me! I don't know where they went, but if I did, I wouldn't tell you." And with another scowl, she went back to wiping down the tables and ignored their further questions.

As Jamison and Ethan left the tavern, they didn't notice the wide eyes in a dirty face that watched them from a corner by the fire.

The next week, the Sinti stopped their wagons to trade in a small village east of King Uriah's castle. The sun was just peeking over the horizon when the first villagers showed up, and soon there was a good crowd bartering for wares.

While the other Sinti traded, Jamison and the Vallenland Sinti talked with the villagers about whether they'd seen two tall strangers. One of the village men, a muscular brute with hard eyes, gave them a suspicious look, but admitted he'd seen a couple of men who fit that description the night before in one of the fighting dens he frequented a few miles south.

"Good fighters they were," he grunted. "Smart, too. Their first couple of fights, they'd act like they weren't too good. Seemed kinda clumsy, you know? But then they'd go for one more fight, and they were in for blood that time. One, two punches, maybe some kicks for fun, and the other guy was down for the count. Down for good, some of 'em. Had to carry 'em out of the ring. I didn't make any money off 'em that first night, but after that last knockout I found out what town they were headed to next, and I followed 'em. Made me a nice packet of money on their fights that time. Seemed like they were getting a little tired of the weakling act after the first two fights that day, though. They put the other guys down pretty quick, but still made it look like it was more luck than skill. I would've followed 'em on to the next town, but couldn't spare the time."

Jamison tried to seem unconcerned when he asked, "Where were they headed next?"

"Buglesville, they said. Small town west of here about twenty miles."

Jamison and Ethan thanked him, and were saddling up their horses ten minutes later.

Greene's Rage Overflows

The only good thing Elaria could say about the journey to Buglesville was that Greene was completely silent. It was obvious that even Jacobson was barely holding onto his temper, and Elaria had a feeling that if Greene opened his mouth, his rage would pour out on her and Jacobson so harshly that Jacobson would've responded in kind.

When they stopped on the side of the road for lunch, Greene stomped away from them, huddling down on the other side of a tree with his meal. Jacobson apologized for him in a low voice. "The woman he was supposed to marry ran out on him a couple of weeks ago, and I'm sure that's what's making him so angry."

Elaria nodded, but she thought to herself that the woman had been smart to get away from a man with that much rage inside him.

When they arrived in Buglesville, Jacobson tried to persuade Greene not to fight that night. Greene didn't bother to reply, just started off for the fighting den and left them to follow or not. Jacobson did and Elaria, feeling sick to her stomach, was right behind him.

Through the haze of red rage in his mind, Greene vaguely noticed that the feeling in this particular den was even darker than the ones they'd patronized in previous days.

They'd been traveling north toward King Uriah's castle the last few days, and as they traveled ever closer to the castle, the haze in Greene's head had increased until he almost couldn't see straight. The only time the fog seemed to dissipate was in the fighting ring.

Greene felt like he was fighting a losing battle with himself. He was filled with all the rage and despair he saw around him, but a small part of him begged him not to give in to it. It was such a small voice, though, so hard to hear in the chaos of his mind.

All Greene wanted was to get out of this terrible land, to get back to the peace of the northern kingdoms. Even if Charla wasn't there, still didn't want to marry him, at least he wouldn't be bombarded on all sides from the despair of the Arleslanders. He and Jacobson had learned about the training barracks Uriah and King Albert had set up on the border between Arlesland and Reimsland. Maybe that was enough information to take back home to King Richard. Jacobson had been trying to convince Greene to abandon the mission, but Greene had stubbornly refused to agree. It was like his mouth was determined to say the exact opposite of what his heart longed for. Maybe tomorrow, though… maybe tomorrow they could start for home.

But they still had this day to get through, in a village where all the despair of Arlesland seemed concentrated. The emaciated people with dead eyes, the starving children with swollen bellies, the meager supplies for sale in the market. A small part of Greene rebelled at taking any kind of money, even gambling money, from such a desperate populace, but then he'd seen the fighters swaggering through the village square on their way to the fighting den.

These men didn't even look like Arleslanders. They had oiled muscles that bulged from sleeveless shirts, powerful hands that shoved at the poor villagers unlucky enough to cross their paths, and sneers on their faces as they made disgusting remarks to the cowed women shepherding their terrified children past them.

Watching the men as they pushed past him, Greene's heart began to pound and pressure built in his head as his vision narrowed to a red tunnel. He didn't notice Elaria's look of concern or Jacobson's plea that he not go to the fighting den tonight.

Without a word, Greene started after the swaggering men, and Jacobson and Elaria ran to keep up with him.

When they reached the floor of the den, a fight was well in progress. One man was holding his opponent by the shirt and pounding him with a fist the size and color of a smoked ham. The other man's head lolled, blood flying from a broken nose and split lips. The victor dropped the loser onto the dirt floor and cheers went up as money exchanged hands.

Normally Greene and Jacobson would observe a few fights, picking their targets carefully, planning the fight in their minds to make sure they didn't give away their expertise.

But Greene didn't do any of that. As soon as the victorious fighter dropped the other man, Greene was leaping toward the ring.

All the rage he'd been holding back since Charla left him exploded. He didn't hear the surprised yells of the gamblers surrounding the fighting floor as they scrambled to get out of his way. He caught a glimpse of the smirk on the fighter's face turning to abject terror as he caught sight of Greene, and then he was on him.

He had no thought except that he wanted to hurt this man as badly as possible, smash his face and break his body. He didn't care what the consequences were.

Nothing mattered except *rage*.

Within him, he felt a furious beast rise, a creature that unfurled wings of power, suffusing his mind with the absolute certainty that *nothing* could defeat him, nothing could come close to stopping him, nothing could protect the puny human before him.

He ripped and tore the world to pieces, slashed and savaged, his usual strength increased one hundredfold by adrenaline that turned his muscles to stone, his fists to granite smashing through the soft flesh beneath him.

After a long, long time, Greene became vaguely aware that someone was screaming. He felt someone trying to hold onto him, but he didn't realize it was Jacobson who was trying to pull him off the man who lay bloody and pulped beneath him, or that it was Elaria screaming for him to stop.

It was the silence that brought him back to himself. The cheering mob around him had fallen completely silent when they saw the mess on the floor that had once been human. Someone was panting in Greene's ear, struggling to pull him away from the man, and Elaria's screams had turned to sobs of despair.

In the silence, the creature within him furled its wings, sated.

"Leave off, man! You're killing him!" The words barely penetrated Greene's hazy mind.

As the red rage dissipated, Greene finally saw the man beneath him, his face unrecognizable now that every bone in it was crushed. Another memory flashed through Greene's mind: his father crouched over a bloody and unconscious princess. Appalled, Greene let himself be pulled from the man, almost falling because his knees were suddenly too weak to hold him.

"You were killing him," a voice said beside him.

Greene turned with a jerk, his eyes wide and unfocused, still fixed on the horror of what he'd done. "Killing him…" he mumbled, swaying as he tried to regain his footing.

The man who'd spoken was holding onto one of Greene's arms while Jacobson clung to the other. "But he is not yet dead," the man said calmly, and Greene swayed and fainted as relief turned his knees to water, blessed darkness taking him away from his sin.

"Leave Off, Man!"

Jamison was relieved that the Buglesville fighting den was easy to find. All he and the other Sinti had to do was watch for a scrum of men heading in the same direction, and follow them down an alley, through a peeling door, and into one of the most foul-smelling buildings Jamison had ever been in. Bile rose in his throat at the smell of blood, urine and sweat that oozed from the very walls. He couldn't stand the smell, but even less did he want to breathe through his mouth and taste the noxious fumes, so he covered his nose and mouth with the scarf around his neck, and followed the yells ahead of him.

After a few rounds, the other Sinti gave up and escaped to the cleaner air outside, but Jamison and Ethan watched fight after bloody fight, the raw vitriol of the spectators flaying their ears until they were numb. They were just starting to shift restlessly from foot to foot, wondering if they should join the other Sinti outside, when Ethan nudged Jamison and nodded toward the door.

Silhouetted against the bright sunlight outside, a couple of men were entering who towered over the others. Jamison couldn't see their faces, but he expected to have plenty of time to do so. From what the village man had told them earlier, the Archenlanders were careful fighters, smart enough to judge their opponents before entering the ring, so he expected them to observe a few fights.

But he was wrong.

As the men made their way to the edge of the crowd, the fighter in the ring delivered his final knockout punch to his opponent and raised his arms in triumph as the crowd roared.

And one of the tall men attacked him.

Jamison's jaw dropped. He'd never seen such a vicious fight before, and the outcome was obvious almost as soon as it began, with the attacker pounding the other's face with a fist of stone, the breaking bones audible. Judging by the silence, the spectators, blood-thirsty though they were, had never witnessed such rage before, either.

Jamison was leaping forward before he realized it, grabbing onto the enraged man's arm. "Leave off, man! You're killing him!" he said in the man's ear, grunting as he tried to hold him.

The tall man didn't seem to hear. He struggled and yelled and almost yanked Jamison off his feet. But Jamison dug in and *pulled* and, with the help of the other tall man, he managed to drag him out of the ring.

"You were killing him," he repeated, and the tall man swung his head toward him, unfocused blue eyes looking past Jamison to a horror only he could see.

"Killing him…" the man said faintly as he stumbled.

Jamison felt a stab of pity. "But he is not yet dead," he finished, and caught the tall man as he fainted, lowering him carefully to the floor.

Looking at the slack face, Jamison felt a moment of disappointment. This wasn't the man they'd been searching for. This man was haggard, his eyes sunken, hollow cheeks covered with a scruffy beard, head covered with dark bristles and peeling skin, like he had some kind of skin disease. He was so dirty that Jamison could smell his unwashed body even over the smell of the fighting den.

Jamison glanced at the man's friend, who was staring down at the unconscious man with fear on his face. He, too, was dirty and haggard, and looked nothing like the sketch of Greene, either.

Jamison was starting to rise to his feet to give Ethan the bad news when a thin boy shoved his way between Jamison and the fallen man, sobbing and crying "Timmy! Timmy! What have you done?"

Timmy.

Timothy Greene?

Jamison frowned at the boy, then glanced again at the man who was kneeling beside Timmy, rubbing a hand across his face and glancing fearfully at the sharp eyes around them.

Gently, the man shook his unconscious friend and slapped his face, whispering, "Greene! Greene! Wake up! We have to get out of here!"

Jamison's face cleared. He nodded at Ethan and reached down to grab the man's sleeve. "Are you Jacobson?" he asked in a low voice.

The man gaped. "How do you know that name?" he whispered.

"King Richard sent us," Jamison murmured.

Tears started to the other man's eyes. "Oh, thank God!" And he dropped his head and cried.

Joy

As Charla and David stepped through the cleft at the top of Mount Ciel, they found themselves in a small hollow surrounded by sharp stone peaks, as if someone had taken a scoop out of the mountain top.

To their surprise, there was no snow in the hollow. In fact, there was no winter, or even autumn.

Outside the cleft was ice and swirling snow and fear of death. Inside was warmth and springtime and hope, because inside was the Strength of Oynos: a tree full of the fruit grew on the far side of the small hollow, its branches dappled with white flowers.

And under it sat a woman on a wooden bench.

They would've known immediately who she was even if they hadn't been expecting her, because she looked just like Old Dan. A younger, feminine version, to be sure, but the same black face, the same wide, sweet smile (although hers had teeth in), the same love in her eyes.

She stood up and held out her arms with joy, and they ran to her with wordless cries, hugging her neck and sobbing. Being in her arms was like coming home, full of the peace and safety and comfort which they desperately needed. They clung to her until she laughed and fell back onto the bench, pulling them down so that Charla sat on the bench beside her, while David sat on the ground.

Amiet, their mother, gazed at them with wide eyes, happy tears streaming down her cheeks, reaching out with both hands to touch their faces, run her fingers through their hair, cup their cheeks, and then pull them to her in joyful laughter, holding them with all the love in the world.

They talked for the rest of that day and half the night. Amiet wanted to hear all about their lives, and they wanted to know about their father and the life they'd had before Amiet became the *skaeweer* and Charla's dream as the daughter-bird sent them into exile. Amiet shed some tears when she told them how their father died of a weak heart soon after David's birth, and then she cried again when they told her of Old Dan's death, but most of their words brought her joy.

When Charla told her that a caravan of Sinti had brought them to Mount Ciel, Amiet nodded. "You are speaking of Mother Tarni, aren't you?" She smiled at Charla's exclamation of surprise. "Yes, I know Mother Tarni. She has been a good friend to us for many years, helping us when we ventured into the world to find husbands and wives. It was she who helped Father make his way north to Archenland when he escaped with you."

Charla looked at David. "That's why Mother Tarni said Grandpop was an old friend. It all makes sense now."

Amiet nodded and said, "Mother Tarni is trustworthy. She will help you in any way she can. Don't be afraid to ask for help when you need it."

When they'd exhausted the topic of their past, and Charla and David's lives in Archenland, David looked around at the beautiful hollow.

"But... how do you live here?" he asked. "What do you eat and drink? What do you *do* all day?"

His mother laughed and motioned to the tree above them. "The Strength of Oynos is my food. The snow outside the hollow is my drink. As for how I occupy myself each day, for year on year..."

She paused for words. "It will seem odd to you, but I commune with Oynos."

She shrugged. "In my life before the calling, I was busy, busy. Planting crops, harvesting, cooking, cleaning, making clothes, repairing our huts… There was always something that needed doing. Here, all is accomplished. I am in the presence of God, which is *everything*. Being here, close to Oynos, feeds my spirit." She thought another moment. "The only thing I *do* is pray for the well-being of my family, for all who live in Bryten, all who live throughout Eoroe. And that is… enough." She smiled, regarding them with calm eyes.

Charla pondered her mother's words. She couldn't imagine sitting around all day with nothing to do but pray. It sounded rather horrible, actually. But she had to admit that her mother seemed peaceful in a way that Charla had never felt.

Finally, they fell into a sort of sleep, with Amiet leaning back against the tree trunk, humming as she held her children, her right arm around Charla's waist and her left arm draped over David's back as he sat with his head in her lap. The stars in the dark sky above them twinkled as if in celebration as they slept.

Charla and David woke with the coming of dawn to find their mother standing at the edge of a cleft in the mountain, where the rising sun could be seen. Amiet was singing a wordless song of joy, with her face and arms raised to the sky. As she sang, the white blossoms from the Strength of Oynos tree above them swirled toward the sun as if in a strong wind, and as the blossoms left the tree, they turned to snowflakes and fell onto the mountain.

Once the sun was well and truly risen, Amiet lowered her arms and stopped singing, turning to face her children with a smile. She came back to them, took them in her arms and held them as they had longed to be held so many times.

They broke their fast with the Strength of Oynos, and Amiet stepped outside the hollow with a large bowl and brought it back packed with snow, which quickly melted in the warm air.

When they had eaten the fruit, and drank the purest water they'd ever tasted, Amiet took their hands and smiled with all the love they had ever desired. "Now, my children," she said. "You must not be sad, but our time is coming to an end."

Charla had been dreading this moment, and tears started to her eyes. David didn't say a word, simply leaned his head into his mother's neck and clutched at her like a child.

Amiet spoke softly to his bowed head. "I know, my darling. Time has been taken from us, but it will be given to us again. This is not the last time we will see each other. There is an entire world beyond this one."

"Now," Amiet drew away from David and stood up, squeezing their hands as she did so. "It is time." She drew Charla up from the bench, and reached into a hollow in the Tree of the Strength of Oynos to pull out a large flat jewel bound with gold. It was blue, with shifting layers of darker blue and green. As Amiet pulled it from its hiding place, it caught the rising sun and the layers of color blazed while a streak of pure white raced across it like lightning. Charla and David exclaimed and stared, then the stone faded back to dull blue as Amiet lowered it.

Amiet held it out to Charla and said, "You are the *skaeweer* now. The Eye is your responsibility. It has been safe, hidden here for countless generations of our family. But Oynos has revealed that there is a great war coming, and soon it will be needed. You must take it from the mountain to a new place of safety. Oynos will help you find such a place."

Amiet pressed the Eye into Charla's hand and said "Guard it well, better even than your life." Her face was intent, very serious.

Charla hesitated, then asked, "Mother… what is the Eye? Is it really worth my life?"

Amiet stroked her cheek. "My darling, the question you must ask is, 'Is *my* life more important than the survival of *humanity*?' For *that* is what destruction of the Eye would bring about. It is the Eye of God, the most precious thing in the world."

Charla stared at her, then finally nodded, and looked down at the Eye. As she watched, it seemed to shrink and diminish until it was merely a pretty stone, rather than a fiery jewel. She carefully put it away in an inside pocket and fastened it securely.

"Now we must say goodbye," Amiet said, smiling with love at them both. "You will not see me again in this life, but I am going to live with Oynos, and *he* is with you always. Be strong and courageous, children. Dark days are coming and true hearts are needed." She pulled each of them to her in turn, holding them and kissing their cheeks, and then she gently pushed them toward the break in the peaks where they had first entered the hollow. As they reached it, Charla and David turned back for one more look.

Their mother was sitting on the bench beneath the Tree of the Strength of Oynos, smiling at them with such love that Charla felt her heart swell. She stared at her mother, determined to never forget how she looked… and then gasped as all the blossoms on the tree suddenly fell, completely covering Amiet in white so they could no longer see her… then the blossoms swirled up into the air like a whirlwind, and with them went a sound like Amiet's morning song as they fell in snowflakes over the edge of the mountain.

And Amiet was no more.

The Tree of Strength, too, was gone. All that was left were dead branches. The fruit had dropped from the tree along with the blossoms, and as they looked at it where it lay on the ground, the fruit shriveled up and disappeared.

Overwhelmed, Charla and David just stared for a long moment. Then they shook their heads as if coming out of a dream, and turned to the piles of warm clothing they had left waiting beside the cleft.

On top of each pile, laying on a bed of white blossoms, was one perfect Strength of Oynos fruit.

Charla and David tucked the fruit safely into their pockets and got dressed, then began the long descent.

Uriah Issues an Invitation

King Uriah was writing a letter. His stomach still churned when he thought of the last letter he'd sent *her*, the one where he'd told her the sword could not be found. He'd assured her he was still assiduously trying to find it, and begged that she be patient with him.

He'd decided not to tell her that he'd killed the man who was the last known possessor of the sword. He was still sure he'd done the right thing, even though a tiny voice whispered that it had actually been a very *stupid* thing, but he'd decided there was no need to tell *her* about it since the man hadn't had the sword after all.

Her scathing reply to his note had made him very glad he'd refrained.

You may be ruler of your country, but you are nothing but a dog to me. You have your uses, but I will put you down without a second thought if you don't give me what I want, and what I want is the sword.

I advise you not to test me further.

Prove that you will do whatever it takes to please me, or give up all thought of my support.

Uriah wasn't sure the note he was writing would qualify as proof that he was worthy of her support, but it was all he had to offer, and, like the dog she said he was, he couldn't help crawling back to beg for affection.

Disgusted, he realized she was doing exactly what she'd taught *him* to do to his people, but knowing how she was manipulating him made no difference to his compulsion to be back in her good graces. He continued his letter, hoping it would bring about a change in her mood for the better.

I've just returned from visiting the training grounds for the army. We're using one of the techniques you taught me years ago: subverting the need to be loved. We've taken that need and twisted it to create our soldiers. Everything they do is for our praise. They live for nothing else.

I humbly invite you to visit our training grounds and see for yourself the kind of men who will be fighting on our behalf. I believe you'll be pleased. I assure you I am your most faithful servant, and will do whatever it takes to win your support.

A few days later his captain of the guards brought a letter to Uriah.

She'd responded. But she wasn't bothering to be polite.

One of my Queen's Men is on his way to judge your soldiers. Make him welcome.

"Make him welcome." He, the king, was supposed to worry about the feelings of a mere soldier. Uriah sneered, but he knew he'd do whatever he had to, to gain her support, even if it meant asking her soldier to sup at his own table.

Nervously, he re-read the short note. She hadn't bothered to start the letter with a greeting, or end it with her signature. She was still whipping her dog.

Scowling, Uriah wadded the letter up and threw it in the fire, then went back to reviewing the progress reports from the soldiers at the new barracks.

The Queen's Men

Uriah paid the queen's soldier the ultimate respect by awaiting the man's arrival himself down in the courtyard, which was something Uriah had been known to refuse to do for other royals, much less a lowly soldier. But he needed the queen's backing, so he gritted his teeth and did it.

Besides, he was interested to see the type of soldier she considered worthy to be in her service.

The clip-clop of horses' hooves was heard in the outer courtyard, and a moment later a phalanx of men on coal black horses rode through the archway.

Uriah watched through narrow eyes. The horses were some of the largest he'd ever seen, easily bearing on their backs the men, their weapons (a sword and dagger each, along with axes hanging from some of their saddles), and the suits of armor the men wore. Uriah pondered the men as they drew to a halt in the courtyard. Had they stopped outside the castle to don the gear, or did they ride fully armored at all times? Surely not. The temperature in Arlesland wasn't nearly as hot as that of Sutherne, though, so maybe this heat wasn't uncomfortable for them.

Although any heat inside a suit of armor was brutal.

The horses spread out in a fan formation, and a soldier with blood-red feathers waving atop his helm stopped his horse directly in front of Uriah. The king couldn't see the man's face, but he could see cold eyes staring at him.

Uriah waited for him to speak, waited for his due obeisance, but the man just stared.

Seething inside, the words pulled from his mouth like teeth, Uriah ground out, "You are welcome here in the name of your queen."

The soldier descended from his horse and gave a quick nod to Uriah before motioning for his men to dismount. Fighting back rage, Uriah asked brusquely, "What is your name, soldier?"

"The Queen's Men have no names, no identity outside her service. You may call me Six Seven Five. That is my number." The voice sounded bored and hollow, echoing behind the face shield he still wore.

"Your number?" Uriah questioned, and added, "You may remove your face shield."

675 ignored the comment and answered the question. "I am the six hundred seventy-fifth soldier in her Majesty's service."

"What was your name before you entered her service?" Uriah asked curiously.

The armored man paused a moment, then said, "The Queen raises her soldiers from birth so they have no goal except to protect her Majesty. The queen's soldiers must be willing to kill anyone who threatens the queen, so we are assigned numbers rather than names to remind us not to form attachments with each other."

Uriah was stunned, not because the queen's methods were abhorrent, but because he'd never thought to do so himself. He felt a moment of annoyance. Surely she could've shared her methods. What an army he could have by now! Instead, he had dregs.

Uriah scowled and turned away, the Queen's Men following him into the castle.

They entered his throne room, where Uriah seated himself and motioned for a servant to bring a chair for… 675. Uriah sighed inwardly.

The soldier ignored the proffered chair and stood stolidly before the throne, hands hanging loosely, one close to his sword and the other his dagger.

Irritated, Uriah said clearly, "You can take off your helmet now. You're among… allies." Claiming they were friends was stretching it, so Uriah didn't bother.

"The Queen's Men are proud to wear her armor at all times," came the hollow voice, the eyes steady on Uriah's.

The king stared. "You never take the armor off?"

"A soldier's armor may be removed for sleeping and bodily care." The voice was bored, the helmeted head turning side to side to observe the servants and soldiers attending Uriah.

Lost for words, Uriah glanced at the Queen's Men behind 675 and saw they were also scanning the room. They'd arranged themselves in two semi-circles around 675, with those at the back turned outward toward any danger that might follow them into the room.

Uriah felt a flutter of panic. He was proud of the army he and Albert had built… but it was obvious his homegrown fighters wouldn't impress the Queen's Men. He needed her support, though, desperately. Was there anything he could do to get it?

An uncomfortable thought fluttered into his mind. She *had* asked for one thing…

As if he'd read Uriah's mind, 675's helmet snapped back to face him. "Have you found it?"

Uriah stuttered, "F-found what?" and tried to surreptitiously wipe the sweat trickling down his cheek.

675 was silent, staring at him from within the armor.

"Oh," Uriah said, "*that*." He squirmed. "One of my soldiers supposedly had it, but he insisted he'd destroyed it. Don't worry, though," he hastened to add, his desire to reassure the soldier pushing him into an unwise admission. "I punished him well for his lack of help." As soon as the words left his mouth, Uriah winced.

675 repeated slowly, "*Punished him well?*"

Uriah hesitated, then said, "My men set fire to his house. Killed him and his whole family." He tried to make the words sound bored, as if there were nothing exceptionable in his action, but he was afraid his fear came through.

His mouth barely had time to fall open in a graceless gape before 675 was on him, the armored hand clenched around his neck. The Queen's Man yanked Uriah up and held him dangling in front of the throne, the king's legs kicking helplessly.

Uriah was vaguely aware of his guards shouting and attempting to rush to his assistance, but the Queen's Men easily held them off.

The eyes glaring at him from the helmet were silver, almost colorless, but they held the ferocity of a burning sun. 675 snarled, *"You killed the man who had the sword?"*

The blood pounded in Uriah's head and his sight grew dim. He gagged, the kicking of his feet dying away as his heart labored to pump blood past the iron fist around his neck. Just before he passed out, he felt 675 drop him to the hard marble floor of the dais, and heard the sharp click of retreating armored feet.

When Uriah regained consciousness that evening, he found his captain of the guards seated by his bedside. The man's mouth was grim as he watched the doctor attend to Uriah. As soon as the doctor left, the captain gave his king the bad news: all Uriah's soldiers were confined to their barracks, herded there like terrified sheep by the Queen's Men.

A rush of fear came over Uriah. He'd never, *never*, been powerless in his own kingdom.

"How dare they?" he fumed, his voice coming out as a raspy croak through the crushed tissues of his throat.

His captain shook his head in frustration. "There was nothing we could do, Your Majesty." He leaned closer and whispered, "I don't think they're human, sire. They overpowered us, ten Queen's Men to one hundred guards. Treated us like children. Some of my men were able to armor themselves while the Queen's Men were attacking the others, but even they had little to no chance. I tell you truthfully, Your Majesty, *they aren't human*." He regarded Uriah fearfully, well aware he'd failed his duties abysmally.

"Fool! Of course they're human! What else could they be?" Uriah scowled, the fear and humiliation within him screaming for him to kill the man. But a more sane and logical part of him argued wearily that his captain was the smartest soldier he had. Uriah depended on him for duties no other soldier was trained to do. Killing him would make Uriah feel better in the moment, but it would have long-term consequences that didn't bear thinking about.

Uriah had learned his lesson long ago about consequences for rash actions. He took his rage out on his nobles quite often, and even more often on the commoners, but he was always careful to do it when he had no more use for them.

So he put his anger aside, sealing the captain's fate in a box to be destroyed some other time.

Instead, he wearily nodded his head and gave into the inevitable.

The Queen's Men had been staying in Uriah's castle for three days, but no one, not Uriah or his captain or any of his soldiers, or even the servants who tended to the needs of the Queen's Men, had seen the soldiers out of their armor. After the first day, Uriah realized that it reinforced the idea that the Queen's Men were undefeatable if you never saw their faces.

When he'd gotten out of bed after 675's attack, he'd found the Queen's Men comfortably ensconced in his most comfortable guest bedrooms, the ones used for his favorite nobles. Uriah had been outraged, but he'd bitten the insides of his cheeks and managed to give 675 a tight smile and say without any visible sarcasm that he hoped the men were comfortable.

675 didn't bother to reply.

Uriah mulled over the idea of growing his own army, raising them with no goal other than his protection. Maybe, if things went well, the queen would unbend enough to share her techniques with him after he'd conquered all of Bryten.

Traveling with the Sinti

When Greene awoke, he was in a small room with an arched ceiling. He was covered with brightly colored blankets, and lying on a feather mattress that swaddled him like a child. He felt safe, and reveled in the sensation for a moment, unaware of why he needed the comfort so much.

He heard a click and saw a shaft of sunlight on the floor as a door at the end of the room opened and a man stepped in. As soon as Greene saw him, the memory of another face came rushing back: the face of the man he'd beaten to a pulp, bones shattered so the shape of the face was a bloody blob.

With a cry of anguish, Greene curled into a ball, clutching the blankets over his head and weeping at what he'd done.

He felt a firm hand on his shoulder and the calm voice he'd heard at the end of that terrible fight said, "Peace, friend. The man lives. Our healers are with him now. He feels no pain."

Greene's sobs of fear turned into cries of relief, but he remained tightly curled. He heard the door open again and Jacobson's voice said softly, "How is he?"

"Grieving," came the reply.

Greene heard Jacobson and the stranger talking, but he was too focused on the thing he'd done to listen to them. He continued the mental flagellation he'd begun the night before: ripping his self-respect into tatters, jeering at himself for ever believing he could be a decent human being.

Reminding himself that Charla had fled from him.

Eventually, the emotions wore him out. He couldn't continue; it took too much effort from an exhausted mind.

Numbly, Greene knew it was time to face what he'd done. He uncurled under the blankets and rolled over, resolutely swinging his legs out of bed and sitting up. He stared down at the floor, unwilling to raise his head and look at the waiting men.

Finally he sighed and looked up, still unable to meet their eyes.

Jacobson said "You didn't kill him. It's going to be alright." The sympathy in his voice made Greene's face twist and he dropped his head into his hands.

"Oh God," he whispered, the self-revulsion strong in his voice.

Jacobson sat down beside him and gripped his shoulder. "He's not dead!" he said fiercely. "He's going to be alright! Believe it, Greene!"

"It doesn't change what I did," Greene said dully as he shook his head and glanced away from Jacobson, noticing that the other man was sitting in a chair attached to the wall with chains. Curiosity finally overcame his mental anguish as he realized the chair, as well as the bed he lay upon, was made to fold up flat against the wall. Puzzled, he looked around.

Arched ceiling. Windows draped in velvet curtains, with another curtain half hiding the door through which Jacobson and the stranger had come. Cunningly designed cabinets. It was a small house rather than a room.

Frowning, he turned to Jacobson, who motioned toward the other man. "Greene, this is Jamison of the Sinti people."

He'd heard of the Sinti, but never met one of the nomads before.

Jamison had long black hair twisted back from his face and tied with a leather thong. Multiple rings pierced both ears and one nostril of his straight nose. Dark eyes studied Greene from under heavy slashes of brows. His jaw was square, his lips full. He sat completely still in the chair, no fidgeting of the hands or tapping of the feet. Only his eyes moved.

The calm voice said, "You must forgive yourself, friend. You were not completely responsible for what happened yesterday."

Greene stared at him incredulously. "Not responsible? Are you crazy?"

"There is a sickness in Arlesland. We Sinti have felt it for many years, but now it grows rapidly, infecting both the southern kingdoms. The kingdom itself has been working against your attempts to remain calm."

Greene frowned. "What do you mean, the *kingdom* has been working against us?"

"As the king is, so is his kingdom. This king has a spiritual sickness that spreads from his castle in a miasma of despair."

Greene edged forward on the bed, his attention caught. "What's causing it? What happened to Uriah"

Jamison was shaking his head. "It is not my story to tell. It is simply my lot to help you on your journey."

Greene frowned again and was about to ask him more questions when the door opened once more and Elaria peered in.

"Jacobson..." she whispered, then saw that Greene was awake. She stepped inside, searching his face intently. "How are you feeling?" she asked, coming to sit beside him on the bed.

"Like I barely escaped the fate of my father," Greene said bitterly.

Elaria glanced at the other men. "Jacobson told us last night about what your father did to Princess Aurora..."

Greene gave a bark of humorless laughter. "When Da was taken away by the other King's Guards, I knew it could've so easily have been me! But I was so sure that I would never let it happen after I saw the devastation it wrought on our family. And then..." He clenched his fists and dropped his head in anguish.

Elaria gently touched his arm. "But Jamison says there are bigger forces at work here. You can't completely blame yourself."

"But I should've been able to control it!" Greene gritted out.

"Friend, this is profitless," Jamison said. "What has happened is done. Continuing to excoriate yourself will only distract you from the work that needs to be done now."

Greene was still a moment, the despair within him warring with the need to escape his dark thoughts. Finally, he raised his head, desperate for any distraction. "What work?"

Jacobson said, "The Sinti are taking us to see Uriah's new training barracks."

Greene stared at him in astonishment.

Traveling with the Sinti meant that Greene and Jacobson had to change their appearance slightly. Instead of the bandages around their scabby, still-healing heads, Jamison decreed that both men should wear headscarves, which Greene and Jacobson donned with grins. Part of Greene was astonished that he could find humor in anything, but since he'd awakened in the Sinti wagon, he'd begun feeling much better than he had since they'd entered Arlesland. He felt *safe*.

"If Charla could see me now," Greene muttered, then wished he hadn't when his heart gave a lurch.

Watching him and Jacobson, Jamison asked, "Charla is your love?"

Greene nodded hesitantly, trying to decide whether to share his story or just leave it be.

Jamison smiled, but didn't ask any questions.

That was something Greene had discovered about the Sinti. They weren't nosy. If you wanted to talk, they let you. But they were perfectly happy sitting in silence for hours if you preferred, although the Sinti didn't spend many hours in silence normally. It was rare to walk around the camp without hearing some kind of music, even if it was only a lone voice warbling from an unseen area.

Besides their headscarves, Jamison gave them leather vests that were intricately stitched with colorful thread in a pattern of trees and flowers, and insisted that they swap their boots for some with slightly upturned toes like the ones he wore.

"Well, that's quite a disguise!" Greene said, admiring his reflection in the polished bronze mirror in Jamison's wagon.

"There's one more thing you need," Jamison said. Greene and Jacobson turned around to see an amused smile on the usually placid face of the Sinti man.

"Uh oh," Jacobson said, eyes wide.

And that's how Greene and Jacobson came to be sporting not one but *two* earrings in each ear. Jamison had given them a challenge they couldn't refuse: "Sinti men are strong, without fear. I see that you are also strong, so this will not be a problem." Greene was pretty sure there was a laugh in the Sinti man's voice, but Jamison looked nothing but reasonable.

It didn't seem so reasonable to Greene when the needle went through his ear, though, and even less so when it plunged back through for the second earring, but he and Jacobson did have to admit they looked pretty dashing in their earrings, painted vests, and Sinti boots.

"Have a hard time now telling we're Archenlanders, that's for sure," Jacobson said at the campfire later that night just as one of the Sinti women came up to offer them their choice of guitar or tambourine. Greene grabbed the guitar, leaving Jacobson with the tambourine.

"I'm gonna remember this," Jacobson growled as Greene tried to hide his laughter. The Sinti men laughed at Jacobson's dismay, too, but then one of them, a young man named Ethan, took the tambourine and showed the Archenlander how to create intricate music. He showed Jacobson thumb rolls along the edge of the drum, then bounced it against his knee, elbow, and even the heel of one foot as he sprang into the air to the time of the wild music the Sinti were playing.

By the end of the evening, Jacobson was playing the tambourine with enthusiasm if not finesse, and Greene had graduated from the simple guitar tunes he already knew. Both men felt inadequate when the Sintis took their instruments back and showed them what real Sinti music sounded like, though.

"But it's something to do while we travel," Jacobson whispered to Greene, who nodded although most of his attention was on the guitar playing. *I want to play like that,* he thought, watching the Sintis' flying fingers as the guitars dueled.

As he listened to the music, a thought occurred to him. He wasn't exactly happy, but he was no longer fearful and full of rage. It seemed to go beyond the simple feeling of safety that he'd noticed earlier, though.

Thinking about it, he decided it was because he'd gone almost as far as he could down a very dark path, the same one his father had trod, and it had shocked him so much that the anger had leached out of him completely. If he'd killed that man in Buglesville, he thought his soul would've been completely lost. He'd never have been able to show his face in Archenland again, to his family or Charla.

But he'd survived the darkness and never, ever wanted to go back to it. He was purged of that evil. He felt it in every bone of his body.

The Sinti women had taken Elaria in hand for a Sinti transformation as well. They'd insisted that she dress like a woman instead of a boy, and Greene had been amused to see them generously praising Elaria's spare figure, making the girl blush as she hesitantly gave herself over to their ministrations.

When she reappeared, being pulled along like a sheep to the slaughter by one of the Sinti women, her unevenly cut hair was covered by a Sinti headscarf, with thick black kohl rimming her eyes. Her ears were already pierced, but the Sinti had pierced them a few more times and added a piercing to her nose as well. Elaria kept touching the nose ring, wincing a bit as she did so, but she bore up well overall.

One thing about her hadn't changed, though, and that was the ever-present belt that held her daggers, and the sword sheath on her back. The Sinti questioned her about her sword, but she explained it was merely a broken remembrance of her father, and they began questioning her about the knives instead. Greene saw her attempt to shrug their questions off, but when they persisted, she grudgingly pulled out the daggers and handed them to the Sinti. The men examined them, weighing and testing the balance.

One of the Sinti women came over to handle the knives herself. After asking Elaria some questions, the woman handed her back one of the knives and motioned toward a nearby tree. Elaria shook her head, laughing off the request, but the woman insisted.

Blushing, Elaria finally threw the knife, taking a moment to aim before drawing her arm back. There was a flash of metal, and the dagger landed with a solid thud in the wood. Cheers went up from the Sinti and Elaria grinned deprecatingly, shaking her head as they clapped and pounded her on the back.

Grinning along with Jacobson, Greene looked around at all the smiling faces and felt a deep well of thankfulness wash over him. They'd been rescued just in time.

Uriah's Barracks

A couple of days later, Jamison's Sinti caravan reached Yaegertown. It was a proper town rather than a village, and the market was packed with people. The Sinti did good business that day, and afterward some of them took their money to the closest tavern. Greene and Jacobson tagged along, hoping to find out some more about Uriah's barracks.

Jacobson fell into conversation with a tavern owner, who seemed to accept him as one of the Sinti. When Jacobson casually mentioned the rumor that Uriah had new training barracks somewhere nearby, the man shook his head and said, "Well, I don't know anything about that! But I'll tell you this," he said, virtuously wiping down the bar as he spoke. "There's been a very steady flow of men coming through here who say they're heading for the Southern Road. It runs close to the Reimsland border, you know, so if'n there *were* new training barracks… well, that might be where they'd be." And he winked knowingly at Jacobson before he went to serve another man.

When the Sinti caravan came to the Southern Road at midday two days later, they stopped at a stream to refresh their horses, and Jamison sent two scouts down the Southern Road. The men returned to report that about a mile south there was a well-worn track off to the west, toward the Reimsland border.

"There are signs of many men and carts having passed that way recently," the scouts said.

Jamison nodded thoughtfully and said to Greene and Jacobson. "The Sinti do not take sides in wars between the kingdoms of Bryten. I will not go out of my way to spy on King Uriah's barracks, but I will assist you as I can."

Greene and Jacobson had discussed it the night before and decided to make the sortie without Sinti assistance anyway. For one thing, they wanted to make sure Elaria was safe. They were sure she would insist on being involved in anything that might help to bring about Uriah's downfall, but if the Sinti were staying behind, it would be much easier to convince her to do the same.

So Greene nodded and told Jamison, "The only thing we ask is that you keep Elaria safe, and send word back to Archenland if we don't return tomorrow."

The Sinti nodded. "We are near the home campsite of the Arlesland Sinti. We will await you there. Follow this road north and you will find us." He motioned, and two of the Sinti led horses over for Greene and Jacobson.

Greene and Jacobson mounted the horses and slipped away from the camp without saying anything to Elaria.

As the sun rose high in the sky, Greene and Jacobson moved silently through the woods, staying off the Southern Road but still in sight of it. When they came to the track the Sinti had found, they slowly walked their horses through the forest parallel to it until high cliffs loomed ahead of them. There was nothing for it but to climb, so they walked their horses well away from the trail, looping their reins around tree limbs, then began scaling the cliff, digging the turned-up toes of their Sinti boots into rock outcroppings as they gripped sharp protrusions with their gloved hands.

Jacobson had pulled ahead of Greene and was scrambling over the top of the cliff to his left. "See anything?" Greene called softly as he searched for the next handhold.

Silence.

Greene glanced up, but Jacobson was gone. When Greene reached the top of the cliff, though, a strong hand reached down and hauled him over. Jacobson put a finger to his lips and led Greene through some shrubby trees to an overlook.

Before them was a vast valley, ringed all around with cliffs like the one on which they stood, and right below them was a large building ten times the size of the guard barracks back home.

"How many soldiers is Uriah training?" Greene said in astonishment.

Jacobson just shook his head, his wide eyes on the activity below.

About mid-morning, they heard the sound of many horses and the wheels of a carriage on the Southern Road. They'd been hearing faint noises from the road all along, usually when an empty wagon went rattling and clattering over the holes in the road, but the sounds had been background noise. This level of sound was sufficient to make them pay attention, so they quietly crept across the top of the cliff to peer back toward the road.

The trees were too thick to allow them to see much, but they could tell there was a large party moving south on the road, and every once in a while they got a glimpse of a brightly colored coat.

"Are those guard uniforms?" Jacobson asked in a low voice.

"Hard to tell," Greene replied. "But it looks like some of them are wearing full armor." That was puzzling. Soldiers didn't wear full armor even when guarding royals, unless they were at war.

As they watched and listened, the party seemed to move toward them rather than continuing south on the main road. In a few moments, they saw people on horses moving along the trail toward the cliffs where they crouched.

In silence, Greene and Jacobson counted them: fifty uniformed men on horseback, ten of whom were wearing full armor, and a well-sprung carriage pulled by a team of black horses. As the carriage passed a gap in the trees, a crest was visible on the door.

"Is that Uriah's crest?" Jacobson asked incredulously.

"Looks like it," Greene replied. They stared at each other in a combination of rising hope and fear, and scrambled to get safely back to their viewing spot on the cliff above the barracks. Just as they settled in, the first of Uriah's guards rode through the trees at the top of the cliff to their left, and could soon be seen in glimpses as he rode along a hidden road that switch-backed down the cliff to the valley floor. The rest of the company followed, the carriage going slowly in order to make the turns.

Eventually, the company rode out of the trees on the valley floor and across the grass to the large barracks. The guards spread out, some going inside the barracks while others led the horses to a nearby water trough. The guards wearing full armor stayed on their horses, but they had spread out to encircle one of their own as if guarding *him*, rather than whoever was in the carriage.

Greene and Jacobson's attention returned to the carriage as the door was opened by one of the uniformed guards. A tall man with bronze skin and dark brown hair stepped out, the thin golden crown on his head catching the sunlight. Greene and Jacobson nudged each other in glee as King Uriah stepped down from the carriage and stood talking with his guards.

Greene was wondering how long the king planned to stay, and whether he or Jacobson should go back to let the Sinti know they might be delayed, when the armored man in the middle of the others swung down from his horse. Puzzled, Greene was trying to figure out his role when he realized King Uriah was walking toward the armored man and motioning toward the barracks as if inviting him in. The armored man gave a short nod and walked alongside the king, while the other armored men pushed aside the king's guards so they'd be close to their leader. Astoundingly, the king's men didn't put up a protest, although they glanced at each other in a way that made Greene sure they weren't pleased.

"What in the world was that about?" Jacobson said in wonder.

"No idea," Greene said thoughtfully.

Gaemedden

Uriah and 675 stood on the parapet on top of the barracks, observing the men training below. Uriah proudly watched one screaming man with a dislocated arm pick up his sword in his off hand and hack away quite effectively at the man across from him. "We train them to wield both sword and dagger with either hand, of course," he said deprecatingly, as if the accomplishment were nothing, speaking as one trainer of killers to another.

675 stayed silent, giving the impression that his men would hack away while clutching a sword with bloody stumps.

Suppressing a sigh, Uriah decided if he couldn't impress the Queen's Men, maybe they could at least be of service to him. They'd probably love the chance to brag about their methods.

"How would you suggest we handle the men who can't seem to win a fight?" he asked as politely as he could.

"Use them to teach the others how to kill effectively," 675 said in his bored voice.

Uriah had to admit it was an efficient solution. And, really, they'd already been implementing it, since at least eight men died every day before the section guards called a halt.

But 675 wasn't done. He seemed to actually be thinking the question over, and abruptly motioned to one of the Queen's Men who was always at his side. The man held one gauntlet up and pushed on the palm with the armored finger of his other hand. A small flap popped open on his palm, and Uriah could see a vial resting in the cavity behind it.

At Uriah's look of confusion, 675 said impatiently, "*Gaemedden*. All the Queen's Men and high-ranking soldiers carry it."

Uriah's mouth dropped open in a silent O. He'd heard of *gaemedden*, the juice of a poppy that only bloomed during the full moon, but he'd thought it was just a myth. "It's real?" he said incredulously, bending to peer at it. "Are the stories true?" he asked in a hushed voice. "Can it really bring the dead back to life?"

"Not back to life, no. But it can invigorate a dying soldier to make one last stand for the Queen," came the answer.

Uriah was ecstatic. He'd never dreamed of such a weapon.

"Is it hard to acquire?" he asked.

"Not if you know where to look, but it is time-consuming to make. It takes boiling and condensing repeatedly for three months," 675 replied. "And it only grows in one place, the location of which is known only to the Queen, who gathers it herself."

"Ahh." Unlikely that Uriah would be able to get his hands on any, then.

But it was here now.

"Might I…" He hesitated. How to ask for such a thing? "Might we see a demonstration of such an amazing weapon?" he said with all the respect and humility he could dredge up.

675 regarded him for a moment. "Very well. This *gaemedden* is old and must be thrown away soon, so I will allow you to use it."

Uriah came as close to jumping for joy as he ever had, and swiftly turned to lead the Queen's Men across the parapet, down the stairwell and along the hallway to the sickroom, where he motioned to the doctor to join them in the hallway.

"I want you to bring the sickest soldier you have, the one who is expected to die any moment, out into the training ground," Uriah ordered.

The doctor started to protest ("Can't you give him peace in his last moments?") but Uriah snapped at him. Frowning, the doctor ordered two men to do as the king had requested.

Moments later, the men returned, bearing a sheet between them. On the sheet lay a man with a severe chest wound, through which his broken sternum was easily visible. His left arm ended above the elbow in a blood-soaked bandage. The man's eyes were closed and his head lolled. He was obviously unconscious.

Excited by the sight, Uriah motioned the men to carry their burden through the door to the training grounds. Once outside, he directed them to take the man to one of the training rings. Uriah started to order one of his soldiers to step into the ring with the dying man, but 675 stopped him and stepped into the ring himself. "Your men are not used to *gaemedden*. They would be killed even if armored," he said.

Uriah was quite happy to allow him to take on the task, and the thought flitted across his mind that possibly the fear of *gaemedden* being used against them was another reason why the Queen's Men were always armored.

675 motioned for the servants to bring the sheet with the dying man on it and lay it at his feet. Looking down at the unconscious man, he motioned to the Queen's Man who held the vial of *gaemedden* in his gauntlet. The soldier used his mailed hand to smash the glass vial against the dying man's chest so the liquid mingled with the bloody mess.

For a moment, nothing happened except that 675 unsheathed his dagger.

Then the dying man leapt to his feet with a scream. His bulging eyes fixed on 675 and he threw himself forward, clawing with his bare hands at the armor. The Queen's Man stood still, only leaning back against the weight of the man, who was groping for a hold on the slippery metal. The man was screaming obscenities as he leapt onto the Queen's Man's torso, wrapping his legs around 675's waist to anchor him. Deep cuts appeared in the man's hands, and blood streamed from them like water as he ripped at the hard edges of 675's armor, but he didn't seem to notice. He somehow managed to tear away part of the heavy metal neck guard to bare 675's chainmail cowl, a feat that made Uriah's mouth drop open. Without hesitation, the dying man bit into the cowl with his teeth and attempted to rip the chainmail away. Instead, his teeth ripped away, but he managed to get his fingers under the cowl and slide his hand up to grip 675's neck, his fingers closing like a vise.

675 had barely moved during the assault, but now he silently slid the dagger between their bodies and into the man's heart. There was a soft sigh, and the man dropped to the ground, limp and still.

"By all the fires of Heol," Uriah breathed, the curse springing to his mouth without thought. "I've never…" He wiped his hand across his eyes. "I've never seen anything like it! He could've killed you with his bare hands!"

675 corrected him, "He could have tried," and bent down to clean his dagger on the dead man's clothing. Standing again, he said, "Now you see that the queen's army cannot be defeated, even though dying." For the first time, Uriah heard a hint of emotion in 675's voice.

Pride.

Well-deserved pride, the king had to admit, turning with a sigh to lead 675 back inside.

An Unstoppable Army

Greene felt his blood run cold as he and Jacobson watched the dying man leap to his feet and attack the armored man. They watched the scenario play out in silence and marked Uriah's triumphant reaction. Uriah and the armored men went back inside the barracks, and Greene and Jacobson watched as a couple of boys were called over to haul away the dead body, which they slung onto a cart bearing heaped piles of trash.

Greene and Jacobson were silent for long minutes afterward, and then Greene spoke. "Whatever they gave that man would make Uriah's army unstoppable."

Jacobson nodded, his eyes wide.

That afternoon, as the king's caravan loaded up and headed up the trail to the cliffs, Jacobson asked, "Do you think we should stay any longer?"

Greene shook his head. "What we've seen needs to be reported to King Richard as soon as possible."

Greene and Jacobson climbed down the cliff and watched until Uriah's caravan had turned onto the main road, then they mounted their horses and slipped away as quietly as they'd come, talking in low voices as they made their way through the forest.

When they rode into the Sinti camp hours later, they caught Jamison's eye before the rest of the Sinti saw them, and he immediately motioned for them to meet him behind the wagon in which they'd been sleeping.

Once there, Jamison asked, "Did you find what you sought?"

Greene said grimly, "Much more than we thought."

Jamison raised his eyebrows and looked at Jacobson, who just shook his head, unable to speak.

Greene said, "We need to get back to Archenland as quickly as possible. It's imperative that we tell the northern rulers what's happening here."

Jamison looked at them for a moment. "I can see that your need is great, but I would caution you that to leave this area in haste is the worst thing you can do. You must act as if nothing is wrong. All things are in the hands of Oynos. Honor his wisdom."

Greene stared at him, frustrated. It was obvious that the Sinti's faith was important to him, whereas it was mostly something Greene didn't think about. He respected the Sinti beliefs, but he couldn't respect a delay at such a time. The entire fate of three kingdoms rested on the knowledge that he and Jacobson had, and they had to get back to Archenland with it as soon as they could.

He exchanged a glance with Jacobson, who murmured, "I think we should tell him what we saw."

Greene thought for a moment, then turned to Jamison. "Today we saw Uriah with a group of men dressed in armor. They weren't his guards, though. He treated them like honored guests. They walked around the training barracks with him, and then they gave a demonstration of a drug that turns dying men into raging warriors."

Jamison frowned. "What kind of drug?"

Greene said, "We were too far away to see much, but the dying man had his chest almost completely cleaved open. One of the armored men had the drug in his gauntlet. He smashed the drug into the wound and the dying man jumped up and attacked the leader of the armored men. He tore the man's armor off with his teeth and bare hands. If Uriah has access to such a drug, we must let King Richard know as soon as possible. That's not a weapon we can fight against."

Jamison's eyes lost focus. After a moment, he murmured, "*Gaemedden.*"

Jacobson repeated, "*Gaemedden*? But that's just a myth, a gift from Oynos that brings dying men back to life so they can fight on his behalf."

"Not a myth, my friend, as you've seen," was Jamison's reply. He nodded and stood up. "It is another omen. This threat affects Sinti as well as other citizens of Bryten. We will ride hard for the northern kingdoms. Eat your supper quickly and then return to your wagon. We will ride through the night."

After supper, Greene and Jacobson headed for their wagon, but Jacobson suddenly said, "Elaria! We have to say goodbye to Elaria!"

Greene drew a breath. In all the excitement of the day, he'd completely forgotten about her. He nodded and followed Jacobson back to the campfire.

They found her and explained they had to return to Bagginsland immediately. Eyes wide, Elaria asked, "Can I come with you?"

Greene hesitated.

"Please! I have to get Hyranstrene away from Uriah. It would be much safer in one of the northern kingdoms." She searched his eyes, intent on convincing him of her need.

Greene remembered how he'd once wondered whether taking the sword back to King Richard would give them a bargaining chip with Uriah.

He glanced at Jacobson, who nodded. Elaria's face lit up and she ran off to pack her things.

When Jamison realized Elaria was coming with them, he directed them to bring their bags to a larger wagon with four single folding beds in it. That night, Greene and Jacobson slept in the beds on one side of the wagon, while Elaria and a Sinti woman slept in the other two as the wagon rolled through the night.

When Greene woke the next morning, Jacobson and Elaria were already awake and the wagon was shaking beneath them.

"We're still traveling?" Greene asked in surprise. He looked out the window next to his bed and saw the sun was well up. "They haven't stopped for breakfast?"

Jacobson motioned to a sack on the end of Greene's bed. "The Sinti woman who slept here last night is up front with Jamison. She tossed that bag through the driver's panel a little while ago."

Greene pulled the sack toward him and found it contained fruit, nuts and some dried meat, along with a flask of water.

Just as Greene finished eating, the wide driver's panel at the front of the wagon slid open and Jamison poked his head in. "Friends, we will stop soon to change horses. You are well?"

They nodded and Jamison slid the panel back in place. A few minutes later, the wagon slowed and finally stopped. When Greene, Jacobson and Elaria stepped outside, they were surprised to see that their wagon was the only one in sight. The large Sinti caravan they'd been traveling with had disappeared. There were a few Sinti men and women swapping saddles from one horse to another and harnessing new horses to the wagon, but all told there were only seven of them.

Greene recognized all the Sinti except two. While he was puzzling over who they were, Jamison motioned him, Jacobson and Elaria over.

"Where are the rest of the Sinti?" Jacobson asked the Sinti leader.

"They were Arlesland Sinti. They remain at their home campsite," Jamison answered.

Puzzled, Greene asked, "Aren't *you* Arlesland Sinti?"

He shook his head. "No, we are of the Vallenland tribe."

Greene and Jacobson exchanged surprised glances. "What were you doing in Arlesland?"

He smiled. "We were looking for you."

Greene asked in astonishment, "Why were you looking for us?" He glanced around, again noticing the unfamiliar Sinti. "And where *are* we?"

"We crossed the border into Bagginsland while you slept." He nodded toward the two strangers. "These are Bagginsland Sinti who brought us fresh horses. You must have patience for your other questions."

Greene had come to trust the Sinti leader over the past few days, so although it was frustrating, he nodded and kept his questions to himself. After a few moments to stretch their legs and settle the horses into the harness, they returned to the wagon and set off northward.

Second Thoughts

After witnessing the power of the *gaemedden*, Uriah found himself having serious doubts about joining with the queen of Sutherne to attack the northern kingdoms of Bryten.

He sat in front of his fire late that night, biting his thumbnail as he stared at the leaping flames, thinking about an army of Queen's Men, fueled by the unstoppable *gaemedden*, coming into his land. Uriah liked the idea of his own men having access to the drug, but 675 had dismissed his tentative inquiries.

"I allowed you a taste of Her Majesty's power to show you how unstoppable she is. Your pride in the men you're training is unfounded. You must work harder if you wish the queen's support, but you will never be granted access to *gaemedden*."

That was when Uriah realized 675 hadn't been showing him what the queen could do to help Uriah in his venture; 675 was showing him that if she wanted, she could smash the entire continent of Bryten. Annihilating Uriah's kingdom would take only a snap of her fingers.

As Uriah had stared at him in dawning fear, 675 had informed him that he and the other Queen's Men would start back to Sutherne at first light, and dismissed him (dismissed *him!*).

Now Uriah pondered the ramifications of letting the queen and her army loose on his continent. She claimed that the only reason she wanted to assist in his takeover of the northern kingdoms was so she could share in the bounty of trade with them. She'd assured him that once he accomplished his goal, she would return to Sutherne.

Uriah wanted all of Bryten for himself. What if the queen decided she wanted it, too?

Was there any way to defeat the northern kingdoms without her help? And was there any way to stop her crossing the Ocean of Faer if he no longer wanted her help?

He had a sinking feeling that the answer to both questions was no.

"The Thing You Want Most"

Greene saw the might of the Sinti put into action over the next two days.

He'd never seen horses with the stamina of the Sinti animals, and every time the horses began to flag, Jamison would pull the wagon over and an unfamiliar Sinti would appear from the woods with fresh mounts. The wagon allowed the group to sleep in shifts, so there were always two people driving the wagon, two in the back sleeping, and another five mounted, two riding in front of, and three riding behind, the wagon.

Greene soon realized that one of the Sinti was always missing, and eventually realized they must be riding ahead to arrange for fresh horses.

They traveled day and night, stopping only long enough for the horses to eat and drink, and then came the morning they crossed into Archenland. A cheer went up from the two Archenlanders, making the Sinti smile.

Greene drew a deep breath of the air of his home kingdom, feeling peace flow through his veins. He hadn't realized how tightly he'd been wound over the past weeks, and the relief of feeling that tension drain away was overwhelming.

He finally allowed himself to think ahead to what awaited them at Kingham Castle. The thought of being home, the possibility of finding out why Charla had left him, made his breath catch in his throat. He wasn't sure if he wanted to know, or if he'd rather continue believing there'd been some terrible mistake, that she hadn't left him after all.

When they stopped next, it was near an overgrown path off the main road. Jamison suggested Greene, Jacobson and Elaria might like to remove their Sinti garb. "There is no need for disguises now that you are safe in Archenland."

Elaria was happy to keep her Sinti clothes on, but Greene and Jacobson immediately pulled their headscarves off and ran their fingers through the stubble on their heads. Their burns were fully healed but it would take a while for their hair to grow back.

"The other King's Guards would never recognize us," Jacobson laughed.

Jamison smiled as he said, "And perhaps you would both enjoy a shave?"

Greene ruefully scratched at his scruffy beard and said, "Absolutely!" He'd lost a lot of weight in Arlesland, but at least he could clean himself up so he didn't scare his mother and sister when he finally arrived home.

Or scare Charla.

Greene inspected his newly bare face in a silver plate. He and Jacobson had divested themselves of their Sinti boots and other gear, but they'd decided to leave in their rakish ear piercings. Grinning, they left the wagon and went to find Jamison.

The Sinti leader was talking with some other Sinti a few hundred yards ahead of the wagon, near a big rockslide that blocked the overgrown trail. Jamison looked up at their approach and smiled.

"Greene, please help us."

Puzzled Greene walked over to the Sinti, Jacobson following.

"You are feeling much better today, friend, more like yourself?" Jamison asked Greene, who smiled. "Good, good. That is good." He nodded, a mischievous grin lightening his usual stoic face.

He continued, "There is something I believe you will want to see on the other side of these rocks. Climb up and take a look." He motioned toward the landslide.

Greene frowned and darted a look at Jacobson, who shrugged. Hesitantly, Greene walked toward the landslide and looked around. "I don't see anything," he said.

"Whenever you are in doubt, friend, look up," Jamison said and pointed to the top of the pile of rocks. The other Sinti laughed and urged Greene to climb up.

Greene was a little annoyed. Was this another of Jamison's references to the providence of Oynos? Greene hoped not. He'd been having a good morning, but comments about the will of Oynos weren't what he wanted to hear. Sighing, he turned to face the rocks and began to climb.

Halfway up, he turned around and said, "I don't see the point of this!" not bothering to hide his annoyance.

Jamison laughed. "Have faith, friend. I assure you that the thing you want most in the world is on the other side of those rocks." He motioned Greene on.

Greene rolled his eyes and turned back to the rocks, muttering under his breath, "How could what I want most be on the other side of these rocks?" He said loudly, "I don't think that's possible, but if you insist, I'll take a look," and finished to himself, "but the thing I want most is… Charla."

He took a deep breath and dashed a hand across his eyes, glad the Sinti couldn't see his tears, and finally reached the top of the rock pile. Bracing himself, he leaned over and looked down…

…and saw a small crowd of people looking up at him.

"Hey!" he said in delight, then turned to tell the Sinti behind him, "There are people here!"

The Sinti laughed and Jamison called out, "Look with the eyes of your heart, friend!"

Greene barely heard him as he turned to ask the people below who they were… and saw a familiar face staring slack-jawed at him.

Reunion

When Charla and David reached the foot of Mount Ciel, Mother Tarni and her Sinti were waiting for them. Charla and David hadn't spoken a word on the descent, too overwhelmed by the reunion with, and parting from, their mother, as well as Old Dan's death.

Mother Tarni greeted them each with a kiss, but didn't speak, for which they were grateful. Neither she nor the Sinti asked where Old Dan was, but as Charla and David followed the Sinti queen to her wagon, many hands reached out to touch their shoulders and heads in silent condolence, and they were strengthened.

They rested in the village the next day. No one asked what had happened on the mountain, which was a relief. Charla needed space to process it all before she could talk to even David about it.

At the midday meal, Mother Tarni announced it was time to take Charla and David back to Kingham Village. Charla felt tears start to her eyes at the thought that soon she would be safely back home, with Greene's arms around her. She wondered how she could explain her absence to him, how she could explain everything that had happened, how she could explain Old Dan's death, and her mother's reappearance.

How she could explain the Eye and her role in protecting it.

The Sinti packed up and the caravan started out that night, Mother Tarni driving her wagon herself while Charla and David, who were still exhausted, slept inside.

When they woke the next morning, they were surprised to see that, instead of heading south on the road they'd come in on, they were heading north, with the rising sun on their right.

"But… the northern road is blocked," Charla said in surprise. "That's why we had to come such a long way around!"

Mother Tarni smiled and said only, "I have sent one of my people to get help. Oynos will provide."

Charla hesitated, and then nodded, no longer disbelieving such a statement.

That afternoon, they came to a great landslide, with rocks too large for one man to move. David whispered to Charla, "That's what Grandfather and I found when we tried to get through."

Charla whispered back, "I wonder what Oynos will provide," but the mocking tone she might have used a week ago was missing. Now she was genuinely interested to see how Oynos would change the situation.

The Sinti stopped their wagons and made camp beside the rockslide. The next morning, as they were stoking up the fire in preparation for the midday meal, odd noises were heard from the other side of the rockslide. All the Sinti stopped what they were doing and went to stand by the rocks. Following them, Charla was surprised to hear faint voices on the other side. The voices got louder, and Charla heard someone say, "I don't think that's possible, but if you insist, I'll take a look…" and a head with short, bristly hair popped over the top of the rock pile.

Charla stared and her mouth fell open. The blue eyes under the hair widened in surprise as the man saw the Sinti below him looking up, and he turned to shout to someone behind him, "There are people here!" Then he turned back around, a delighted grin on his face. He started to say something to the Sinti…

And then his eyes fell on Charla, who was still staring at him in shock. A look of astonishment crossed his face.

Charla finally found her voice. *"Greene?"*

An Evergreen Love

Greene threw himself over the barrier of rocks, scrambling on hands and knees to get to her. Behind him he heard laughter and shouts from the Sinti, telling him to wait until they dug through the rockslide, but there was no way he was waiting.

Apparently Charla felt the same, because she was clawing her way up the rocks to get to him, too.

He reached her and fell back onto the sharp rocks without feeling a thing, pulling her into his arms, hugging her with all the desperate love in his heart. "You're alright, you're alright," he kept whispering.

"I'm so sorry, so, so sorry, my love," came the muffled answer against his chest, where her head was buried. "I never would've left you like that if I'd had any choice."

A sob burst from Greene and he squeezed Charla so tight she almost couldn't breathe, but she didn't push him away. She couldn't get close enough to him after these weeks apart, couldn't tell him enough how much she loved him.

They kissed, their hunger for each other overwhelming them so they didn't hear the whistles and teasing from the crowd below them. Finally, Charla dropped her head onto Greene's chest, her tears of happiness flowing onto his shirt, his heart beating hard beneath her ear.

They lay there a few more minutes, Greene rocking her in his arms, until Greene shifted against the sharp rocks and said, "My love, I suggest we remove to somewhere more conducive to hugging."

Charla laughed and leveraged herself off him, then held his hand tightly in hers as they carefully climbed down the rocks they'd scrambled heedlessly over earlier. Seeing only each other, hearing nothing of the activity around them as the two groups on either side of the rocks proceeded to clear the trail, Charla led Greene to a fallen log, where they sank down and just stared at each other.

Neither was thinking of the journeys they'd been on the past few weeks. All they cared about was drinking in the sight of the person they loved most in the world, of feeling that joy that comes from loving and being loved. And so they sat, almost silent, wrapped in each other's arms, filling up those wells in their hearts where their love lived. The only words they spoke were assurances that they'd never stop loving each other, that nothing, not even death, could kill their love, that no one had ever meant as much to them as the other did.

They promised their love would never die, that it would always remain "Evergreen," Charla said, laughing as she gently stroked Greene's cheek.

And that they would absolutely, positively, get married as soon as they got back to Kingham Village.

Eventually, they came to themselves and noticed what was happening around them. The rockslide was significantly smaller now, so the heads of Jamison's group could be seen clearly as they called back and forth to the others. Watching the people around them, Greene was surprised to realize that Charla was traveling with another group of Sinti, this one led by a vigorous woman Charla called Mother Tarni.

"She's amazing, Greene. You wouldn't believe the power she has. Just being around her… it makes me feel like I can do anything.

And she's so calm, like nothing ever bothers her, like there's nothing she can't handle."

Greene nodded excitedly and said, "That's just like the Sinti man we've been traveling with! His name is Jamison ..."

Charla's eyes widened and she exclaimed. "I know him! He's part of Mother Tarni's tribe! He was there when they rescued us, but then he disappeared..."

Greene said, "Wait... *rescued* you? Rescued you from *what*?"

Charla opened her mouth to reply, then shook her head. "That is a *long* story!"

A voice above them said, "And one that can wait until tonight, when we can all hear it."

Greene looked up to see Mother Tarni standing before them, smiling. "You are welcome here, Greene. I look forward to hearing your story soon. But for now, I invite you to help us prepare the midday meal."

Laughing, Greene and Charla went to find a task they could complete without letting go of each other's hands.

The rockslide had been cleared, Jamison's group had joyfully reunited with the rest of their tribe (including a small girl who squealed "Daddy, Daddy!" as she ran to Jamison), camp had been set up, the evening meal eaten, and they were relaxing around the fire.

Earlier, during the midday meal, Greene and Jacobson had told the story of their mission to Arlesland, and the ramifications of what Uriah was plotting against the northern kingdoms had been talked over thoroughly.

Charla had held Greene's hand while he and Jacobson told their tale. Greene had bravely left nothing out of his narrative, even the parts that shamed him deeply, the parts where he'd given into the darkness of Arlesland.

Charla had said nothing, but her grip on his hand had tightened, and she'd put her other arm around his waist and leaned on his shoulder, holding him together while he fell apart.

Now, Greene and Jacobson were eagerly awaiting Charla's story. Greene knew she hadn't left him willingly, and that was all he'd cared about earlier, but now he wanted the full story. He'd noticed during the midday meal that Old Dan was missing, and Charla had told him he'd died, but she'd been unable to continue. Greene had just wrapped his arms around her and rocked her, soothing her as much as he could.

Now, when the quiet rustles of night creatures were the only things that broke the silence, Charla ignored the others sitting around the fire and fixed her gaze solely on Greene as she said, "It all started one night when I was looking in Old Dan's trunk for something of my mother's that I wanted for the wedding. I found a metal box wrapped in cloth, and when I opened it, I saw it was full of a strange, bitter-smelling sand. Suddenly, I had a vision…"

Greene's eyes were wide all through the telling. He'd been furious when she talked about the torture of the Dark Ones, tempted to cover his ears at one point because he couldn't bear to hear the words; he'd wrapped her securely in his arms when she told of the death of Old Dan; and he'd exclaimed with amazement when she told how she and David had reunited with their mother.

"And that's what happened to us," Charla finished her tale.

Greene, Jacobson and Elaria stared at her in amazement. Jamison and the Sinti who had traveled with him were regarding her thoughtfully, which Greene thought was probably the Sinti version of amazement.

"So… you're now the protector of some kind of jewel that is key to the survival of mankind, and evil beings are trying to steal it?" Greene asked hesitantly.

Charla smiled ruefully. "I know it sounds insane… but if you'd been with me, you wouldn't doubt the story."

Greene was shaking his head. "No, no! I don't doubt it one bit. I'm just shocked at everything you've been through. Honestly, I thought you were back at Windham Village telling all your friends what a jerk I was." He tried to laugh, but it didn't fool anyone, least of all Charla.

"I would never have let them keep me from you if Grandpop hadn't convinced me it was of vital importance. I am so, so sorry," she ended on a whisper, leaning over to kiss him on the cheek. "You are so important to me, and I hate that you were hurt."

"Well, honestly, it might have been good for me," Greene shrugged. "I needed to do some soul searching."

"No. I don't think us being apart is ever going to be a good thing," Charla said firmly.

Greene sighed and hugged her. "Yeah, me either. Let's never do it again."

"Never again," she whispered.

On the other side of the fire, Jamison's eyes were on Greene, who was staring at the ground as Charla clutched his arm. As Jamison watched, she slid her arm around Greene's waist and leaned against him, murmuring comfort, kissing his cheek softly.

Jamison had once had that kind of love, *given* that kind of love, before his wife died. He looked away from them, his heart hurting, and noticed that Elaria was watching Greene and Charla, too. There was a sadness, a hunger, on her face, and Jamison wondered if she'd ever felt that depth of love for someone.

Looking back at Greene and Charla, Jamison saw Greene staring at him with something that looked like hurt and anger in his eyes. Puzzled, Jamison walked around the fire to him.

Staring up at the Sinti man, Greene said slowly, "Charla said that Mother Tarni sent Ethan to Kingham Village to tell me she was safe. But Ethan was with you when you rescued me and Jacobson, and neither of you ever said a word." His eyes searched the calm face of the man he'd come to think of as a friend. "Does that mean that the whole time Jacobson and I were traveling with you, you knew that Charla was safe, yet you didn't tell me?" His eyes burned into Jamison's.

Jamison knelt before him and put one hand on Greene's shoulder and one on Charla's. "It was not a decision I made lightly, my friend, but King Richard told Ethan that you should not be distracted until your mission was finished. When you told me how close you were to finding the information about Uriah that you sought, I feared the message about Charla would make you lose focus when you needed it most. I knew Charla was safe, and that you would be seeing her soon, so yes, I chose not to tell you while we were in Arlesland. When we crossed the Arlesland border, we received word that our brethren were trapped by the rockslide. You had just begun to lose the haunted look from your time in Arlesland, so I made the decision to delay telling you once again. I knew you would be reunited with your love very soon, and that made my heart glad. I hope you can forgive the delay, my friend."

"And," he continued, peering closely at Greene, "I believed that you needed more time to heal from the damage Arlesland had done to your soul before you could meet your beloved with a clear conscience."

There was a long silence, then Greene sighed and nodded, squeezing Charla tight against him. "Yes. You were right. It hurts me that I didn't know sooner that she was safe, but I understand your reasons, and I agree with them. Thank you for doing what I *needed*, rather than what you knew I *wanted*."

Jamison smiled and squeezed their shoulders, then went back to his place on the other side of the fire.

"Charla…" Greene said hesitantly, his eyes on their linked hands. "There's something you need to know."

She squeezed his hand, but said nothing.

"When I thought you left me because you didn't trust me to be a good husband, I swore I'd become a better man. But when Jacobson and I were in Arlesland, I lost my way and turned into the person I swore I'd never be. I'm so ashamed, and so scared that I'll never be the man I want to be, a man you can respect and love with all your heart."

Something Greene loved about Charla was that she didn't tell him things just to make him feel better, and she didn't let him down this time.

She said thoughtfully, "I think you'll probably struggle with this all your life. I *know* who you are. I know your challenges. But I also know your heart, and that you are trying your best to change. When you almost killed that man, you lived out your nightmare. You spent almost three weeks in Arlesland, slowly becoming the man your father was, and I think you'll do everything in your power not to fall prey to that again. You were weak because you thought I'd left you, and you weren't expecting the effect Arlesland would have on you.

"If you should ever be in a position like that again, you'll have a better idea of what to expect, and I hope you will always know that, even if the unimaginable happened and I *did* decide to leave you, I would never do it without talking to you face-to-face. So until then, you need to fully believe that I love you with all my heart. I hope that will give you the anchor you need to hold onto in those moments of weakness.

"Besides," she said with a laugh in her voice, "If you ever became a horrible man, I've got a good friend whose father would be happy to lock you in his dungeon until you came to your senses."

He knew she was teasing, but that thought actually made him feel better, made him realize that he and Charla had a whole host of family and friends to help her, help *him*, if his anger ever put Charla in jeopardy. They weren't alone. Charla would be safe, and so would he, even if the unthinkable happened.

So he held the woman who held his heart, and focused on how loved and thankful he was, and tried to forget the bad things in the world. As long as he had this core of goodness in his life, he could survive.

The fire was dying down and sleep was creeping into tired minds, many of the listeners getting to their feet to ready themselves for bed. Mother Tarni and Jamison went to find Greene and Charla.

"Come with us, *skaeweer*. We must discuss your future," Mother Tarni said, her face serious.

Inside her wagon, Mother Tarni took a seat on the small wall bed, while Charla and Greene sat on the larger bed, and Jamison gracefully lowered himself to a floor cushion.

"You have the Eye?" Mother Tarni asked.

Charla nodded and started to take it out of the pocket of her Sinti dress, where it had resided since she'd returned to the mountain.

"No, *skaeweer*. Do not show it to anyone, as you value your life. It is not meant for human eyes except under extraordinary circumstances. You may view it because you are its guardian."

Charla hesitated, then carefully refastened the pocket.

"You must take the Eye north as soon as possible."

Charla and Greene glanced at each other. "Ma'am… we'd planned to be married when we return to Kingham Village," Greene said.

Mother Tarni nodded. "This is good. The *skaeweer* will need support and protection. Many will seek to possess the Eye. As soon as you are man and wife, however, you must go north."

Charla asked hesitantly, "Why must we leave Kingham Village, leave our home?"

"There are deep forces at play, ones you cannot understand. The Dark Ones are on one side of that hidden battle, and the Eye is part of the other. The evil forces are strongest in the south, so you must go north to protect the Eye."

Greene asked, "How far north?"

Mother Tarni said, "You will be safest with trusted friends or family around you."

Greene and Charla thought for a moment, then Charla exclaimed, "Dellham Village. Martin's Aunt Grace lives there!"

Greene grinned. Martin's Aunt Grace had one of the sunniest, most optimistic attitudes of anyone he knew, and her village was in the far north of Archenland. If they would be safe anywhere, it would be with her. He nodded. "That's a great idea. I'm sure she would welcome us with open arms."

They turned back to Mother Tarni, tacitly asking whether she approved.

She nodded. "A wise decision. Now that you are *skaeweer*, you must learn to listen to your intuition. The Eye is a gift from Oynos. You must let it guide you. If you journey to Dellham Village but do not feel safe there, you must continue your journey."

Charla asked, "How will we know where to go if Dellham doesn't feel safe?"

"The Eye will guide you." Mother Tarni was unconcerned with specifics.

Listening, Greene realized he no longer questioned the Sinti's complete belief in Oynos. After hearing Charla's story, knowing her as he did, he fully believed in this strange new view of the world. He also completely trusted Jamison and Mother Tarni, even though he'd just met her. She had a deep peace about her, as though she'd seen the worst the world had to offer, but steadfastly believed in the good.

Mother Tarni continued, "Now you must rest. We leave early tomorrow."

Charla and Greene grinned at each other. In a couple of days they would be home!

"And you know what that means…" Greene whispered in Charla's ear as he pulled her close.

"Lots of kissing!" she laughed against his mouth.

"*Married* kissing," he said with satisfaction, making her laugh again.

Darkness Comes to Archenland

Mother Tarni woke them in the predawn hours. The Sinti had broken the camp down the night before, so all that was left was to make a quick meal of the dried meat the Sintis carried in vast quantities. This took place in silence, the darkness slowly lightening so they could see the Sinti moving about like wraiths in the newly graying world.

A few of the Sinti caravans were missing, since the most vulnerable of the tribe, including the elderly and children, had been directed by Mother Tarni to return to Vallenland. The Sinti queen had told everyone the night before that they were approaching the most dangerous part of their journey.

"When we leave the safety of Mount Ciel, the Dark Ones will be able to sense the power we carry with us. They have been unable to penetrate as far north as Archenland thus far, but we know their power has grown." She looked at Jamison.

He nodded. "The Dark Ones I encountered in Reimsland were many, many times more powerful than the ones we fought when we rescued the *skaeweer*."

Mother Tarni said, "We must be prepared for another attack. The power we carry with us now will draw the Dark Ones like a lightning rod. However, the power will also work on our behalf. Even these powerful Dark Ones will fall if we keep faith in Oynos."

Jamison had full faith in Oynos, but he was glad his daughter and the other children were safely on their way back to Vallenland. As he glanced around the remaining group, Elaria caught his eye as she stared at the ground in front of her. Jamison had grown fond of the young woman on their journey, and had liked her even more yesterday when he'd come upon Elaria playing a game with his daughter. The little girl's giggles had brought a brighter smile to Elaria's face than he'd seen before.

Jamison knew Elaria could handle herself, but he'd stick close to her today anyway.

Charla was riding with Mother Tarni on the seat under the overhanging roof of the Sinti queen's wagon, while Greene rode on the front bench beside the driver. Mother Tarni had asked if Charla would prefer to ride inside the wagon, where she would be more protected from a potential attack, but Charla had said no. Ever since her mother had given the Eye into her keeping, Charla had felt her strength and confidence growing beyond anything she'd ever felt. The thought of hiding in Mother Tarni's wagon made her heartsick, as if she didn't trust Oynos.

Mother Tarni had searched her face for a moment, then said, "The Eye will protect you, but it will also draw the attention of every Dark One if we are attacked. It will be much worse than anything you experienced at their hands previously."

Charla had hesitated, then nodded. "I trust Oynos," she'd said simply, and Mother Tarni had smiled.

So now she rode beside Mother Tarni, trying to ignore the rapid pace of her heart.

It was a misty morning, the trail obscured beyond ten paces, so the company rode slowly, alert for danger. But they were still taken without warning.

One moment they were riding along, then they were surrounded by silent and motionless cloaked figures.

Charla would have sworn that the Dark Ones appeared out of thin air. There must have been forty of them, certainly enough to enclose the Sinti caravan. Charla could barely see the Dark Ones, blocked in as she was in the middle of the Sinti wagons, but she could *feel* them.

She'd never forgotten the terrible fear she'd experienced the two days she'd been tortured. Never forgotten the horror of the writhing, glowing writing under the skin of her tormentors. And she'd never thought she'd feel anything worse.

But she was wrong. The terror and despair that flowed over her now felt like thousands of insects creeping under her skin and into her mind.

She seemed to hear moans and screams of fear, and her body shook with chills so that she could barely keep her seat on the wagon. Greene scrambled over the seat to hold her, but his warmth did nothing to stop the freezing hopelessness that gripped her. There was a fog in front of her eyes, a mist like the one around the Dark Ones, but it surrounded Charla herself. It shut the world out, shut out Greene and his love. The despair overwhelmed her and her body went limp.

Mother Tarni stood up, placing her hand on Charla's head. Charla saw the black mist in front of her eyes begin to dissipate as a slow warmth crept down her body.

Mother Tarni was staring over the tops of the wagons toward the trail ahead. Through a gap in the wagons, Charla could see one of the cloaked figures in the middle of the road. The awful power, the terror and despair, spilled from it in waves that Charla could *see,* waves of paralyzing black mist.

"Begone! Let us pass!" Mother Tarni cried.

Nothing could be seen below the hood of the cloaked Dark One, but "Give us the *skaeweer*," came a whisper drifting on the black mist, surrounding them on all sides.

"You will *not* win this battle!" Mother said sternly.

"You will not win this *war*," was the reply.

With yips and ululations, the Sinti leapt from their wagons and horses, landing crouched with knives and sword blades raised.

After one breathless moment, the Dark Ones rushed them.

Near one of the wagons surrounding Mother Tarni's, Elaria fought alongside Jamison, doing their best to press the Dark Ones away from the caravan.

When the hood fell off one of the Dark Ones, the moving letters under his skin hypnotized Elaria with fear long enough that the Dark One almost slid past her defenses, but she came to her senses at the last minute and pressed back, her daggers blocking his expertly.

She'd been holding back all the rage, pain, and hopelessness she'd felt since her family had been murdered, but now she let it burst free, turning her world into pure vengeance.

The Dark One was more than a match for her, though, even fueled as she was by fury. After several minutes of fierce battle, Elaria managed to dispatch him through luck more than anything, going in for the kill when he was knocked off balance by one of the battling Sinti nearby.

As she raised her daggers again, ready for the next attack, she looked around and began to despair.

Many Sinti were fallen, either motionless on the ground or moaning as they died in pain, while only a handful of Dark Ones had been felled.

As she watched, a Dark One stabbed a Sinti woman, forcing the knife under her ribcage and twisting it as she screamed. The Dark One pushed the dying woman down and turned toward Elaria, a grin on his face.

Elaria fought hard, but soon realized she was losing. The Dark One was too strong, too fast, too vicious. He was bleeding from half a dozen deep cuts, many of which he'd made himself by refusing to back off when she stabbed at him. Instead, he leaned into the knife to get close enough to hurt her.

Elaria was bleeding from several deep cuts herself, the loss of blood making her woozy. If something didn't change, she was going to fall, and the last of her family would be gone.

Renewed rage coursed through her and, taking a note from the Dark One's book, she pushed against him with all her force, earning herself another deep cut but also overbalancing him so she could rush past and stand clear for a moment.

The Dark One was on the ground, but soon he would stand, and turn, and kill her. She had no doubt of it.

There was only one hope left. *Only use it in the darkest moment,* her father had whispered.

As the Dark One began to rise, Elaria swiftly slid her blood-covered daggers into their sheaths and reached behind her head with both hands. Hyranstrene rasped against the scabbard as she drew it forth, and she saw light from the crack in the sword glowing on the face of the Dark One before her.

He gaped at the sword, the moving words under his skin fading beneath Hyranstrene's glow. Elaria slashed it through the air between them, and it *hummed.*

The Dark One's eyes widened and he *sniffed* at the air through which the sword had passed. His moment of distraction gave Elaria her chance, and she whirled, Hyranstrene singing as it cut through the sinews and bone of the Dark One's neck.

She had a moment of pure exultation before the face of every Dark One near her turned as though pulled by a string. There was a frozen moment as the power pulsed from the sword… and then they came. She braced herself, her body thrumming with the power she held.

Elaria danced with the sword, releasing her terrible anger and reveling in the carnage, and when she was done, a pile of Dark Ones lay at her feet.

The weight of her last strike spun her around to face the main part of the battle, where the Sinti and her friends were still dying as they tried to protect the *skaeweer*. Elaria raised Hyranstrene in the air and screamed a challenge.

Greene heard the shout and raised his head from where he knelt on the ground, his knife buried in the neck of a Dark One who had almost pulled Charla from the wagon. He saw Elaria standing with the sword above her head, saw the fallen Dark Ones at her feet. A trick of the sun shining through the fog made the sword appear to glow, the metal of the long blade almost too bright to look at. From it came a hum that set every cell of Greene's body vibrating, bringing him to his feet with renewed energy.

But rushing him from every direction were the remaining Dark Ones, intent on getting the *skaeweer*. As he fought them off, Greene saw Elaria running toward him and prayed she'd get there in time, but from the corner of his eye he saw the Dark Ones swarming up the other side of the wagon and heard Charla's screams.

Charla fought back-to-back with Mother Tarni on the wagon, the Sinti queen's daggers flying as she hacked at the Dark Ones, but they were being overwhelmed.

The long daggers Charla held in both hands didn't seem to have any effect on the Dark Ones pulling at her. She stabbed and they grabbed, and they were winning. She kicked their faces with her boots, sliced the hands reaching for her, and still they came.

"Charla!" came a scream.

Charla's eyes darted sideways and she saw Elaria running toward her, a glowing sword in her hand. For a moment, Charla felt a rush of hope, but the Dark Ones pulled at her and Charla knew Elaria wouldn't arrive before they overwhelmed her.

She sobbed, desperation in every move as she fought the clutching hands and arms. Then, as she began to fall toward the Dark Ones, she saw Elaria throw the sword. At first she thought the girl was trying to impale one of the Dark Ones, but then the sword was hurtling straight toward Charla, and she suddenly realized it was going to impale *her*. She stopped moving, staring at the sword, unable to look away from the glowing tip. As it came nearer, the sounds of the battle faded, and a humming filled her mind.

If I catch the sword, I can fight my way free.

One part of Charla knew it was crazy to attempt such a thing, but the rest of her was sure it was completely logical. As the blade flew toward her, Mother Tarni slashed viciously at the arms holding Charla and screamed, "*Now!*"

Charla was able to yank her arms free and, as the blade sliced past her, she reached up and grabbed the leather-wrapped hilt with her bloody hands, turning in one motion to slice through the horde of Dark Ones reaching for her. Heads, arms, hands, all came off, and the horde collapsed as one.

She looked around and saw the tide had turned. Elaria was pulling her dagger from the heart of one of the Dark Ones, while Jamison grimly surveyed the fallen bodies around him. Greene and Jacobson still battled, but Mother Tarni, daggers in each hand, jumped from the wagon to cut the throat of the Dark One Jacobson grappled with, and then turned to plunge a dagger into the neck of the one Greene was fighting off.

Then all was silent, save for the heaving breaths of those still alive, and the moans of the wounded.

Greene, wiping blood from his eyes, turned desperately to find Charla, afraid that the Dark Ones had her.

But, no. There she stood, a glowing sword in her hand and her breast heaving with effort, a grim smile on her face. Then she looked up and saw him, and her face softened in love and relief.

The Sinti healers helped the most grievously injured of the survivors, then turned their ministrations to the others. Greene insisted on binding Charla's wounds himself before he accepted help for his own wounds.

As Greene turned to survey the fallen, who were being attended by the other Sinti, he saw Elaria standing nearby, cleaning Hyranstrene. He walked over and said with a smile, "I think I understand why Uriah wants that sword now."

She gave him a shy smile and nodded.

"It's not broken, is it?" he asked, looking down at it. He could see the crack in it, but a faint light still glowed from the fissure.

She shrugged.

Mother Tarni said from behind him, "Sometimes broken things are the most powerful, if they break in the right way." She strode past him to Elaria. "May I see it?" she asked.

Elaria handed her the sword wordlessly.

"It is Hyranstrene?" Mother Tarni asked, balancing it in her hand.

Elaria nodded.

"We thought it was lost."

Elaria said, "My family was charged with keeping it safe." She looked at Greene. "We were sworn to tell no one, and to use it only in our direst need."

Mother Tarni said, "You have done well," and handed it back to her. "We will speak of it to no one. It must remain safe."

Elaria nodded, and Mother Tarni switched her gaze to Greene, who also nodded.

Greene said, "That was a lot of excitement."

Charla agreed and fell into his arms, the tension and shock of the battle catching up with her.

"You are well? The Eye is safe?"

Charla looked up to see Mother Tarni. "Yes, I'm fine and it's safe," Charla assured her, her hand gripping her tightly laced pocket just to be sure. Yes, the familiar bulge was there. She'd known it was there all through the battle, because it had grown oddly hot against her skin, but now it was cool again.

"We must waste no more time," the Sinti queen said, beckoning them toward her wagon.

"But," Charla began to motion toward the injured Sinti on the ground.

Mother Tarni shook her head. "Jamison will take care of them, but you must come with me now." She beckoned to Jacobson, David and Elaria as well. "Come. You will ride inside my wagon. We have many miles to go, so you must rest now."

Charla didn't argue further, just followed Mother Tarni to her wagon and climbed inside with the others.

They'd barely closed the door when the wagon lurched and began to roll, gathering speed. Charla and Elaria claimed the big bed, while Greene and Jacobson argued over who would get the smaller wall bed, only to turn around and find David sitting smugly on it. Jacobson immediately protested, but Greene said, "Watch out, *Johnny!* That's my future brother-in-law you're mauling!"

"Johnny?" Charla laughed, making Jacobson roll his eyes.

"What do *you* call him?" Elaria asked, surprised.

Charla said, "The Guards are normally called by their last names. I still haven't gotten used to saying 'Timothy' instead of 'Greene.'" She grinned as Elaria laughed.

Laying back on the bed, Charla stared out the window. The sun was high in the sky now, so she was pretty sure she wouldn't be able to sleep, but she wasn't about to pass up the chance to rest after dealing with the Dark Ones. Her exhaustion was mental as well as physical.

Jacobson said, "Those Dark Ones… they're pretty… *interesting*, huh?"

Shivering, Charla said, "That's an understatement. Did you notice their skin?"

Greene asked, "Yeah, what was that? Some kind of weird tattoos? It almost seemed like it was moving, but I couldn't get a good look."

Charla glanced toward David, who grimaced and turned his head away. She said, "We unfortunately had the chance to observe their skin closely on numerous occasions, so I can tell you that the lettering *does* move across their skin somehow. Weirdest thing I've ever seen, and it makes them hard to look at, like you can't focus your eyes."

"But all that stops when you kill them," David interjected. "The letters almost disappear and they look like regular men." The others nodded slowly. They'd all gotten a good look at the dead Dark Ones.

Suddenly, they were overcome with exhaustion. The rocking of the wagon soothed them, and they slept.

Home

When Mother Tarni's wagon next stopped, they were well along the road to Kingham Village. "We'll send a pigeon in the morning to let King Richard know to expect us," Mother Tarni said. "We should be in Kingham Village by mid-morning."

Charla felt a huge weight lift from her. Almost home.

But without Old Dan.

The thought made her heart hurt and tears start to her eyes, and she clung to Greene that night, her other arm around David, as they sat by the fire watching Jacobson practice his tambourine skills with Ethan.

Greene whispered as he pulled her close, "Old Dan and your parents would be so proud of you, of the way you fought the Dark Ones. You truly are a worthy *skaeweer*." He pronounced the word carefully and almost correctly.

Charla gave a soft laugh and pulled his head around for a kiss.

The sun was high in the sky when the Sinti caravan was spotted on the road to Kingham Village. The signalman in his tower at the top of the gate rang the bell once to let the gatekeeper know friends were approaching.

As the Sinti wagons wound their way through the gates, the King's Guards called greetings to Greene and Jacobson, making rude comments about their appearance as men are wont to do when showing affection to each other. Greene and Jacobson were still wearing their Sinti earrings, and they'd donned their Sinti scarves again to cover their burned heads, so there was a lot to make fun of.

But when the guards turned their eyes to Charla, who was sitting on the wagon seat next to Greene, their comments turned to sincere words of welcome.

Charla smiled and gave them her thanks, but her heart was running ahead to the castle where her best friend would be waiting. Greene had comforted her when she cried about Old Dan's death, but Charla longed to share her loss with Princess Aurora.

As she mentally urged the horses to go faster, she heard pounding footsteps and saw a figure running toward them, skirt caught up in one hand so the booted legs could move freely, red braid bouncing with each step.

Princess Aurora arrived panting. "Oh, thank goodness you're home! I was so glad when the pigeon from Mother Tarni arrived yesterday saying you were both fine, but I've still been desperate to find out where you've been!"

She ran on in this vein for a bit, absentmindedly accepting the hand Greene gave her so she could mount the wagon. Then, "I love the dress!" she exclaimed, grinning at Charla's Sinti garb. "And Greene, those earrings are… interesting!" She nodded emphatically, her wide eyes making the sentence something less than a compliment.

They all laughed, and then she turned to Charla again, her face becoming serious. "I say this with all the love in my heart: you'd better have a *really* good explanation of why you went missing."

Charla said, "Well, I found out that our family has been protecting a magical object for generations, and I climbed a snow-covered mountain to retrieve the magical object, and I met my mom right before she died, and I was almost killed by magical beings…" She shrugged and awaited Aurora's verdict.

The princess stared at her for a long moment, then said emphatically, "Explanation accepted, and full recital of events expected!"

Charla laughed and she and Aurora hugged, then the princess drew back and asked, "I see David, but where is Old Dan?"

Charla's eyes welled with tears and her throat closed so she couldn't speak. Aurora's questioning look turned to horror and she turned to Greene.

He shook his head. "He's dead, Princess. He died while climbing the mountain with Charla and David."

"Oh, *no!*" the princess exclaimed, but then she stared from Greene to Charla in confusion. "Old Dan was *climbing a mountain? How…?*" She shook her head and managed to focus on the important part. Putting both arms around Charla, she kissed her cheek and whispered, "I'm so sorry, dearest. Old Dan was such a wonderful man. I'll always remember his kindness and wisdom. He is a true loss to us all." The princess kissed her again and whispered, "I'm so glad you're back. Never, never disappear again."

Charla nodded, tears leaking from her eyes.

A New Mission

King Richard called a meeting immediately after the travelers had changed their travel-stained clothes and partaken of food and drink.

The king sat at the head of the long table in his weapons room. On his right were Princess Aurora and her husband Martin, along with Charla, David and Greene. Jacobson sat across from them with Captain Anderson of the King's Guards, and Princess Morgana of Vallenland, who had remained in Archenland to hear the outcome of Greene and Jacobson's expedition.

The others were slightly surprised when Queen Maribel walked in with Mother Tarni and said to her husband, "The queens have arrived; you may begin," as she and the Sinti queen took the remaining seats amid laughter.

The group listened intently as Charla and Greene related shortened versions of their respective stories, with occasional input and clarification from David and Jacobson.

King Richard said rather cryptically, "Things are coming to a head," and Mother Tarni nodded. The king continued, "If the drug that was demonstrated for Uriah is indeed the legendary *gaemedden*…" He looked at Mother Tarni. "Is there anything we can do to mitigate its effects?"

Mother Tarni shook her head. "Unfortunately, no. But I have been thinking on this, and I do not think it will be offered for Uriah's use."

The king frowned. "Why not?"

"This Sutherne power that your men heard of… We Sinti have also heard rumors of a queen on the southern continent who has united all the tribes. It's my belief that her alliance with Uriah is merely a move in a larger plan. I do not think she would risk her warriors, and certainly not the precious *gaemedden*, to help him achieve his aims in Bryten."

King Richard asked, "You don't think she wants to take over Bryten as she has Sutherne?"

Mother Tarni said, "She would surely take it if it came easily into her hand, but I think she is looking for something more powerful than even these kingdoms, something to give her power over all of Eoroe… as well as the *Ungesewen Weraldi*."

"Power over the Unseen World?" the king asked in surprise.

Mother Tarni nodded. "Uriah is the immediate threat, but there are signs that the *Grauta Beadu* approaches."

"The Great Battle," Queen Maribel breathed.

Mother Tarni said, "Elaria told Greene and Jacobson that Uriah is seeking Hyranstrene. I believe this Sutherne queen told him to search for it. Fortunately, it is now safe with us." Then, motioning toward Charla, she said, "And the *skaeweer* has the Eye. All the strength is on our side. This queen of Sutherne would be unwise to attack unless she knows she will prevail. But you are right to fear an attack from Uriah, because the Eye and Hyranstrene have important parts to play later, and their power must not be squandered. If Uriah attacks, you must try to defeat him on your own, even if the queen of Sutherne puts all her might behind him."

Queen Maribel glanced around the table. "Perhaps we should discuss those topics later?"

King Richard followed her eyes and realized from the puzzled frowns on the other faces that no one else had understood the conversation about the Unseen World and the Great Battle. He nodded. "Of course. No need to go into all that now. We have more timely decisions to make. Uriah must come first."

Looking around the table, he said, "We need to get someone close to Uriah. Mother Tarni believes the Sinti may be able to help us." He motioned toward the Sinti queen, who addressed the group.

"Every few years, the Sinti caravan visits the monarch of each kingdom. The Arlesland Sinti are due to visit King Uriah this year, and I suggested that King Richard send a request to the Arlesland leader of the Sinti that some of King Richard's people be allowed to join them when they enter Uriah's castle. Sinti do not take sides in wars between kingdoms, so we will not spy on Uriah ourselves, but we are willing to help you in this way.

"The people King Richard sends will join the Arlesland Sinti when they begin their journey through Arlesland. The Sinti are currently at their home camp, replenishing the wares they sell, so you have some time to prepare."

Mother Tarni turned to Princess Morgana.

"King Uriah is unique among the monarchs in that he insists that only Arlesland Sinti enter his court. In order to get someone inside the castle, that person must look like an Arleslander. You have the coloring."

Morgana's golden eyes widened. After a moment, she said, "My birth father was from Arlesland." One hand hesitantly brushed the dark hair out of her eyes. "What are you asking me to do? I'll have to talk to King Rudolph first, of course," she said to King Richard.

He nodded. "I've already spoken with him. He does not want you to go into potential danger, but you would be safe traveling with the Sinti, so he is willing to leave the decision up to you. It is your choice. I'm asking you to travel with the Sinti for at least twelve days, which is the time it normally takes them to trace their usual route through Arlesland. They have another week or two before they begin their loop through Arlesland, so I'd like you to join them as soon as possible. That will give you time to absorb enough of their culture to pass yourselves off as Sinti in front of the king.

"When they arrive at the king's castle, I'd like you to try to get close to Uriah. Mother Tarni says he usually invites his most favored nobles and allies to join him when the Sinti arrive, so you may be able to overhear something of interest."

Morgana asked, "You said 'pass *yourselves* off as Sinti.' Is someone joining me?"

The king's eyes turned to his Captain of the Guards. "Captain Anderson, I'm assigning you to be Princess Morgana's protector. She'll be safe with the Sinti, but her father would skin me alive if I didn't have at least one King's Guard with her. Your hair is not as dark as most Arleslanders," he said, glancing at Anderson's light brown hair, "but your eyes are the right color and you can wear a Sinti scarf to cover your hair." The king turned toward Jacobson. "I also plan to send you back to Arlesland with the captain and Princess Morgana. I know you must be tired from your trip, and I'm sorry to send you right back, but it would be good to have another Guard there, and you're the only one we have available to send. You don't look like an Arleslander, so you won't be allowed to enter King Uriah's castle with the Arlesland Sinti, but it will ease my mind to have two King's Guards on the trip."

Jacobson nodded hesitantly.

King Richard asked, "Do you have reservations, Jacobson? Speak freely."

Jacobson glanced around. "It's just that Arlesland..." He glanced at Greene. "It was hard for me to be there..."

Mother Tarni spoke up. "The difference this time is that you'll be traveling with the Sinti, rather than being on your own. Did it make a difference when you joined Jamison's group last time?"

Jacobson's face cleared. "Yes! I felt... safe."

She nodded. "You will not be at the forefront of the mission this time, which will also make a difference." She smiled suddenly. "Your main objective will be to master the tambourine, for which I'm told you already show an aptitude."

Jacobson laughed with the others and nodded. "Alright, I'll go. I know it's important, and I want to help."

Captain Anderson clapped him on the back. "Good man. I'm glad to have you along. You and Greene did good work, even with the strain you were under."

Jacobson and Greene exchanged a glance. The pain of the past few weeks was fading now that they were back in Archenland, but it still hovered like a half-remembered nightmare.

King Richard was addressing Princess Morgana and Anderson. "Greene and Jacobson had a hard time earning the trust of the Arleslanders, but you may be able to pick up gossip from the commoners since you look like natives yourselves."

Anderson nodded, glancing at Princess Morgana, who was studying him. She gave him a brief, impersonal smile, then turned her attention back to the king.

Jacobson asked hesitantly, "Will Elaria be coming back to Arlesland with us? I know King Uriah is looking for her sword, but it was certainly good to have it during the last fight with the Dark Ones."

"Yes!" Charla said emphatically. "I couldn't have escaped without it."

Greene asked, "What *is* Hyranstrene? It's not just a regular sword, obviously. Mother Tarni, you said you thought it had been lost…"

The Sinti queen said to him, "I can tell you nothing except that it is an important instrument, too important to risk falling into Uriah's hands. It has been decided that Elaria and the sword will accompany you and Charla northward with the Eye. I cannot go with you, but Jamison will travel with you as well."

Charla gave a deep sigh of relief. "I feel much safer knowing that," she admitted. "I know the Eye has power of its own, but those Dark Ones… they were almost too much."

Mother Tarni nodded. "It is not time for the full power of the Eye to be revealed. But, in conjunction with Hyranstrene, it will afford you much protection should the Dark Ones again attack you."

King Richard asked, "Any more questions?" As everyone shook their heads, he said, "It's settled, then. Anderson, work with Princess Morgana to pack what you'll need for the journey. Mother Tarni, if you would assist Captain Anderson in determining what they'll need to bring, I would appreciate."

The Sinti queen nodded, and they were dismissed.

Delaying the Storm

The day had finally come. Greene and Charla were to be married.

Charla had been terribly disappointed that all the friends from Windham Village that she'd expected to be at her wedding had returned to their village during her absence, but after weeping over it with Aurora, she'd dried her eyes and gone back to planning, with Aurora assuring her they could plan a later celebration in Windham Village itself.

Aurora knew the real reason Charla was so upset was because Old Dan wouldn't be there to ceremonially join her and Greene's families as one, and she was sure there was also a part of Charla that mourned the lack of her mother and father. That thought might have been only a twinge of regret if the wedding had taken place when planned, but now that Charla had met her mother, the wound was fresh and raw.

So Aurora spent as much time with Charla as she could, and made her laugh after she cried.

Charla and Greene had decided to pare the wedding to the bare necessities. It would just be them, Greene's mother and sister,

David, and the royal family. Greene had also invited Jacobson. "You're like a brother to me. I want you to be there," he'd said.

Jacobson had been surprised, but accepted gladly. "Maybe wedding cake and wine will make up for your lousy attitude in Arlesland," he mused.

Greene gave a shout of laughter and clapped his shoulder in relief. He and Jacobson had easily returned to their usual camaraderie once they were back in Archenland, for which Greene was grateful. That dark time was behind them. He hoped.

Greene had questioned Charla when she'd said she wanted to have a simpler ceremony. "Are you sure? I know you're sad about your friends from Windham Village not being here, but we have a lot of friends here in Kingham Village who would love to come."

Charla had thought about it, but, "No," she'd finally said. "I just don't feel right about having the party we'd planned. Something has changed. Something feels… wrong now. Almost like I don't want to draw attention to ourselves. Does that make sense?"

Greene had nodded slowly. "Do you think it's because of the Eye?"

Charla said, "Partially. But a lot of it has to do with what we discovered over the past few weeks. Now we know there's an entire… what did Mother Tarni call it? Unseen World? We know the fight between good and evil is real, and we have a part to play in it. It just feels like there are much bigger things happening now, and I don't think I could relax and enjoy the wedding the way I wanted to. I'd rather wait to have a celebration after things calm down… if they ever do."

Greene had kissed her and made her laugh and the moment had passed, but that was the moment that everything changed, much more so than the moment when Charla had the first vision of Mount Ciel, or even when she met her mother and took over protecting the Eye. All that time, she'd always had the thought of her love for Greene and their wedding to keep her grounded while everything around her was thrown into the air and disarranged.

But now she'd disarranged their wedding plans, too; now there was a shadow over their celebration. It was like planning a picnic while ominous clouds gathered on the horizon. You couldn't possibly ignore it, so you just prepared as best you could and waited for it to strike.

The day of the wedding, Princess Aurora, along with Greene's mother and sister, spent the morning braiding Charla's hair and carefully gathering the heavy mass to wind around her head, pinning it in place with some of Aurora's enameled hairpins.

Greene's mother and his sister then carefully placed fresh sweet pea blossoms and roses in the bride's hair, leaning down to kiss her on the cheek when they were done. Greene's mother said, "I'm so proud to have you as my daughter, Charla. I couldn't imagine a better wife for Timothy." They hugged her one last time, then slipped away to make their way down the hill to the white tent by the old apple tree.

Princess Aurora sat down beside her dear friend, the first girlfriend she'd ever had, and said, tears pricking her eyes, "Your parents and Old Dan would be so proud to see you today. You are beautiful, the best friend I could imagine, and the best wife Greene could ever have."

Charla said emphatically, "Don't make me cry!" and laughed a little shakily as she hugged Aurora.

There was a soft knock at the door, and David came in. "It's time," he said, a big smile breaking over his face. "You look beautiful."

Charla stood up, smoothing into place the dress that Madeline, Aurora's seamstress, had created from a simple cream-colored scarf that had belonged to Charla's mother. The scarf was creamy silk with an embroidered border surrounding a pattern of flowers and vines made from white and pale pink beads. Madeline had turned the scarf vertically to form the front of the dress, embroidered another panel the same size for the back, and added the panels to a simple cream-colored dress.

The dress had been created before Charla met her mother, but now it had special meaning. Another item with special meaning was the small beaded bag that hung from Charla's wrist, the one she'd been looking for the night she found the bitter sand. Now it reminded her not only of her mother, but of the journey that had changed her life.

Charla put her hand in her brother's, and held her other hand out to Aurora, who was taking Old Dan's place at Charla's side.

And heavy against Charla's stomach, where it lay in a leather pouch suspended from a strong silver chain, was the Eye, which she now wore at all times. Mother Tarni had told her, "It is your burden to carry until it is needed."

"When will that be?" Charla had asked.

But Mother Tarni had merely said, "Be ready."

Greene watched breathlessly, heart pounding, as Charla appeared, flanked by David and Princess Aurora. All he saw was Charla, though, her brilliant smile shining with love, her eyes firm on his as she walked toward their future together. Her eyes were full of tears, and he knew she was thinking about her parents and Old Dan, but the tears dried as she drew closer.

And then she was there beside him, and they said the words and made the vows, and were joined for the rest of their lives. Greene's smile was so wide he thought it might break his face.

But, as he leaned in for their first kiss as husband and wife, he had a fleeting moment of fear that the rest of their lives…

Wouldn't be long at all.

Enthralled

King Uriah stood alone at the window of a stone tower in south Arlesland that overlooked the Ocean of Faer. The coastline of Sutherne was too far away to see, but he imagined Her Majesty seated on the red velvet throne as he'd last seen her.

He'd been so young then, only nineteen. It was the first trip out of the kingdom that he'd been on, and he'd been determined to be everything a young prince should be: chivalrous, kind to commoners, princely but not arrogant... all the things his father wasn't.

Uriah frowned. He'd been so different then, so naïve about true power. That had all changed when he met *her*.

Queen Rusulka.

He'd been planning to go to the Twenty-Fifth Birthday celebration of King Rudolph of Vallenland, his first trip outside Arlesland. His father had always refused to leave Arlesland, which to Uriah seemed paranoid. When Uriah received the invitation to King Rudolph's celebration, he'd accepted it, only informing his father of his plans a week before he planned to leave.

At first his father had been angry, raging at him for days. But, as the time for the trip had approached, the king had grown quiet and finally given his consent for the trip. He'd even insisted on sending Uriah in his spacious traveling carriage, so Uriah could sleep in comfort on the journey instead of staying in dubious inns along the way. He'd also sent his captain of the guards to ensure Uriah's safety.

Uriah had slept well that first night on the road, and it was only when they arrived at a seaport at mid-morning the next day that he'd discovered his father's men weren't taking him northwest to Vallenland. Uriah had demanded to know where they were, and his father's captain of the guards had calmly informed him that they were taking him to Sutherne, to meet with the queen of a small kingdom there.

Uriah had tried to fight his way through the guards surrounding him, but he'd known it was useless. So he went to Sutherne.

Her castle had been small, little more than a defensive tower. When Uriah walked into her Great Hall the night he arrived, he'd seen two long tables of about sixty people. As the heads turned toward him, he was surprised to realize there were no "nobles," as he thought of them, among them. They were prosperous commoners, to judge by their cotton and wool clothing, which was rather more ornamented than that of most commoners.

But his eye had quickly been drawn to the woman seated at the head table, on a dais above the rest. Surprisingly, she was seated on a red velvet throne rather than a dining chair, and Uriah realized the Great Hall must do double duty as her audience chamber, a theory that was born out the next day when he entered the same hall to find the tables stacked against the wall and the throne alone on its dais.

But that evening, there had been one other chair beside the throne on the dais, and he'd been escorted to it. As he walked between the tables, the commoners bowed to him, but he only had eyes for their queen.

She stared at him unblinkingly as he walked, brushing a lock of her long black hair over her shoulder. Her high-necked green velvet gown had a pattern of vines embroidered on it in gold thread, but from a distance the vines looked like snakes writhing across her body. Her skin was the color of the caramel that was Uriah's favorite treat as a child, her eyes the green of the grass he used to play on.

But the look in those eyes reminded him of nothing from his childhood. It was the look of a huntress spying her prey. A smile curved her dark red lips, the color of dried blood, as he bowed to her. She regarded him for a long moment before motioning him to take the chair beside her.

That first meal with her was like nothing he'd ever experienced. She said not a word for the two hours they were seated at the table. He attempted to engage her in conversation, but if she was listening, she gave no sign of it. All her attention was on the commoners seated before them, and the minstrel band playing at the far end of the hall.

Uriah didn't care for the music, with its skirling pipes and drums that beat without any kind of rhythm. He felt his heart stuttering in his chest as it tried to match the drums.

After a few moments, he gave up trying to talk to her and put his attention on the food the silent servants were setting in front of him. The taste of the food was unusual and not to his liking. The spices made him sneeze and his stomach churn.

She was rude, not even attempting to welcome him, but at the end of the meal, he was disappointed when she stood without a word and disappeared through a door at the back of the hall. One of the servants waited until Uriah had finished his meal, then led him through another door and up a staircase to a small bed chamber.

The next morning, he woke up anxious to see her. As his stay lengthened, his desire for her company deepened, especially when she finally deigned to talk to him that first morning, even though her words were light and teasing, as if to a child or a rather dumb adult.

She was much older than he, but he'd been fascinated by her. Over the next few weeks, he'd listened eagerly as she explained how all the things he hated about his father were the things that made him a good ruler.

Truthfully, he couldn't remember much about *what* she'd said to convince him. It was more about how he *felt* when she explained everything. As he'd knelt on the floor beside the velvet throne for hours, looking into green eyes under heavy lids, he'd felt calm, peaceful, as if all his cares had disappeared, as if he sat at the feet of perfect knowledge. When she gazed at him with her half-smile, he felt like the most powerful man in the world.

He knew that in order to keep feeling that way, he had to do whatever she told him, and what she told him was that when he returned to Arlesland, he must become the heir his father wanted, the strong, powerful prince the kingdom *needed*.

Rusulka explained that only by treating his people harshly could he bring them to the fullness of their destiny. He had to push them, hurt them, in order to make them great, to make the *kingdom* great.

"And you'll see, young prince," she'd whispered, running her fingers with their long red nails through his hair. "It will all happen just as I say. Trust me," she'd murmured in his ear, sliding her lips over his cheek in a light kiss.

And so he had. He'd never once doubted her wisdom from that day forward, and he'd completely changed himself from that romantic, naïve fool into the prince his father and Rusulka wanted.

Thinking about those days long ago, King Uriah stared out the window of the prison tower and frowned.

There had been that one episode, though.

The girl. The one from Vallenland. He didn't like to think about her, but sometimes he couldn't help it.

She'd arrived soon after he returned from the trip to Sutherne, and as soon as he saw her, he knew she was meant for him. Unfortunately, she was promised to someone else, and Uriah had never been able to accept that.

Here was where it had all ended, though… where *she* had ended. Uriah leaned out the window of the stone tower to look at the dark rocks below, where the surf churned and swirled. For a moment, he could see her lying broken on the rocks, the waves washing over her, then he blinked and she was gone, just as she had been that night so many years ago.

He sighed heavily. That had been painful, had almost destroyed him… but with her passing, he'd once again been able to focus on the vision Queen Rusulka had placed in his head.

The vision of a strong, unbreakable Arlesland, a kingdom before which all other kingdoms crumbled.

And now, the dream was coming true.

Uriah smiled and turned away from the rocks where his love had died.

Epilogue

Queen's Man 675 dismounted from his steaming horse, throwing the reins to the stable boy who ran to meet him. As his fellow Queen's Men headed off to the barracks for some much-needed food and drink, 675 quickly mounted the castle steps and strode through the entrance hall toward Her Majesty's chambers. He knew he would find her there because, unlike most monarchs, she didn't have daily audiences with her people. She made no pretense of having an interest in their daily lives.

She was ruthless and beautiful and terrifying.

But not as terrifying as others 675 had known.

As he approached the doors to her chamber, they were thrown wide by the unarmored guards on either side. 675 gave each guard a nod of recognition and strode in to find Rusulka reclining on a red velvet couch, one elbow propped on the arm as she stared out the nearby window.

He dispassionately noticed what a beautiful picture she made, her dark hair and creamy brown skin set off to perfection against the red couch and white silk curtains behind it.

"Your Majesty." 675 gave her the same nod he'd given to the guards, which he knew she hated.

Her mouth pursed but she forced herself to smile. "One of these days, dear, you'll give me my proper homage. I'll bring you to your knees, you'll see."

675 ignored the comment, merely stating, "I've come to report on King Uriah."

She waved impatiently for him to continue.

"He and King Albert have about a thousand soldiers, which might be enough to subdue one northern kingdom at a time, but the army is weak, made up of starving commoners. They are vicious however, fighting until their bodies give out."

Rusulka's face lightened. "Ah. He's using the techniques I taught him, I take it?"

675 nodded.

Rusulka turned to the window once more, staring unseeingly at the cloudless azure sky. "You think I should support him, then?"

675 said, "No. He has not yet proven his loyalty to you."

Rusulka's head snapped back to him. "He hasn't located the sword?"

"He killed the last man known to have it."

Rusulka screamed in frustration and stood up to furiously pace the room. "I must have that sword! Is there no word of it at all?"

"None that I could trace. The man's entire family was killed, his house burned, and no one besides the soldier who gave the information to Uriah seems to have even heard of it, never mind seen it."

"You searched the man's property, of course?"

He nodded. "I took thirty of Uriah's servants and had them dig up the entire property, as well as sifting through the charred rubble of the house. There was no sign of it. I personally questioned the man's closest neighbors, but they were too stupid to do much other than nod when I asked them to confirm that the man's entire family had perished, and that none of them knew of any weapons he had at the house."

Rusulka said sharply, "You didn't tell them the sword was valuable? They might sell it!"

675 said, "I told them the man had stolen the sword when he left Uriah's employ, and that the king would be grateful if it were returned to him. They won't sell it."

Rusulka scowled.

"There's one more thing," 675 said. He'd pondered whether to tell her this or not. She had a habit of rushing into situations where a more reasoned approach would be advantageous.

But he was concerned about how the situation might affect his long-term plans. As long as he worked for Rusulka, he needed her support to move openly in the world. If he wanted to find out more about this new situation, he'd need her permission to look into it, so he had to tell her.

"I detected traces of a… malevolent presence in Bryten."

She stared at him.

"One which is working against your plans. Against *our* plans."

She froze. After a moment, she whispered, "Heolcnihts?

675 nodded.

The blood drained from the queen's face.

The End

Visit AuthorJoCook.com to sign up for her newsletter and be notified when book four of the World of Eoroe: Bryten series is released.

Acknowledgements

I got a bit derailed by life in 2023, so when 2024 rolled around I was <u>determined</u> to write the third book in the Eoroe:Bryten series!

I announced to my family that I was going to "disappear" from life for a month while I banged out the first rough draft, and they were incredibly supportive and understanding.

My Prologue Writing Group was also integral to my completion of the story. Every month, I'd set a new goal in our meetings, which is about the only thing that got me focused enough to get this book done. Shout out to Autumn, Katie, Shana, Donna and Laura for making me laugh, making me work, and giving me lots of understanding ears to pour my frustrations into.

No author can turn out a decent book without decent beta readers, and mine are great. Ying Gao, Nina Boaz, Rebekah Murray, Cory Witt, Carolyn Lance, and Carol LaTurno: thank you, thank you, thank you! Your input was invaluable and helped me shape the final product. By the time I finish the final draft, my brain is whirling with all the scenes I deleted, the ones I added, and the ones I added in my mind, but forgot to put on paper! You point out the good, bad and ugly, and I need that tough love!

My friend Dr. Brown always wants me to base a character on him, but he never reads my books *eye roll* even though he supports me in theory *double eye roll* so once again I haven't bothered. Dear Dr. Brown: Stop being a picklehead and maybe you'll get a character!

My readers are my greatest inspiration. Every good review, every email telling me how much you enjoyed the books…

they are food and drink to a writer. I've had lots of jobs, but never one that filled me with delight on so many levels. Thank you for giving me a reason to keep going!

The last shall be first, so lastly I want to thank the one who is first in my heart. I called him Oynos in this book, but no matter what his name, his power is mighty and real. I prayed over this book many, many times, and the inspiration always came through. Sometimes it took me a while to listen to the promptings, but they were always there, and I am grateful.

-Jo-

About the Author

Jo Cook dabbled with writing her whole life, but it was only during the World Upheaval of 2020 that her writing angel deigned to dictate something more than a novella.

Jo has been a flight attendant, copy editor, and small-business owner, and she spent a couple of very hot months bouncing around in a Tigger costume at Walt Disney World. She has a bachelor's degree in psychology, and a master's degree in conflict management.

Jo's perfect day would involve thrifting, a good book, movies, and lots of lemonade.

Visit Jo Cook's website and subscribe to her newsletter to receive a FREE novella, A Rose for Carter, as well as news about upcoming releases!

AuthorJoCook.com

www.ingramcontent.com/pod-product-compliance
Lightning Source LLC
Chambersburg PA
CBHW032053050726
47590CB00001B/252